All Who Came Before

All Who Came Before

SIMON PERRY

An EMERALD CITY Book

ALL WHO CAME BEFORE

Resource Publications
An imprint of Wipf and Stock Publishers
199 W. 8th Ave., Suite 3
Eugene, OR 97401

www.wipfandstock.com

ISBN 13: 978-1-60899-659-9

Manufactured in the U.S.A.

For
Willem, Lewis, Alice, Stefan
and Edwige

Acknowledgments

ABOVE ALL, THE WRITING of this book has been enabled by the generosity of Bloomsbury Central Baptist Church, who in 2008, granted me a three month sabbatical. At the end of this, several members of the church also read and very helpfully critiqued the first draft, most notably, Brian and Faith Bowers, Jean Harrison, Seth Stephens and Robert Doty. Great encouragement for this project also came from my colleague, Ruth Gouldbourne, our church secretary, John Beynon, and three members, Shona Scanlan, Jordan Tchillingirian, and Emma Langley. A former minister of the church, Brian Haymes, also offered invaluable insight, as have several other friends.

Ali Hale and Carys Underdown helped the idea to take shape in my head over lengthy conversations after chapel services at Fitzwilliam College, Cambridge. Others who have committed time to reading and helping with various stages of the Manuscript are Stephanie Brock, Simon Woodman, Dien Wooller, Roy Bagley, Kae and Rachael Rake, Mike and Belinda Smith, Bill and Joan Perry, Richard James Perry, and June Brotherton.

My own children, Willem, Lewis, Stefan and Alice, have heard various versions and summaries of the plot, and their competing cries for justice have helped to inform the story. Lastly, my gratitude goes to Edwige, whose constant encouragement, ridicule, and love, have ensured that the book was completed and the story heard.

THE DAGGER SLIPPED FROM Yeshua's grip, tumbling into darkness and taking with it all hope of justice. Warm blood trickled from his empty hand. Silently the drops fell, until their collective voice would gather to cry from the ground. Yeshua—God will save us—had not saved his people, and his God had not saved him. Facing his final moment, he lowered his eyes and the fear he had so recently shaken returned with mortal force. The clash had lasted only seconds, but the build-up had seemed endless as he lay concealed in the grass, waiting for it to begin.

"Right on time," he had heard his brother call from across the track as their targets emerged from the city.

"Be ready, Theudas," Yeshua the Egyptian replied in shallow breath. "They'll be here before we know it."

The dark western horizon was crafted by Roman hubris. The cut stones, mounted as legionaries in rank and file, silently forbade any hope of resistance: the city wall, standing like the tip of a colossal blade sunk deep into the heart of the Promised Land; the aqueduct, bleeding the milk and honey from that land to fuel its oppression; the amphitheatre, celebrating the human body by enslaving it. The empire's capital was incarnate in Straton's Tower, conquering the sky to monitor all that passed by sea or land.

The intent of this almighty stonework reached far beyond its practical purpose. This was a spectacle to invoke astonishment and fear, and in so doing to radiate the divine power of Rome. Where once the sky would meet the land, magnificent structures now intervened. Heaven and earth could meet only through Rome.

The shallow chill of the Judean summer night still clung to Yeshua's limbs, but he lay motionless, hidden in the scrubland outside the eastern gate of the great coastal city, Caesarea. Two Roman soldiers had emerged from the gate and begun the shallow descent along the southerly track that in two minutes' time would bring them within six paces of the would-be assassin. At sight of their approach, Yeshua was seized by a momentary paralysis, which spread from his bowels and ordered his entire body to abandon its absurd intentions. Every limb and organ agreed this was an insane scheme: the son of a merchant, lying in wait to attack soldiers of Rome. A split second transformed these soldiers into immortals. They would surely hear his approach and fall on him long before he was within striking distance. No professional soldier, hardened in battle and sharpened through constant training, would fall prey to such a misguided amateur.

The glint of helmets and spear-points flickered toward them, still over a hundred slow paces away, but an infinite distance to the wavering Egyptian, overawed by the mortal consequences to be determined by the skill or failure of his own hand. Someone's blood would soon cry out from this dry patch of ground. He looked at the veins carrying a quickened pulse to his fingers and wondered whether that blood would be his.

"No safe path to victory," Yeshua snarled in an effort to buttress his resolve.

"You alright?" his younger brother asked, in a tone suggesting he himself was not. Yeshua could see, even from the loose curls of Theudas' hair, silhouetted against the skyline, that his entire body was tense.

The elder brother paused to control his breath before responding in a stage whisper. "We've watched them every night for a week. We've rehearsed this move to perfection." His quiet words were packed with determination. "Theudas. We are ready."

The Romans were protected by carefully designed amour, yielding little in the way of exposed flesh. So the assassins would attack from behind, hands gripped over the pommel of the dagger's hilt. They had practiced their move repeatedly upon one another using whittled wooden play knives, and even tied scarves around a tree to see whether the real blade would cope with the knot protecting the throat.

Theudas said nothing. Can he go through with this? Yeshua thought, but could hardly ask. "Theudas," he said, "think of Yotham. Think of Saul. Murdered by these pagans."

Silence made an eternity out of three heartbeats. Eventually Thuedas grunted. "These pagans will taste justice tonight," he said.

Yeshua sighed in relief, and with this reminder of why they were here, fear gave way to a stab of grief followed by a deeper blood rush of seething anger towards these troops. His eyes lifted as he offered an embittered prayer. "My brothers' lives ended the day they went to Your holy city to worship at Your holy Temple. . ." He paused to glance at the approaching soldiers ". . . And so did mine."

Yeshua inhaled the salty air as if to draw energy from all around him. Lightly moistened by the Mediterranean breeze, small trees and thick grass defied the sandy earth, freckled across a dry landscape where the jackal would hunt the hare. The raging calm of the predator descended upon Yeshua. He looked down at the wiry grass that had been his companion all night, and up at the heavens through a few patches of clear sky. The Egyptian's cynical prayer had done its job. He knew well enough that it was offered only to himself. He knew this God was merely the convenient name of his own projected anger. But by deceiving his own spirit with the conviction that some greater Other was being engaged, he broke the stranglehold of self-doubt.

The genuine otherness of the prayer was the recollection it brought of his father's friend, Caius. The legionary's tales were treasure to a wide-eyed adolescent eager for stories of war. Whatever the story, the same moral would mark the climax: "you can't fight well 'till you let go of your life." Only then can you be totally consumed with the task in hand. "No safe path to victory!" was the old soldier's refrain. The logic seemed to work, and to work its way into Yeshua's prayer. His supplication had certainly pulled some handle, released some demon to kindle the fiber of his frame.

Even more heartening was the thought that his target was no legionary. No elite troops were assigned to Caesarea, only civilians with ill-deserved military uniforms. "Remember, Theudas—these are not real soldiers. They're just auxiliaries."

"Auxiliaries, p'ah," Theudas scoffed, mimicking the old soldier's scorn for any troops but legionaries. His brother's response lifted Yeshua's spirit. He was ready. Creation had taken his side and bestowed upon him divine status for his righteous duty.

The auxiliaries, basking in their delusions of divinity, were about to discover they were all too human: mortals, unworthy of all reverence or respect. Yotham and Saul had been worthy, before they were crushed under the might of the empire. His brothers' lifeless faces; his father's undignified wailing. The inescapable memory of them fuelled the Egyptian's resolve as he considered the justice of his motives. If his targets were gods, he would be an angel of revenge. Appointed and anointed by whom, he was unsure. But he was an agent of justice, a justice that must be served if the world were not to crumble under the weight of unrighteousness.

The facial features of the soldiers were now visible and their conversation audible. Yeshua held his dagger in the predetermined grip, his hands ice-cold, the only remnant of fear his body now retained. Confident, he ran his left hand through the loose gravel scattered across the harder, sun-baked texture of the ground. Looking up, he found himself commanding a heightened sense of all he could see. Every stone and tree, every cloud and star was in on the plan, feeding his determination, but he would not move as a wild savage. As the soldiers ambled slowly towards the assassin's position, the Egyptian's nerve was utterly calm. His fury would be measured, disciplined: no war cry, no raised arms, only a simple task to fulfill. He had become a machine, waiting to be activated the moment his targets crossed the line between the trees under whose shade he lay.

"No more talking now. Stay calm. Hold your nerve."

"This is it," Theudas replied.

The soldiers arrived within ten paces as Yeshua loosened his limbs and prepared to move. But across the track, Theudas sprang to his feet in full view of his targets. The soldiers turned towards him. And there he stood: motionless, speechless.

Yeshua acted instinctively. Theudas' departure from the plan had created a decoy. The soldiers had walked side by side along the track but by turning towards Theudas they presented their backs to his brother. He moved in on the first target. Neither feeling nor calculating his attack, he merely rehearsed his move. By the time he registered the smell of the leather and oil rising from the soldier's metallic amour, his target's muscles had flinched, relaxed and given way. The still upright corpse was abandoned to gravity as the Egyptian closed in on his next mark.

Undistracted by the liquid that dripped warmth from the dagger onto his cold right hand, the assassin repeated the move. He pulled the blade into the scarf. But the resistance of the knot protecting the soldier's throat forced the dagger handle, now lubricated with blood, to slip through Yeshua's fingers.

Instantly, the alerted soldier became as solid as Roman marble. A statue quickened with life, he twisted sharply to the left, throwing off his assailant's embrace with his right elbow. Yeshua, in the knowledge his life was now forfeit, stepped back towards the fallen body of his first target. The second soldier had dropped his spear but had also now turned fully. Yeshua sank to the ground to retrieve the first fallen spear. The Egyptian cotton merchant, who before that moment had never laid his hand on a spear, prepared to face an infantryman, fully trained, fully armed and ready for combat. The soldier's right hand reached for the hilt of his sword, but the terrible chime of his unsheathing blade was never heard. Another face had appeared at the Roman's left shoulder. The soldier froze, gurgled and coughed. Theudas had finally completed his mission. A heavy thud concluded the action.

Theudas began to shake his head. "Yeshua. I am so, so . . ."

"Late? . . . Or was it early?" grinned Yeshua.

"Better late than never," Theudas grimaced as he answered his older brother. "I don't know what happened, I just . . ."

"Theudas. . ." Yeshua frowned as he embraced his younger brother, before turning toward his fallen victims, mesmerized by their lifeless bodies.

"Now what do we do?" Yeshua heard his brother's words, but was immersed in an involuntary prayer of thanksgiving to the God he did not believe in . . .

"Yeshua!" came the whispered shout.

The Egyptian waited a moment and, without change of expression, the command, "search them!" escaped his mouth before his brain had chance to hinder it.

Stooping in compliance, Theudas offered an obligatory but meaningless protest: "Robbery was never part of the plan."

Stepping towards the other body, Yeshua replied with equally casual tones, "Well, neither of us have followed the plan that well."

Killing a Roman soldier did not feel like a crime, but fumbling around his dead body . . . "Forget it. Let's just hide them, take their swords and go." But as Yeshua dragged his victim from the sandy track, he noticed a small bag, full of coins. A purse was removed from each soldier, their bodies pulled into the long grass and sand kicked over the deep red patches underfoot. Within three minutes of the soldiers' appearance at the gate of Caesarea, the companions were on their way.

Armed with a sword, a surplus of ego and an unknown sum of cash, the newly graduated assassins ran silently towards the dawn, stretching the ground between themselves and the Mediterranean.

As the Egyptians fled, the distant stonework of Caesarea, still visible as an ornament upon the sea, finally found its voice. It called after them, proclaiming that the escape attempt would fail, that their victims would be avenged. The creation, which so recently had been their ally, now became an enemy who condemned their righteous act. Every tree and bush breathed out its scorn as the assassins hurried by. Each panting breath of fresh morning air filled their lungs with the toxic of contempt, slowing their escape.

The quiet town of Narbata was only eight miles east, but every anxious glance over the shoulder saw Caesarea no more distant than the last. Each new stretch of the track ahead drew Yeshua's frantic visual search for the nearest means of cover should the thunderclap of angry hoof break from the track behind. Occasionally, the runners would quicken their pace to cross chasms of open road that offered no hiding place. Soon after the run would drop to the slow jog demanded by an exhaustion that seemed to draw them back towards the coast as they recovered their breath.

The sun had not yet risen above the distant ridge but the clamor of birds was beginning to fill the sky. Scattered patches of woodland that passed all too quickly echoed with the songs of the earliest lark, while the thin, exposed pastures hosted grazing sheep, too lazy to take heed of the murderers who rushed by. A raven squawked in a nearby bush, disturbed by the noise of the Egyptians as they ran. It sent a cold shiver through Yeshua, who was still convinced that all God's creatures were pointing the finger of guilt towards him and his brother as they fled for the anonymity of the town. Before the assassins, the silhouette of the Samaritan mountains was sharpening, as daylight was about to break. From behind, the Mediterranean haze pursued them along the dusty track that crossed the

Plain of Sharon. Gradually the climb towards the foothills began to take its toll on Egyptian limbs and the brothers' pace began to drop.

"Stop!" Yeshua panted. "Can you hear that?"

"Above the sound of your breathing?" Theudas gasped, "I wouldn't hear if they were chasing us on elephants!"

Yeshua held up his hand and gazed back along the track that had begun to wind itself around the contours of small hills, hiding itself from full view. "I thought I heard horses," the Egyptian heaved as he gathered his breath.

"Only because you're expecting to hear them," his brother replied. "They'll be lucky if they've found the bodies yet."

"We need to keep moving," said Yeshua, narrowing his eyes and facing east. "I don't want to take any chances."

Yeshua had been so obsessed with preparing for the worst outcome imaginable that it had become the *only* outcome imaginable. Every minute of his escape brought further disbelief that he was still alive. After countless further glances behind and several pauses to listen, the town of Narbata eventually unveiled itself through the widening gaps between hills that filled the view ahead.

"We're going to do it," Yeshua muttered to himself.

"Of course we are," Theudas puffed as they ran. "Ten minutes and we're there."

Yeshua turned to notice with gratitude that the coastal haze had, at last, visibly retreated. No one had been passed on the road, and the companions reached the little town before the sun's rays and prefect's horses.

The assassins circled through the dry landscape south of the town so as to enter from the east, as though they were journeying toward rather than away from Caesarea. Today was market day, leaving the brothers to mingle easily in the early morning crowds. The plan was simple. Having collected their supplies, they would make the two-day journey south to Joppa from where they could take their return voyage to Alexandria.

Still, it was too early to enter Narbata without suspicion so the brothers sat under a fig tree, out of sight from the town's eastern approach and hidden from the road behind the bumpy landscape.

"Er, Yeshua. Have you looked inside here?" Theudas was gazing into his newly acquired purse. "A week's wages!"

"So you're buying breakfast?" said Yeshua as his sweaty fingers explored the purse he carried. The coins were accompanied by a small piece of wood, which was brought out for inspection.

"What is it?"

"A figurine! Looks like a boy."

"Money?"

"Yeh, ten denarii, probably about the same as you."

"We are going to have such a party tonight."

"Let's get through today first." He paused, and caressing the coins he had robbed asked Theudas, "You okay?"

Theudas shrugged his shoulders, as though the inconvenience of killing someone had merely robbed him of a little sleep. "Ask me over a cup of wine this evening."

"They must have found the bodies by now. Do you think they'll know where we're going?"

"Yeshua! It could have been anyone from anywhere. We've done it. The prefect's bowels are bursting. Justice is served. Job done." With that, Theudas lay himself down, closed his eyes, and sighed.

"Don't tell me you're going to sleep!"

"We need rest. It'll help us to think straight."

"We're not in the clear yet."

"Yeh, well we can't do anything for at least an hour."

"Theudas! We are assassins. As far as Rome's concerned, we're murderers."

"Tired murderers." yawned Theudas, adjusting his back on his patch of stony ground. "Wake me up in an hour."

"You're not praying?"

"Suppose you're right." Theudas sat up and closed his eyes, "Lord of hosts, God of Israel, Almighty maker of heaven and earth. I beseech you, in your manifold and great mercy, close my brother's mouth and let me sleep." With that he reclined, placed his hands behind his head and after relaxing for a second, lifted his head just off the floor and added, "Amen."

Yeshua smiled, shook his head and returned his attention to the figurine of the young boy. Had he made an orphan of this boy? Whoever he was, he would weep many tears on account of Yeshua's deed. Before remorse could take root Theudas' snoring interrupted him. The Egyptian glanced at his younger brother, sleeping just as he had since childhood.

Eyebrows slightly raised, eyelids looking poised to lift, mouth open, his whole face relieved of all care and his limbs scattered at random. Yeshua sighed in envy and laid back to stare into the heavens.

The laughter of distant farmers and traders began to rise through the song of birds and the yawning of Theudas. The scent of fig leaves above, forced into transparency by the bright morning sky, fell upon Yeshua like a drug. As his breathing slowed, his spirit lightened. His brothers had been avenged. He didn't feel it yet, but at least he knew it. All that now remained was the journey home.

Sleep would not give itself so readily to Yeshua. The weight of those amour-laden bodies still weighed down upon him. The horror he felt as the dagger had slipped from his hand. The relief he had encountered as his right hand grasped the fallen spear. And his brother's rescue, redeeming himself from his apparent failure. He opened an eye to glance at Theudas who by now lay like a corpse himself. The sight carried Yeshua back to the moment that spawned this quest for vengeance. The sight of his older brothers' lifeless bodies in the temple precincts. The final kiss he placed on their foreheads. But their memory brought little relief from the turmoil he felt at taking life in return. The two incidents were entirely disconnected. If only he could link them in his mind he would feel relieved, justified, unburdened. But it was too early for these fatal events to be wed to one another, or for the Egyptian to be reconciled to himself. These thoughts were not for today, he decided as he attempted the descent into sleep. In his agitated state he threw himself on the mercy of the fig tree to bring shelter, calm and rest. But the comfort brought by the tree was shallow and short lived. It did not approve of the foreigners' actions, and yielded little to the assassin.

Yeshua rose from his unrest, seeking mental refuge instead in the practicalities that had now to be addressed. He concealed the swords in their rolled up cloaks, strapped and ready for carrying, and walked the several paces toward the ridge of a shallow hill. From here he could observe the business of the market, a mere five minutes' walk away. The sweat of his hurried journey had turned cold but still clung to his skin, texturing his limbs with goose bumps while the growing warmth of the day was as yet too weak to penetrate his garments. He stood and watched and shivered. Another nervous prayer was offered as the prospect of entering the town as a murderer dawned on him. It was time to move.

Yeshua tapped his brother's leg with his foot. "Feeling rested?"

Theudas screwed his eyes tight, drew an extended breath and puffed it out just as laboriously. "Mmmmmm" his voice spanned several pitches in random sequence. "What's for breakfast?"

"Prison food if you don't get a move on."

The two returned to the road and Yeshua tried to look as unlike an assassin as he could. He glanced at his brother who harbored no such concerns. The road surrendered readily to the heel of Theudas' sandals, which bore a conquering spirit through this piece of the Roman Empire. His feet crunched the gravel, as Adam's accursed foot would crush the serpent. His unshaven face bristled with the suggestion of recent heroics. His dark hair was reddened by the early sky that brought it to life. Even the garments he wore hung about him in admiration. Undaunted by the risk of capture, Theudas entered Narbata as though he were its liberator.

Yeshua did not share this optimism. "Sacks, food, water, then we're on our way."

"So you don't want breakfast?"

"We can eat outside the town. Let's just get a move on."

Narbata's market was just like any other. No purpose built square as in the larger cities. Just busy streets cluttered with stalls, every trader's voice dragged into disharmony by every other. Although Yeshua had no desire to linger in this place, there was something strangely welcoming about busy streets and human company.

The warm smell of fresh bread mingled with salted fish freshly brought in that morning. Children weaving their way through adults preoccupied with finding the best fruit, the finest wine, the choicest grain. Dozens of chickens waiting to be sold added their voice to the clamor, contributing to the anonymity that Yeshua so gratefully felt. Sunlight had still not penetrated the corner of the busiest streets where there stood a gathering of laborers who had so far failed to find their day's work.

Theudas stopped to collect the bread for his breakfast while Yeshua gathered fruit for the journey. Within a few minutes the companions were fully stocked. All that remained was a quick visit to the well to fill new skins for the long walk south.

As Yeshua inspected his fruit, the noise of the market traders was drowned beneath a nearby commotion. His bowels plummeted the moment his eyes lifted. Cavalry. The market was surrounded by at least fifty horsemen. Every escape route was closed off. A dark-skinned centurion dismounted and climbed onto a low roof.

"People of Narbata!" A hundred busied individuals immediately became a single anxious crowd. "People of Narbata. Early this morning two soldiers were murdered in Caesarea. Shepherds on the plain saw two men fleeing for this town." Expressions of horror echoed through the crowd, not so much at what *had* happened as at what *would*. "Your prefect, Pontius Pilatus, wishes it to be known that such acts of barbarism cannot be tolerated." With that, a grey-haired market trader, still clinging to an earthenware jar, was thrown to the ground beneath the centurion's platform. His face was full of pointless protest, but his eyes resigned to his fate. The chime of an unsheathing blade was followed immediately by the gasp of the spectators.

"It wasn't me . . ." he sobbed. Yeshua hid his eyes. The now trivial sound of the ornamented jug, almost unnoticed as it smashed onto the gravel, spoke just loudly enough to foretell the horror that would inevitably follow. The marketer repeated his sentence with more emotion, but it was cut short. A moist thud echoed around the market. After a moment's silence it was followed by another, and then a third and a fourth. The Egyptian's eyes opened to see the soldier picking up the severed head by its curly grey hair and lifting it for the crowd.

"Let it be known, if you harbor murderers you share their crime and will suffer their fate." He nodded at one of his soldiers, who brought forward another random crowd member. A young man, barely in his twenties, was dragged from the queue of would-be laborers and thrown onto the floor near the corpse of the market trader, his shattered jar and the reddening sand. His eyes declared that he was unable to comprehend what was happening to him. The crowd, still in shock, irrupted in a chorus of muted disbelief.

Yeshua couldn't bear to watch the atrocity and scanned the people, every one of them innocent of his crime. In an instant, the spirit of the crowd became visible: its younger members had not yet learned the futility of a hope that had abandoned their elders, but all had been overcome by the same dark silence. Even the children's previously carefree faces had aged an entire generation in a single moment. Their hollow gaze forced the Egyptian's eyes back towards the soldiers.

Yeshua found himself possessed by a physical urge to confess his crime, but his body along with his tongue were paralyzed by the spectacle before him. The executioner's sword was raised, but the soldier was distracted by a scuffle in front of him. A robed figure had burst through the mass and into the makeshift arena.

"Me for him," shouted the Pharisee. "Me for him!" As silence spread through the crowd, he lowered his voice for one last offer. "Me for him."

The centurion was as stunned as every other onlooker. This young Pharisee had momentarily seized control of the scene and glared up at the centurion in defiant humility. The executioner also looked up at his commander, who closed his eyes and threw his head to the right to gesture the laborer's release. His attention then turned to this Pharisee whose childlike eyes looked as though he had merely issued a mischievous dare. He promptly dropped to his knees before the executioner.

"You for him?" he smirked. The centurion descended the rough worn steps to ground level, looked at the lowered head of the substitute, and addressed the crowd. "No deal." With that, he mounted his horse, "Bloody Jewish market traders," he grinned as his feet found their place. "Is there nothing you people won't barter for?" The horses were gone as quickly as they had arrived, leaving the townsfolk to grieve their victim and celebrate their Pharisee.

Immediately the market became a place of wailing. The body of the fallen trader was swamped by companions, but one face remained painfully visible through the mass. A young girl, maybe ten years of age, was screaming. With one hand she caressed the chest of the severed corpse, the other clung to the side of her head. Screaming, screaming at the crowd, at the corpse, at the sky, at Yeshua. The girl's wailing penetrated the Egyptian's inner being, causing convulsions in his stomach. Yeshua's body forced his hands to his knees, his stomach tensed up against his will, and he vomited.

He turned and, grabbing his brother by the arm, picked his way through the crowd that swept against them, away from the screams, away from that girl. No words passed between them as they hurried towards the eastern gate of the town. Before they emerged from the market stalls that had now fallen silent, they realized that not every soldier had departed Narbata. A hundred paces away sentries had been positioned at their exit point, ready to question those leaving.

Theudas halted, screwed his face up and looked toward the sun. "Now what do we do?" Silence followed. Covering his eyes he looked back towards the center of town. He sighed, paused, and spoke again. "That man. You know it wasn't your fault."

For the first time since this incident, the brothers made eye contact. Yeshua let his eyebrows express what he thought of Thuedas' attempt to absolve themselves of this crime.

His little brother was undaunted. "It wasn't our fault: an eye for an eye. We have not spilt one drop of blood too much. That man died because of Roman cruelty. They killed him. We didn't."

"Great. So what do we do next?" asked Yeshua. "Avenge that market trader as well to balance the books?"

"Well," Theudas jested, "we are merchants!"

Yeshua grabbed Theudas by the shoulders, and bored his brown eyes into his brother's. "From now on, I killed both of those soldiers! Do you understand? It was I."

"Well, that's *almost* true" Theudas frowned in confusion.

"I'm serious." Yeshua shook him with covert violence. "If anything happens, if anyone asks us, it was me who killed them both. You had no part in this. Do you understand?"

Theudas looked vacant.

"Do you understand?" he repeated, trying to conceal his alarm from all but his brother.

"Yeshua!" Theudas looked embarrassed, and leaned forward to whisper. "I understand."

"The next thing we do is dump the swords," said Yeshua.

"Er—didn't you want to keep them? Souvenirs of revenge . . ."

"What do you think'll happen if we're caught with them here?" The elder brother frowned.

"Fine. Shall we visit the well?" They turned to head back towards the wailing.

"Yeshua? Theudas? . . . Shalom! What brings you this far inland?" The brothers were speechless at being recognized. "Come to see how your cotton is selling? Or have you been murdering soldiers?" A tall, full-bodied, red-faced man clutching a hook full of fish smiled at them quizzically before he laughed and continued. "Not the best welcome to Narbata! Come on, let's get out of here and celebrate being this far from the coast."

"Yudah," said Yeshua, as though he had no care in the world, "it's great to see you, but . . . what's all this about?" He gestured towards the sound of wailing? "Is Narbata always like this?"

"Not much trading here this morning. We can talk over breakfast." The Egyptians looked at each other and shrugged shoulders. "Come on," said Yudah, already disappearing into the crowd. "Come and see the house your cloth has built me!" They walked together through dusty streets still echoing with grief and distant wailing, towards a large house of grey stone turned into gold by the alchemy of morning sunshine. The dwelling was necklaced by a ring of palm trees that teased with the light above and bestowed gentle shade on the home below.

Yudah entered through his gate and sent his guests to sit in a small courtyard. "I won't be a minute." The garden excluded the eastern sunlight, but was designed to offer comfort to all who were invited in. Stone seats were positioned around a cistern containing water brought fresh from the well. This place retained the welcome aroma of the herbs that grew there, imposing a peace that only the most anxious guest could defy.

"Right," Yeshua whispered hurriedly, "we're on our way to Jerusalem to offer sacrifices."

"Oh that's convincing!" Theudas chuckled.

"So what do we say? Oh, we just popped in to murder some soldiers?" Theudas' face emptied itself of all expression.

Yeshua's thought was so frantic it was almost audible. He had failed to concoct an alibi before his host reappeared.

"Breakfast will be here soon," Yudah called, rubbing his hands on a cloth as he marched briskly across the terrace to take a seat next to his trading partners. "Now, did you see what just happened?"

"The execution?"

"All too common with this idiot as prefect." There was a warm familiarity to Yudah's voice. His greying beard and rosy cheeks combined with a body that had enjoyed no shortage of fine food and drink, brought a surprising depth of relief given all that had happened on so young a day. Yudah was a fine host who thrived on the company of others. He perched his excessive body on a low stonewall and leaned towards the brothers.

"Just let me say, I was horrified to hear about your brothers. Please send my sympathy to your Father. That prefect's determined to cause misery everywhere he goes. Still, at least his toilet will be seeing plenty of traffic this morning! Maybe justice is . . ." Yudah paused, and sent a serious but curious frown at his guests.

"What's that wrapped up in your cloaks?"

"Oh, it's . . ." Yeshua knew that there would be no fooling Yudah.

"Swords!" Theudas cut in with a flash of inspiration. Or so he thought. "We took them from the soldiers we killed before dawn," he laughed.

Yudah also laughed, allowing Yeshua to gather his thoughts as he smiled. "We were on our way to Jerusalem," he said "but I don't think we'll be getting there in a hurry now."

"How are things with you?" Theudas asked in a manner so far out of character that even a stranger would have noticed. He knew it, and his eyes attempted to chase after his words and stuff them back in his mouth.

You may as well have asked if we could change the subject, thought Yeshua. It was a sentiment carried on a glance that was not missed by their host.

"What *were* you doing in Narbata this early if you're traveling to Jerusalem? Have you just left Caesarea?" Yudah frowned. "And . . . what *have* you got in those packs?" The brothers exchanged another frown that rendered futile any further attempt to conceal the truth. Yeshua lifted his hands to mark the end of the charade.

"Yes, we left Caesarea long before dawn this morning," Yeshua confessed, leaving Yudah to work the rest out for himself. Every corner of the trader's friendly face was besieged with a confusion, which eventually gathered at the side of his mouth, where a mild but restrained grin was slowly taking form.

"Please don't tell me . . ." said Yudah, who paused again before composing himself. "But they were professional soldiers. You boys are traders."

"Angry traders," Theudas objected.

"Amateur soldiers," added Yeshua.

"No . . . Seriously," Yudah smiled as he shook his head. "You wouldn't do that." Yudah laughed. Then he stopped laughing. "You're not rebels. You're not violent. You're not desperate . . ."

"We're bereaved," Yeshua interrupted, looking a little offended. "Our brothers have been taken from us. An eye for an eye."

Yudah continued to shake his head. "This isn't you," he said, standing up and looking towards the sky. "You don't do this," he said to the brothers but addressed only himself. He turned to look at Theudas, who was losing the battle to contain his pride at the morning's achievements. "Your father's a rabbi," Yudah frowned, "a rabbi who preaches peace . . . He wouldn't support this." He looked back to the brothers, expecting their look to confirm his denials. Their demeanor forced him to pause. "You wanted revenge. And you took it."

Yudah was unable to conceal his admiration, "Mmmarvelous!" he declared with grave sincerity. Immediately the warmth returned to his face, "You'll be sure to let me know if I start to get on your nerves."

"We're on our way to Joppa," Yeshua explained, "but we weren't expecting to get trapped here."

"You really haven't thought this through have you, boys. Our prefect's going to be looking for you. He may be an atrocious prefect, but revenge is one thing he's good at. He excels at it! You've seen that with your own eyes."

"How could he possibly find us?" asked Theudas.

"Well, how long did it take me to force a confession out of you? At the very least you'll need to stay with me and hide until the guards have left. All I can say is that you're lucky you bumped into me." Yudah shook his head and grinned at the heavens. "What is your father going to say about this?" He looked back at the brothers, abandoned his grin and paused. "You're defying him."

The late morning conversation in Yudah's garden was interrupted by shouting from his gate. "Yudah, Yudah," a voice short of breath bellowed from beyond and sent panic bouncing around the warming stonework of the haven.

⟨3⟩

YUDAH WAS IN NO hurry. But then he never had been in a hurry of any kind and had gained too many pounds to start now. His eyes stayed with the brothers as he made an economic gesture towards his gate. "Now, let's see what trouble you've brought with you," he laughed, and touching Yeshua's shoulder, carried his hefty frame towards the commotion. It was more than the depth of his voice. The strength of Yudah's presence, like a tonic, continued to work its magic long after he had excused himself from their company. So present had he been to Yeshua, so inside this intolerable situation, and yet without condemnation or even shock, that a feeling of normality prevailed. Yeshua reclined, closed his eyes and, for the first time in an eternity, drew a breath unpolluted by fear.

Peace came likewise to the garden, with Yudah calming his new guest by waving his palms towards the floor. The conversation at the gatehouse was hurried but hushed, and Yeshua presumed that the agitated visitor was bringing news of events in the market place. The panic-stricken messenger, barely twenty years of age, looked awkward in his own body, which seemed far bigger than the person that rattled around inside it. His spirit and his manners of expression were no more under his control than was his physique, and all conspired to draw Yudah to share their panic. If there existed a negative version of all that their host embodied, it stood before him in the form of this young man.

"Well, we can't be blamed for not planning this part of our journey too well," Theudas yawned.

"Why's that?" asked Yeshua, still transfixed by the gatehouse drama.

"Er—because we never expected to be making it."

Yeshua turned to his brother and felt a burden lift as he chuckled through his nose.

18

"We shouldn't have pulled this off. We should be dead by now. Who knows what we've got to face next!"

"What have we started?"

"I don't know but if it's revenge you want then perhaps we should stick around and see it through"

"See it through?"

"Er—Look at them," Theudas threw his eyes across his motionless head towards the gate, as though Yeshua hadn't noticed the scene. "This morning we watched an innocent man die . . . There'll be repercussions, Yeshua. Look at Yudah!"

Yudah exuded confidence through every pore of his skin. He was clearly in authority over his conversation partner. His guest, already calmed, was now nodding carefully, Yudah waving his hands as though every object around him were awaiting his instruction. They were obviously not simply exchanging market place news.

"Yudah has always had a revolutionary streak about him, you know that. Who knows who he knows and what he might be suggesting? But we're in this now, it's our doing and we must honor our brothers by seeing this through."

"Seeing this through?" Yeshua repeated. "We've played our part in this. The violence started before us and it will end long after us. Our job is done. An eye for an eye."

"We may not have any choice," Theudas shrugged as Yudah returned from his conversation.

"Sorry about that, boys," smiled Yudah as he clapped his hands together. "Just getting an update on your handiwork. I look forward to hearing more about this. But first things first, what do you need?"

"Drink!" they replied in unison.

With that a young woman appeared, carrying a jug of water, several cups and a bowl of ripe fruit.

"You answer me before I call," Yudah nodded with satisfaction. The woman smiled but did not withdraw as would be expected of a servant. He placed his hand insider hers and the two of them broke into a smile. "You don't remember Miriam then?" asked Yudah, as his daughter took a seat beside him.

"But you are only ten years old!" Yeshua smiled, "or at least you were last time we saw you, which must have been years." He thought it best not to inquire after the whereabouts of her husband.

"Fifteen!" she smiled. The only memorable feature to have survived intact the passage to adulthood was her long, dark brown hair. Her face carried hints of a past beyond reach of Yeshua's consciousness. As she looked at him, he recalled her warmest trait. She had an air of mischief about her, poised always on the verge of a warm smile that promised to show itself at the next word to fall from your lips.

"Are you staying long?" she asked.

"No," said Yeshua, oblivious to the disapproval of Theudas. "We're heading back to Egypt at first light."

"Never mind," she smiled as her attention was drawn by Theudas' discomfort with his brother's hasty answer. "Hopefully it won't be another fifteen years before I see you again." With that she withdrew from their company, taking with her the smiles and attentions of all three men, before Yudah regained his more serious demeanor.

"Well, we have plenty of time, and you clearly need to spill your guts to someone so why don't you tell me the whole story?" He had looked through Yeshua's eyes and penetrated his Spirit.

Yeshua took a deep sip, wiped his lips and began. "You know my family, Yudah. My older brothers were always faithful to Moses and the Prophets. But it was only this year that we got as far as visiting Jerusalem. They wanted to offer sacrifices on the mountain where Abraham himself had consented to sacrifice his firstborn. They worshipped the God of Abraham, Isaac and Jacob. 'Adonai is our shield and stronghold,' were the last words Yotham ever said to me. But there was no divine protection from the soldiers hidden in the crowds."

"The crowds were the protesters, right?"

"Yeh, some protest to do with an aqueduct. The demonstration was outside the prefect's garrison, near to the temple, and we had to weave our way through the crowds to make it from the temple to the city gate. The prefect was treating the crowds to a pep talk. But . . . as we were trying to push our way through, he called a magic word that must have been a hidden command for his soldiers." Yeshua puffed out a long sigh as he shook his head.

"They were armed only with canes, hidden under their tunics." At this point Yeshua stopped, realizing he had recounted this event to no one but his father. Unable to continue, Theudas took over.

"I don't know how many they killed, I wasn't even there . . . Yeshua got separated in the crowd . . . He didn't find Yotham and Saul until it was all over." Theudas made several false starts before continuing. The only detail of this story that really mattered to Theudas was the outcome. It was all that interested him, and all he could recall. "He butchered our brothers. Our innocent brothers. Simple as that."

"How did your Father take the news?"

"As you'd expect. By the time we left he still hadn't eaten."

"What did he think of you coming here to do this?" Silence. "It goes against everything he always stood for."

"And still stands for," sighed Yeshua, shaking and then dropping his head in lament.

"So you came to Caesarea . . ." Yudah beckoned.

Theudas obliged. "A week ago. We watched the morning patrol for six nights, and then this morning . . ." He smacked his right fist into his cupped left hand.

"You can say that again," muttered Yudah, who then widened his eyes for a second and let out a controlled breath through his puffed out cheeks. "Didn't you think about what the prefect would do?" he frowned in thought, and smiled a humorless smile, teeth concealed, that expressed gentle disapproval.

"Why do you think we hit them in Caesarea? It could have been anyone from anywhere!"

Yudah chuckled. "Give your brain a chance, Yeshua. Think about what kind of man this prefect is. All he needs is an excuse to spill blood and the feast begins. He's not that choosy about whose blood, or how much of it."

Yeshua drew breath to answer his friend, but Yudah, wanting his point to stand, jumped in quickly by adding a veiled complement. "And targeting his own soldiers? I doubt that's been done to him before." The approval in Yudah's expression was immediately eclipsed by a more somber tone. "You have plenty of admiration here in Narbata, but there are also plenty who would like to see you crucified for what you did." He paused before continuing. "Can I make a suggestion?" Yudah took the silence as an affirmative. "Come to the synagogue this afternoon. Afterwards I'd like you to meet some friends of mine. One of them you'll already recognize!"

"The synagogue? Come on, you know we don't want anything to do with all that."

"A rabbi's sons afraid to go to a synagogue?"

"What, so we can listen to some hypocritical, self righteous egg-head bleating religious purity while the world crumbles around him?"

"If Yeshua goes into a synagogue the walls are likely to crack . . ." Theudas laughed.

"I think you'll find our synagogue a little different from what you boys are used to in Egypt, even in Caesarea. Narbata is a rebel town. And Kaleb, the Pharisee from the market place this morning, has just been invited to speak." One after the other, the brothers shrugged their shoulders in reluctant compliance. "Come straight back here afterwards, Miriam will let you in. I'll need to linger a while, and will bring a couple of friends back with me."

Yudah's synagogue was smaller than the one the brothers had attended. A square hall, each wall about four feet thick and twelve paces long, with a cobbled floor underfoot. Even with so many bodies crammed in, its cool was a welcome relief from the Judean heat. The long central benches were packed with men talking in low and serious tones. The women's end of the hall generated a more hurried brand of chatter, but all was swamped by applause as the young Pharisee entered. Whatever his status had been, this day had heightened it beyond measure.

The ruler of the synagogue stood and the congregation slowly quieted. On having everyone's attention, he uttered a brief, opening prayer, concluding with words, which the whole congregation knew by heart, words which today reached a new depth as the crowds voiced them as one, "For Adonai is our judge, Adonai is our ruler, Adonai is our king. He will save us."

Prayers concluded and the ruler turned to welcome the Pharisee to the platform. Kaleb, robed in dull white, was probably in his early thirties, but what he lacked in years he made up for in his presence. His eyes were bursting with a quiet energy that promised his listeners that, for better or worse, his coming words would evoke some kind of reaction. The attendant handed the scroll to Kaleb who in turn performed rather than merely read its contents, feigning disagreement with the prophet who penned them.

"*How beautiful on the mountains are the feet of the messenger who announces peace, who bring good news, who announces salvation, who says to Jerusalem, 'Your God reigns!'*"

Kaleb's voice was not nearly as cavernous as that of Yudah, but it was carefully furnished with a growl to maximize its authority. He read with dramatic poise and handed the scroll back to the attendant. A calm silence had seized the congregation as every eye was fixed upon the speaker.

"Today, this scripture has been turned inside out in front of your eyes!" He paced a few feet across the raised platform, as though he were exploring the Scripture itself from inside. "How detestable on these our mountains are the feet of those who bring *bad* news, who proclaim *vengeance*, who announce *oppression*, who say to us "*Babylon* reigns."

"Babylon?" whispered Theudas

"He's talking about Rome, you heathen," his brother replied.

Kaleb threw his head back as he proceeded to justify playing with the words of Holy Scripture. "How dare we speak of 'good tidings' on this day of wrath, when the blood of our brother cries from the ground? This ground, our ground. Right down to the grains of dust, for centuries we have cherished this land that Adonai gave to us. But is it really ours?"

He scanned the room to make sure that his listeners were hungry for his next words. Yeshua scanned also, and felt like the odd one out. "When it is trampled under the hoof of heavy horse. When its fruit is taken to fuel armies and lavish feasts, while our people go hungry, is it really ours?" The preacher paused, and his voice began to tremble as he gestured towards the market place. "When a pagan sword force-feeds it with our brother's blood? Is the land yet ours? We may live here but our hearts are still in exile, and our God does not seem to reign."

The congregation murmured to register their disgust at the truth Kaleb was highlighting. "When we see heavy taxes forcing farmers off their land, Babylon reigns. When pagan symbols are carried into our temple, Babylon reigns. When soldiers roam freely, forcing us to carry their loads, Babylon reigns. When they take an innocent life, they deface the image of our God, and Babylon reigns. When pagan sentries guard the gates of our town, Babylon reigns. When we trade with coins marked 'Caesar is Lord', Babylon reigns."

So young a preacher would not usually sail so close to the wind by seeming to contradict the words of a holy prophet. But Kaleb was using his current heroic status to full effect. He allowed silence to assert itself again, breaking it only to feed the hum that was filling the air. In a hushed and soft tone, he charged their expectation, "Brothers." After another pause he continued in a stage whisper. "There . . . Is . . . No . . . King . . . But . . . God." A wave of approval was rising rapidly, and with perfect timing Kaleb repeated the slogan with greater volume and passion, "There is No King but God."

The congregation again irrupted into applause, cries of "amen," and repeated shouting of this well-known slogan. Kaleb held a silence pregnant with phenomenal but restrained energy, frowning as he waited for the clamor to die down. "Babylon reigns?" He scanned the synagogue. "Babylon reigns?" he repeated, beginning to shake his head slowly as he slowly opened a floodgate of defiance. "Today I tell you this: Your God reigns. Our God reigns. There is no King but God."

The Narbatans again gave way to shouts, this time with the cry for liberty, "Hoshannah," finding its way into and occasionally above the clamor. Again, the preacher waited calmly until his voice could once more be heard.

"So where is his Kingdom? When will we see the Kingdom of God? When will our God reign in Jerusalem? When will the gods of Babylon bow before Adonai?

"People of Narbata, Israel's God is returning to claim his Kingdom. This land can no longer bear the weight that crushes it. He will not allow this present injustice to go unchecked. We are on the brink of a new era, a new age in which all will see that there *is* no king but God. And we enter this era by sacrifice and struggle and force. You and I must live and breathe God's holy law, so that we become the living enactment of his Scriptures. 'Your God reigns' . . . There is no King but God."

Yeshua's sheer discomfort at the Pharisee's message did not immunize him to Kaleb's charisma. The preacher was as riveted to his hearers as they were to him. He knew where he was going, and carried his congregation with him one step at a time. He was deeply connected to his listeners, communicating with far more than his words alone—but planting his words firmly in their hearts with the quiet force acquired either from his act of self-sacrifice or from some divine source. Whether this divinity was Adonai, the God of Israel or Hermes, the messenger of pagan gods, the Pharisee's eyes discarded their frown and searched the synagogue roof to re-establish contact with eternity. The gaze itself carried with it the promise of supernatural wisdom.

"Today we are still a nation, and today we have a King. How beautiful on the mountains are the feet of those who bring good news. Who say to Zion '*your God reigns*.' Whoever killed those soldiers in Caesarea brings us a reminder that our God reigns. Not that God will one day reign again. Not that God will reign in the future." The frown returned. "Isaiah says that God reigns, today, here and now. Caesar is not God! Adonai is God!" The preacher left more room for silence.

"Brothers! Take up your inheritance! His Kingdom is here. Our God reigns today!" At this point the frown lifted again, and Kaleb looked towards the heavens, apparently trawling his memory. "In the market place this week I saw a small boy with his mother. The boy was crying, shouting, stamping his feet. He wanted to eat one of the apples his mother had just bought. He was making such a fuss, that he could not hear his mother saying, 'Benjamin, Benjamin, Benjamin—here it is!' The child was so worked up that he could not see his mother holding the apple before him, and carried on crying, 'I want an apple.' All he had to do was reach out his hand and take it! The only thing making him wait any longer was his own tantrum."

"Friends. We long and we cry and we demand God's Kingdom. But he is holding it out in front of us. All we need do is take it. He has already given it to us. We must simply take it. Our God reigns!" Kaleb paused to allow his illustration to percolate.

"Babylon has spilt innocent blood in our town today. And this afternoon . . ." Kaleb paused, drawing deep breaths to gather his emotion. ". . . This afternoon, we hear he has done the same in the towns of Dor and Aphek." Gasps of disgust echoed around the synagogue, while the Egyptian brothers cast each other a despairing glance. "Brothers. Here, now, today, the lives of our oppressors are being taken. On our own doorstep the soldiers of Rome are being taken. The might of Babylon is challenged. The Kingdom of God is coming. Not everyone can attack a soldier, but I support those who do." The congregation remained silent. "The centurion says that those who support these people must share their fate. Then let us all share it together."

Across the synagogue a number of heads nodded quietly. Yeshua, terrified though he was by the implications of this Pharisee's rant, found himself reluctantly warming to Kaleb if not to his message. He looked down at his own fidgeting fingers, only to discover in his hands the figurine of the small boy. Whoever it represented, this carving undermined Yeshua's confidence that the morning's deeds were worthy of anyone's support. The Egyptian was transported back to the market place, and for a moment the screams of the grieving child swamped the preacher's own voice. Kaleb's message brought little comfort for his hyperactive conscience.

Regardless of how convincing his message was, Kaleb's oratory skills, combined with the selfless part he had played in this day's horror, had succeeded in keeping the crowd hooked on his every word. He approached his conclusion with measured rhetoric.

"When we came here this afternoon, did we come singing 'Caesar is our judge, Caesar is our ruler, Caesar is our King and Caesar will save us'? Children of Abraham, throughout your lives you have sung this hymn of Isaiah. It is part of who we are. Allow it now to beat its rhythm through your being, as we celebrate together, for . . ." with that, he lifted his hands and with one voice the congregation filled the synagogue with familiar words,

". . . Adonai is our judge, Adonai is our ruler, Adonai is our king. He will save us."

Kaleb's was the right message for the right time. A people whose anger and despair was an open wound had heard what they wanted to hear: a call, issued in word and deed, to defiance and sacrifice, with the promise of divine blessing. Adonai's endorsement of the Pharisee's message had been witnessed in his deliverance at the market place. For Yeshua, the atmosphere was as stifling as the afternoon's thick humidity. As the service ended Yudah disappeared into the crowd while the brothers pushed their way out to seek the peace of his garden.

The Egyptians returned to the welcome of Yudah's daughter, Miriam. "Thank you," said Yeshua as she gestured them to enter. Theudas' attempt to conceal his yawn was no more successful than Miriam's attempt to conceal her amusement at it. But this wordless exchange released the brothers from the lingering influence of that pharisaic frown. The weight of the day's events that pressed down on these Egyptians, whilst not being removed, was nevertheless lightened by the atmosphere of Yudah's home and its hostess. But Miriam offered no escape from the realities that crowded in on them, which only made her comfort all the more valuable.

"I haven't seen Yotham and Saul since I was a child, but I remember them well . . ." Miriam said warmly as she touched Yeshua's shoulder, ". . . and I treasure that memory. I can only imagine how you must feel . . ." She dropped her head. "How your father must feel." She lifted her gaze to Yeshua. "How is he?"

Ely of Alexandria was distraught at the loss of his elder sons, and saw the vengeful quest of Yeshua and Theudas as the loss of his younger sons. He had begged them not to leave Alexandria before having had chance to grieve properly, but Ely's pleas were ignored. You can't spend your whole life preaching about justice, Yeshua had reasoned, and then complain when your sons go in search of it. Justice would be the gift that Ely would receive on his sons' return to Egypt.

"Not well," Theudas answered, jolting his elder brother out of the thoughts that had left Miriam's question unanswered.

"Sorry," said Yeshua as he shook the thoughts from his head. "He'll be okay when we get home. He'll know that justice has been done and his grief will be lessened."

"Well," she smiled provocatively, "when you go back to Alexandria, be sure to take *our* love as well as *your* justice." For a moment, her smile evoked in Yeshua the discomfort that only a prophet could awaken. "Now!" she grinned, having noted their relief at escaping the synagogue. "After surviving the sermon of Kaleb the Pharisee, I assume you're both ready for the vine of Yudah?" Miriam's question was accompanied by a smirk of sympathetic frustration with the sermon she hadn't heard, although she looked as though she had endured it a thousand times before. Her smirk became a smile as she withdrew to bring refreshments.

Furnished with a cup of wine, the brothers found their garden bench and breathed relief at escaping the commotions of the outside world. Miriam perched herself lightly on a large stone, pulled a jasmine leaf towards her nose and inhaled as though her true life-energy were contained in the plant. Although mesmerized by the sight, Theudas was unable to restrain his tongue.

"Yeshua, how come she's allowed to miss the synagogue and we're not?" he grinned.

"You sound like you're talking to my father!" she smiled.

"He sounds more like he's talking to ours!" Yeshua cut in.

"Theudas! If you went because you were forced," she added, "perhaps you shouldn't have gone at all!"

"Maybe," he laughed. "But I'm asking about you! What are you doing, here, waiting upon us? The whole town's in crisis?"

She eyed the brothers, content to say nothing immediately. She allowed a lark singing beyond the courtyard's walls to punctuate their conversation as though she had pre-ordained it. "Someone needs to look after our liberators," she grinned, unconvincingly.

"Miriam," Theudas tried again. "What *are* you doing here?"

The woman's energy left her with Theudas' question. She took another breath of jasmine, emptied her lungs and screwed up her eyes as though staring into the sun. "Believe me," she said, "it's a long story, and you have more pressing matters to discuss—or at least you will when my father returns!" She stood, faced away and lifted her head. Yeshua shook his head at his brother before Miriam turned again to speak softly to them whilst shaking hers. "Don't get dragged any further into our troubles here." With that, she excused herself from their company.

"How do you feel now?" asked Yeshua after a moment, not forgetting his brother's invitation to ask this question again once wine had appeared.

"Bloody stupid."

"I'm not talking about Miriam, you pagan. I'm talking about this morning. You remember, we killed a couple of soldiers, a few more people were killed as a result." Yeshua's laugh was devoid of any joy. "Can you remember that far back?"

"I don't know . . . " he shrugged and frowned.

"Well get your mind out of your loincloth!"

"I don't feel anything." Theudas grinned, and then shut up. Yeshua knew the best way to keep his brother talking was not to respond. Silence was intolerable to Theudas, and he broke it after only a couple of seconds. "I thought I might feel relieved, or guilty, or something. I just don't feel anything." Yeshua still refused to respond, and after a pause Theudas continued. "I guess it's because we're still in the middle of this. Sitting here in the same luxury we enjoy at home. But really . . ." he glanced at his elder brother and paused, ". . . we're at the eye of the storm. Yudah will be back soon with his bandit friends, probably with some scheme to get us crucified for the good of Israel."

"While Yudah watches on with admiration you mean." Theudas' face contorted at his older brother as Yeshua continued. "He's a great guy but he's only ever been an armchair revolutionary. He likes the idea of rebellion, probably as a distraction from his real life. It probably reminds him of his roots."

"That's hardly fair!"

"Yeh, well look around you Theudas. His father was a farm laborer. You and I were born into our comfort; Yudah built his from nothing. A real revolutionary does not build this life for himself." Yeshua used his eyes to point around the garden. "Yudah's genuine enough, and he's well connected. But in his heart he's no rebel."

"Well, I'm glad about that. And I'm certainly glad we bumped into him."

"It's who we bump into next that bothers me." In his mind, Yeshua scanned the countless weathered faces he had seen in the synagogue, wondering how many brigands were baying for Roman blood. Or was it his blood they wanted? His mind's eye settled only onto Kaleb and his one memorable sentence. He sighed to himself before continuing. "We have caused too many deaths . . . in Aphek, in Dor . . . in Narbata."

"Well, our escape route's cut off anyway. You may as well accept it. We're still in the thick of it. I think that's why I still don't feel anything," he added, with another yawn. "Except tired."

4

THE WARMTH OF A booming laugh told the brothers that Yudah had returned with company. His arm was on the back of his companion who emerged almost reluctantly into the light of the garden. A figure who had to stoop as much as Yudah to pass through the archway leaned back as he walked forward.

"Yeshua, Theudas, this is Amram." Yudah's companion was impossible to age, but had the look of someone younger than his appearance suggested. In fact, he seemed to have missed an appointment with his grave. Hades evidently did not consider this too much of an inconvenience. The pursuit of Amram was clearly not worth any expense of energy. He would surely find his way back to the angel of death soon enough of his own accord. Amram eyed the brothers, revealing an ill-favored complexion restrained by dark hairs poised to turn grey at any moment. His smile, though requiring minimal effort, revealed a missing front tooth. Its absence cast upon that smile a trace of warmth that might otherwise have remained undetectable. "The finest marksman in the province," Yudah boomed, handing his friend a large earthenware cup of wine, "when he hasn't been drinking."

Amram released a gutsy belch as he extended his right hand to Yeshua and then to Theudas. A few silent convulsions in Amram's throat and chest passed before his voice was freed to greet them.

"Good work this morning, boys," he grinned before returning to a frenzy of silent belching.

"An archer? With which army?" asked a wide-eyed Theudas.

"Seventeenth legion, under Publius Quinctilius Varus."

Immediately Yeshua's mind raced back to the fireside stories of his father's legionary friend, Caius. This was a legion wiped out in ambush by Germanic tribes. "Were you in Germania?" he asked in awe.

On seeing that Yeshua knew what this meant, he simply replied, "Indeed I was. And I'm pretty sure, I'm the only one that's not still there!"

"He can knock a sparrow off its perch at a hundred paces," said Yudah with friendly pride.

"And that's just with my breath!" added Amram as a prelude the next round of belches.

Yeshua wondered how a professional soldier had become anti-Roman. Had he been a deserter? Or perhaps regarded as such? Had he been spurned by the Romans when he returned from the front as a sole survivor? His mind was full of questions that he dared not ask. Yet, despite this unspoken curiosity, the atmosphere of the garden remained light, bringing further but still much needed comfort to the brothers. No secrets were hidden. Yeshua was surrounded by people who not only knew of his escapades, but who regarded the morning's action as normal, perhaps even commendable. This awareness was deeply comforting. So too was the knowledge that the company who took the news of this assassination in stride were not insane or bloodthirsty criminals, nor were they altogether strangers. It was a comfort superficial and short-lived, and although the Egyptian knew this, it was welcome for as long as it lasted.

Eventually a pause in the conversation, brought about by Amram and Yudah lifting their cups to their mouths in coincidental unison, inexplicably drew everyone's attention to the gatehouse. Another familiar figured appeared as if on cue.

"Kaleb!" Yudah moved from his seat with his oversized equivalent to a leap. The host's free arm extended toward the Pharisee's left shoulder.

Kaleb, radiating untold energy and warmth, acknowledged Yudah and graced his host with formality, but made straight for Yeshua and Theudas as though he were being freshly acquainted with old friends. "Brothers! As I said at the synagogue, you have my support," the Pharisee smiled.

"But you! This morning! You should be dead!" said Theudas with deep admiration.

"Well, Romans are easily confused," he chuckled dismissively, but noticed the momentary lift in Amram's eyebrows. "Most revolutionaries nowadays don't go for military targets," he grinned at the archer.

Yeshua tempered his response with calm. The Pharisee's charisma had immediately overcome his younger brother, but from Yeshua it evoked as much caution as wonder. "We're not revolutionaries."

"Well, whatever you are, you have acted for the sake of justice. What are your plans?"

"Our plans are to enjoy Judean wine on this fine summer evening, in this fine company."

"And rightly so!" laughed the Pharisee. Kaleb's eyes bored into those of Yeshua with an intensity that, whilst partly unwelcome, brought with it an assurance, a confidence that the God of heaven and earth was silently pledging his allegiance. "This wine will bring you the worthiest hangover. But what are your plans when that hangover lifts?"

Yeshua glanced at Theudas and lost his grin. "Home," he announced, "with justice for our brothers and our father."

"Which brothers?" the Pharisee pushed, glancing around at all who were present. "And which Father?" he laughed, as he raised his eyes to heaven. Yeshua was overcome by the sheer weight carried by so few words, so lightly spoken.

"Yeshua doesn't worship the God of Abraham," Yudah interjected.

"But he does seek justice?" quizzed the Pharisee. "And whatever you worship, violence begets violence." Kaleb fastened his eyes again upon Yeshua, who under other circumstances may have given way to their charm. The Egyptian's current state however, left him only too aware of the mortal consequences this conversation might have. Still, he remained overawed by the realization that the Pharisee's heroic deeds were a reaction to the deeds done by his own hand that very morning. Kaleb's searching eyes had penetrated the deepest recesses of the Egyptian's mind. "Your action has resulted in five more deaths . . . So . . . what must you do?"

"We must do nothing!" said Yeshua with a smile that could barely hide his growing fear. He scanned the others to assess how much authority the Pharisee commanded in this miniature congregation.

"Careful," said Amram with a grin. "Don't quote scripture at Kaleb. He'd have you for breakfast . . ." He paused mid-sentence to allow air through his windpipe. The pause was long enough to make Theudas restrain himself from completing the sentence using the very words with which Amram eventually concluded, ". . . if he wasn't fasting."

"Ah, but this is a Rabbi's son!" laughed Yudah with his hand now on Yeshua's shoulder, apparently stirring them up for the contest but lightening the atmosphere as he did.

"Theudas and I just want to get back home. We have lost our brothers. We have avenged them. 'An eye for an eye.' For us it is the end of the story."

"There are plenty in Israel who would disagree." Amram's voice echoed out of his cup as he looked and spoke into it.

"Are you going to stop us leaving?" asked Yeshua, looking at the three men who had begun to look menacing, at least to Yeshua.

"It's cavalry that stand in your way. Not your friends," answered Yudah, in as kindly a tone as he could summon up.

Kaleb leaned forward and continued in the sympathetic vein of his host. "I understand you are grieving. But you must know that you are not alone in your grief . . ." The sympathy felt merciless to Yeshua. The Pharisee spoke gently, calmly. "What those Romans did to your brothers was unspeakable. But have you thought about your brothers here in Judea? Do you know what those Romans are doing to the people who live here? For you, the prefect's actions were tragic. But we," he lifted his arms to his sides, "we live with this tragedy day in, day out. Yudah brought you to the synagogue today so that you could feel something of it for yourselves."

Yeshua looked at his brother who was clearly open to the idea of hearing more from Yudah and his guests. Yeshua was having none of it, but had no desire to debate with a zealous Pharisee whose intent clearly ran beyond winning an argument. "I understand what you're saying. But we've played our part. We've relieved you of two soldiers . . ."

"And robbed us of five countrymen," interrupted Amram.

"Your prefect did that, not us!"

"And why did he do that? . . . Because of your violence," the Pharisee pressed.

"So what you're suggesting is peaceful?" Yeshua asked Kaleb. He restrained himself from asking why the Pharisee had made no reference to peace in his sermon, when that seemed to be the whole point of the scripture he had read.

"Peace is the fruit of justice," Kaleb mused.

Amram belched.

"If we move against the heathens, and move now, God will honor our commitment and come to our aid." The Pharisee's words hit Yeshua with the force of a sledgehammer. The Egyptian was well accustomed to fierce rabbinical arguments over the finer points of Scripture, over the interpretation of Psalms, and the application of Jewish Law. But those debates had taken place amongst privileged Jews, in the comfort of multi-cultural Alexandria. This present exchange of views was not for the sake of better understanding, nor of winning a debate. It was not taking place amongst wealthy scholars, nor in a political backwater. This was a scriptural debate in an oppressed land, amongst aggrieved rebels with violent intent. The Egyptian knew plenty about the text, but nothing of the present context. Who knew where such a debate might lead? He held his tongue.

"Kaleb moved against the heathens this morning, and God came to his aid. It's happening under our noses," Yudah declared.

Neither Yeshua nor Theudas were able to make much sense of what Kaleb might be suggesting, nor of what might be proposed if the conversation continued. Kaleb clearly had a definite set of plans in mind, and seemed to be withholding them while he tested the water to see if the Egyptians would support him. Yeshua's deep uneasiness was impossible to hide, and he hoped that their obvious reluctance to consent to any further violence would be enough to show that they would not be suitable recruits for Kaleb's scheme, whatever it was.

"No one's going to stop you leaving." Kaleb's sympathetic warmth displaced his debating-frown, and began to lighten the atmosphere. "But you must leave in the knowledge of what you've started here. We have to live the consequences of your vengeance!"

"In that case, we thank you for all the kindness you have shown to us . . . kindness we do not deserve . . . and we're sorry for any trouble we've caused, but we must leave in the morning." Yeshua's resolve was intended to appear insurmountable.

Theudas took his brother by the arm and addressed him quietly. "Are you sure about this? We'll never get past the cavalry without being caught."

"Then we'll just have to be careful."

Yudah eyed the archer and the Pharisee before warning the brothers. "If you leave at dawn and stay off the road there might be a small chance of you making it out."

Amram said nothing, but his carefully placed snigger was articulate. He knew well enough about how soldiers worked, and did not need to spell this out to the brothers. Yeshua, however, would not be persuaded to stay.

"Kaleb, say something scriptural!" Yudah commanded, ever trying to keep a light atmosphere.

"Shalom!" said Kaleb, "I hope to see you again soon," he nodded with apparent foreknowledge.

❧

Singing seabirds entered so conspicuously into Yeshua's dream that they carried him rudely out of it. He sat up in bed as the voice of Yudah echoed along the corridor. "Boys, hope you're fully rested."

The brothers left Yudah's home with his best wishes and ample food and water to see them through the remaining two days' journey south to the Mediterranean port of Joppa. The northern wall of Narbata formed a boundary of Yudah's property, and the brothers lowered themselves carefully down the rope that brought their feet into contact with the dusty earth. They bowed their heads in gratitude towards Yudah, who saluted them from the town wall. Within seconds they had disappeared from his sight, into the bumpy terrain that stretched towards the north and east.

The early morning landscape was enlivened by the nighttime humidity that still clung to the ground. "So, you think we'll make it to Joppa?" asked Theudas.

"Who knows, but if we'd stayed around those guys long enough we certainly wouldn't have."

The brothers pushed south for half an hour, deliberately staying off the main track towards the town of Aphek so as to avoid any attention from the town's sentries. As they sank further into the wilderness, they appeared to be borne hopelessly along with the tide of circumstance. The small, steep hills and dips of the landscape became a hostile ocean, as though the waves of a stormy sea had solidified into rocky mounds coated in sand. The young girl's screams echoed through Yeshua's mind as he walked, and he tried to expel them by whispering to himself the number of steps he took to climb each rise.

Half an hour's hurried march had carried the brothers less than a mile south and left them panting for breath. They joined the main road before the shadow of the mountains had retreated eastwards across it. The relative ease of the road made their journey infinitely more agreeable. As their nerves began to settle and their breathing became lighter, they resumed their conversation.

Theudas was relieved at having escaped Narbata, but for the first time voiced his anxiety about making it to Joppa. "Have you worked out how we're going to get into Aphek yet if it's guarded?" he asked, with no expectation of a worthy reply.

"No. But we can't let ourselves be drawn any further into this. You saw what kind of people these were. I don't know if you were aware of the danger we were in."

"Well, we're certainly in danger now."

"At least we're free to deal with our own problems. At Yudah's we would have found ourselves sucked into something beyond our control."

"Yeshua! This whole thing is beyond our control." Yeshua offered an expression that conceded the point. "We had no idea what we were starting when we came here. And Yudah was right. We didn't think it . . ." Noise from the road behind silenced the brothers. A bottomless pit opened up in the depths of Yeshua's stomach. The brothers turned to see two armor-clad horsemen followed by a small dust cloud. The Greek command could be heard clearly enough as it thundered across the four hundred paces that stretched out between them. "Wait!"

"I think it's time to run," said Theudas as the brothers walked backwards with increasing speed towards the cover offered by the hills. Dropping their packs at the foot of a nearby palm tree, they broke into as much of a sprint as the bumpy terrain would allow. They scrambled up the first sand hill in full sight of their pursuers, sliding down the other side to leave a column of dust confirming their position. Ahead of them, the hills only got taller and they realized that they were not going to outrun the cavalrymen unless the terrain forced them to dismount.

The sound of beating hoof was closing in at an alarming rate. Yeshua pointed towards the route where they would be unable to follow. A near impossible climb for the brothers would bring them again within full view of the soldiers. As they neared the top, Yeshua glanced behind him. As he had planned, the soldiers had dismounted and were now continuing the chase on foot. They were a good twenty seconds behind and nicely laden with armor and sword. He and Theudas disappeared over the second ridge. Now that the horses had been abandoned, they made for the shallowest route through the rocky ocean.

Yeshua gestured left and so the brothers doubled back, racing through the deep hollows between the tiny hills. Staying out of sight also kept the soldiers out of theirs, but the Egyptians took the absence of sound as a good sign. A mere three minutes of running through these foothills had left the brothers battling for breath. Having climbed a ridge facing back towards the road, they tried to conceal themselves in the long, thin grass and locate the soldiers. Nothing.

Looking south, the ground flattened into a patch of greenery that crowded around a small stream. The priceless cover of trees was a hundred paces away, just a few seconds of sprinting. The brothers remained motionless. They heard no sound above their own heavy breathing. Had the soldiers given up the chase? Surely they could not have escaped so easily. From the top of their hill they expected to see the cavalrymen come into view at any moment. Yeshua's breath returned, but the fearful pounding in his ears remained. The brothers lay quietly, scanning all directions. The soldiers could have given up the chase and returned to the road, or they could be within fifty paces. They waited.

Theudas gestured towards the open ground ahead of them with a face that wore a question. The brothers looked towards the trees, then back at each other with an unexpected grin, scanned the horizon again for soldiers and rising dust, nodded at each other and moved. But as they slid down the steep slope, they fell helplessly towards and in full view of the approaching cavalrymen.

The soldiers had returned to their horses and emerged from the small ravine on the brothers' left, fuelled now with arrogant superiority. The horses trotted forward with ease to arrive at the foot of this hill at the same moment that the brothers ground to a halt on their backsides.

"Good morning," said Theudas, reclining on his elbows in the midst of a sandy haze, looking up at the soldiers with a defiant smile.

"Not for you," came the soldier's reply as he drew his sword and prepared to dismount. That heart-stopping metallic chime had lost none of its terror for the brothers, but Yeshua's heart had ceased pounding.

So this is how it was destined to end, he thought. Death at the hands of Roman cavalry, who finally would have taken seven lives in return for only two troops assassinated in Caesarea. He felt for his dagger. The slim chance of fighting his way out consumed him. He did his best to look compliant to the soldier, whose superiority remained unquestionable.

The arrest was interrupted by the sound of a loud hammer blow, the dull thud of metal striking metal. The soldier's arrogant air was displaced by a look of sheer confusion, as he leaned forward involuntarily. What was that noise? What had robbed the soldier of his superiority? Within two heartbeats there was another blow, again the identical sound of a heavy, muffled metallic strike. This time it was followed immediately by a deep but distant belch from the western ridge. The second soldier fell from his horse, a long wooden shaft protruding from his back. A third metallic thud struck his hunched-over companion from the saddle to join him on the ground. Again, a belch echoed from the western ridge.

A MRAM HURRIED DOWN FROM the ridge. Still amused by the audacity of Theudas, he looked him in the eye, "Good morning?" he laughed. "Best you boys make for that there hill while I clear up this little mess." He did not wait for the brothers' consent before setting about his fallen victims as though it were his daily routine. On seeing that one of them was not dead he adopted a more serious tone. "Go!" he growled, nodding again towards the hill. The brothers, still stunned, complied without word.

The Egyptians hurried away in silence until Theudas could contain himself no longer. "Do you think tomorrow we might make it as far as breakfast before killing any soldiers?"

Yeshua sighed and shook his head. "It looks like we might be spending the autumn here in Judea after all."

"Amram must have been following us all the way from Yudah's house!" said Theudas, before succumbing to the gravity of his own observation.

Yeshua shook his head as the realities began to sink in. "They all knew this was going to happen! They let us go, *knowing* this would happen." The brothers both glanced back at Amram. No wonder he knew what he was doing, he had probably been planning his attack all night. "What was I thinking? I just wanted to get us home." He stopped near the top of the appointed hill and turned his head towards the sea. A full day and night had not granted them much distance from the coast. "Maybe we should try to get back through Caesarea. We could be on a boat by this afternoon."

"Yeshua. We've tried the safest option and look what happened. We're not going anywhere."

"I don't like this," said Yeshua with a grim determination to do something if only he could think of what that something might be. "We're as captive to our allies as we are to our enemies." He paused for a moment to gather breath as the climb continued. "I'm not sure who's toying with us more. The sooner we can get away from all of them the better."

"But that's just it!" Theudas argued. "We are trapped. Like you say, by our friends as much as our enemies." He looked over at his brother. "And for now I know who'd I'd rather be with."

Yeshua exhaled slowly and turned to carry on up the hill. On reaching the top the Egyptians sat together, looking out towards the coast. "Look at that." Theudas pointed down across the plain towards Caesarea. "Not a single ship has left the port. We're stuck here."

"We're not stuck! We can see the coast, and walk to it from here. We don't have to climb walls or dig tunnels. It's there. We can walk straight . . ."

"But every soldier between here and there is looking for us!" Theudas grabbed his brother's arm. "Looking for you and me, brother. And there are thousands of them."

"But look at the area they have to cover. We could go north and board a vessel to take us to Joppa. They'd have to be extremely lucky to get anywhere near us."

"So how lucky were they this morning, when they found us within an hour of us trying to leave?"

"We'll just have to stay off the road. It'll take us longer but we could do it. Why not? If we just leave now?"

"I know you just want to get home. And I know why. But if you were in your right state of mind you wouldn't be suggesting this." Theudas took his brother's silence as a sign that he was beginning to accept their fate. "When I think of how carefully you wanted to plan our attack in Caesarea, what you're suggesting now sounds like insanity. It's not the same person speaking."

Visibly, energetically, silently, Yeshua cursed at the situation in which the brothers now found themselves. Theudas was right. The attack had been planned so carefully, but their escape? It could hardly have been planned.

"Until yesterday you were in control of this quest. Today this quest is controlling us. Be patient, for our father's sake! Patience is now our safest route home."

"I don't want to be sucked into some hair-brained, half-thought-out, anger-fuelled gang of rebels," he said. "You heard Miriam. If we're patient, we'll find ourselves caught up in something we'll never escape."

"You don't know that for sure," Theudas remarked. "Amram has just saved our lives. As far as I'm concerned that's good news. Now, our journey here has made us dependent on other people, whether we like it or not. And of all the people to choose, Yudah is a lifelong friend and Amram has saved our lives."

"And followed us, knowing that we were walking into a death trap," said Yeshua, still amazed that his brother had not seen this. "Whatever they might be to us, they have not been honest with us. They are toying with us."

"No. I'm sorry," Theudas argued, "they tried to talk us out of running away, and it's you that wouldn't listen to them."

Offering wisdom was far preferable to Yeshua than receiving it. Nor was he accustomed to receiving it from his younger brother. Unable to concede verbally that his brother might be right, he allowed his silence to do the job, before eventually turning to Theudas and nodding.

"Strangers in a strange land," said Yeshua. "Not really the kind of thing a son of Abraham would say when in Israel!" The brothers smiled and lay back on the crest of the hill, wondering what kind of eruption was building below them. Whatever fate was to befall them, Yeshua was beginning to accept that for now it was beyond his control. As he stared up into a sky as empty as his future and his thoughts, he closed his eyes and attempted to escape into sleep.

Images of yesterday's victims flashed across Yeshua's consciousness, joined by the horsemen whose victims they had so nearly become. The cold rhetoric of Kaleb's oration combined with the warm embrace of Yudah's greetings. The screams of a grief-stricken peasant girl merged with the tears of the boy represented by the figurine. The gaunt image of Amram appeared in his mind, whilst not bringing enough comfort to free his troubled mind, it nevertheless released him from the traumas of the Egyptian's full consciousness. The voices in his head overcame other sounds around him, but weaving its way through the succession of pictures that formed the beginnings of a dream, was a single, disturbing constant. A snake, that now paused and recoiled, was ready to bite. The Egyptian was saved from the serpent's attack only by the most unexpectedly welcoming belch as it thundered like a volcano from below. Yeshua sat up from his brief dream to hear his brother's voice.

"Ah, the sweet sound of our salvation," said Theudas as he scrambled to his feet. Yeshua followed his brother downhill before his consciousness had fully returned.

The three assassins met at the foot of the slope, along with two horses, a large bundle, and the brothers' belongings.

"Can you boys ride?"

"We can ride donkeys," Yeshua suggested in reply.

"Do you know what the Parthians call these creatures?" asked Amram, as he threw a blanket over one of the horses.

"Er, Horses?" asked Theudas.

Amram over-pronounced each syllable of his answer. "Mountain donkeys," he declared. "And we're off to the mountains now, so best you make the most of your first lesson."

Theudas addressed Amram, "Yeshua. Do you get the feeling Amram could see this coming and just didn't say anything?"

"Some people just won't be told," said Amram with a grin.

"Where are we off to then?" asked Yeshua, struggling to sound indifferent.

"Somewhere safe," was not a deeply reassuring reply. "We're going into the hills that border Galilee. It'll give you boys some time to adjust to reality."

"And who else is going to be there?"

Amram returned to a few moments of belching before responding. "Oh, one or two familiar faces, a couple of strange faces, and if the Pharisee turns up then you'll have someone who's both familiar and strange."

Amram's clear fondness of the brothers was priceless for Yeshua. Given the events of that had brought them to their current position, he could still not bring himself to trust the archer properly. But any other brigand friends of Yudah they would come to meet in the hills would be unlikely to match Amram's abilities and experience, and the respect these things commanded. To have him on side reassured Yeshua that they need not expect death at the hands of hill-dwelling bandits. Still, the recollection of the look upon Amram's face as he dealt with the fallen soldiers was enough to prevent the brothers from asking him about what he had done to the survivor. There was a seriousness about Amram's character that neither of the brothers nor even Amram himself were keen to access. But Yeshua was compelled to press questions about their fate. "What's the plan?" he asked.

"*The* plan?" laughed Amram. "There are as many plans as there are people. This whole thing would be much easier if there was such a thing as *the* plan. At the moment, everyone has his own plan. And none of them are likely to work."

"Does Kaleb have a plan that might work?" Yeshua inquired, before voicing his disapproval of the Pharisee, "Apart from stirring up violence using scriptures that cry for peace?"

Amram's appreciation of the comment could be heard through his dutiful counter to it. "The Pharisee's charm doesn't work on you does it! But look at what happened yesterday . . . Who knows . . . he might be right."

"About what?"

The question seemed to have dragged Amram from some kind of slumber. He looked the brothers in the eye and sighed. "Kaleb's convinced that we should be able to gather enough people to get rid of the Romans from Jerusalem. They only have a couple of thousand soldiers in the entire province. Technically he's right. If all the tribes of Abraham unite . . ."

"What?" Theudas laughed.

"He's convinced that he's got God on side, and that a resistance movement will snowball as it approaches the capital."

"When was the last time there were snowballs in Jerusalem?" asked Theudas with a frown almost identical to Kaleb's, although on the face of the merchant it suggested a lack rather than an excess of certainty.

"It's his plan, not mine. But I tell you what, boys. That man's faith is so strong you could eat your dinner off it." Amram's tone suggested that he did not share Kaleb's faith.

"It's true. You can't question his faith or his commitment . . ." said Yeshua, before Theudas interrupted.

"Only his sanity," he said, without his frown.

Yeshua shook his head and resumed. "No, he's obviously a good man, he's clever, he's fine a preacher . . . It's just a shame that he's completely misguided. What kind of a plan is marching on Jerusalem? Will he carry a banner along the way—'follow me to certain death'? What is driving that man? Does he have no family?"

"He has no father. Well, not in the usual sense."

"What's that supposed to mean?"

The archer looked at the brothers, whose own exchange of glances evoked an expression on his face that suggested he'd said too much. "You should ask him about it when you see him." He ended the conversation with a gutsy belch.

೩♥

The companions climbed with the sun, the road becoming gradually steeper and dustier. "Gentlemen, we are now entering into the region of Galilee." The Mediterranean glimmered behind them, but ahead the mix of greenery and sand blended into a hazy distance, when it became visible beyond the hills. As the small track joined with a larger road that followed the contour of the hill, Amram slowed to look carefully at the ground and without warning leapt from his horse. Stooping towards the gravel, he ran his finger around the shape of a hoof mark.

"There shouldn't be this many mountain donkeys in these hills," Amram muttered as he gestured the brothers to dismount. Moving toward them his voice was lowered. "These are cavalry tracks." The Egyptian's heart began to pound as Amram continued. "And I can think of only one reason why they'd be up here." He handed the brothers their packs, bundled his own together and hurried off the road and up the hill, bow in hand. The brothers obeyed the unspoken command to follow, not daring to ask what this one reason might be.

Five minutes brought them to the crown, affording them a clear view of the road that wound before them. "We're not far from the house of Eliazar, but we can't see it from here." Amram was too distracted by circumstances to explain to the brothers what was happening.

"Is that where we were heading?"

"It was, and it looks as though someone has beaten us to it."

"How did they know we we'd be coming?" Yeshua asked, before realizing how many times he had been outwitted by the Roman response to his actions. Amram looked at Yeshua and confirmed these thoughts using nothing other than his tooth-deprived expression.

The companions crept down the far side of the hill, staying out of sight of the road. But from that road came the sound of voices and horses. Amram paused to scan the hilltops around them. Sweat was dripping from Yeshua's nose, either from scrambling up another hill, the heat of the high sun, or the fear that had seized his limbs. As the companions reached the crest of this hill their worst fears were confirmed. About a hundred feet below them stood half a dozen cavalrymen. Had the assassins stayed on the road they would have walked straight into them. The cover of the hill's rocks and bushes made it easy enough to follow the track from above and remain undetected.

The sound of Greek conversation and laughter kept the Egyptians' pulses high. Amram's movement was that of a cat stalking its prey. His head staying low and level, his limbs carrying him swiftly and softly across steep, sandy terrain as though he were creeping across Yudah's garden to refill his cup. The belching had ceased.

Amram, Yeshua, and Theudas skirted to the north of the third hill, half expecting to be spotted at any moment. They slowed as the road snaked back into view. Again, the archer scanned the hills that surrounded them. Again Greek chatter could be heard nearby. The companions sank to the ground and crawled through stringy grass to observe the soldiers. A further six horses came into view, three of them with mounted riders. Yeshua's eyes attached themselves to the cavalrymen's swords. The blades seemed to know more than the soldiers who wielded them about the whereabouts of the outlaws. He'd seen these swords a thousand times. He even carried one upon him now. But the Roman short sword looked like a different weapon when hung about a soldier charged with burying that weapon in *your* gut. With this recognition, Yeshua's status as an outlaw began to take root in him.

The soldiers were situated outside a small house of pale stone, barely visible against the hill's own stone of identical color. "Eliazar's house?" asked Yeshua.

"Yeh, but they won't have got him," whispered Amram with little apparent concern.

"Er—how are you so sure?" Theudas asked.

"Because . . ." Amram sung the first word, suggesting that what followed should be obvious, ". . . Eliazar is a shepherd. He's spent his life listening out for predators. And there are few predators that make as much noise on their approach as an armor-clad pagan on a mountain donkey." Amram was still entranced by the commotion at the shepherd's house. "The plan now is to head as far east as we can. It won't be long before they find our horses." He turned to check on the brothers' nerves. His face looked weighed down by their fear as he reached through their packs and produced their swords. "Have them ready to hand, just in case." Amram's obvious concern brought home to the brothers the sheer danger they were in. And yet, for such an unlikely figure he radiated remarkable assuredness. His dark hair was soon to be colonized by grey, which had already established an outpost on his rough-shaven face. The gap of a missing front tooth as he grinned, which yesterday gave him a threatening look, was now part of the reassuring demeanor.

"Boys," he said, with a father's tenderness. "Stay alert . . . Stay calm." Yeshua's whole body was energized by the shiver that came from somewhere beyond him, swept through him, and left, taking with it the fear that could so easily have crippled him. "No safe path to victory," said Amram.

That's my line, thought Yeshua momentarily, before making the connection with the old soldier and his war tales. This was a phrase that the Seventeenth Legion came to treasure, as slowly its numbers were ground to zero at the hands of Germanic tribes ambushing them en route. But the Seventeenth Legion all those years ago had never made it to a battlefield, and any who might have survived would be familiar enough with guerrilla warfare. Amram must have known what it was to be hunted through alien territory.

The terrain was their ally as the assassins made silently towards the mounting hills of the East. The Romans were obviously expecting the companions, and by now would have found the abandoned horses. Within half a mile of them a company of soldiers was on the hunt, although once again, they would not be on horseback. Amram froze, forcing the brothers to do likewise. They followed his eyes to the top of a nearby hill as the archer's right hand felt for an arrow from his pack and placed it upon his bow. The brothers could see nothing. Amram began to strain the bow, and still the brothers could not see his target. Then he loosed. The sound of a distant body hitting the ground was heard before the Egyptians had laid an eye on the arrow's victim. Looking back at Amram they saw that another arrow sat upon his bowstring, as silently they followed him around to the eastern side of the hill.

"Stay here," the archer whispered, as he climbed towards his fallen prey. He was out of sight for only a few seconds, and returned to the brothers as silently and effortlessly as he had left them. The archer said nothing as he pushed further towards the east in the knowledge that the Egyptians would stay close and quiet.

Amram seemed to know exactly what he was doing and where he was going. The brothers continued to scan every ridge and slope, in front and behind, in case Amram's all-seeing eye might fail. As unlikely as that might have seemed, they hardly assumed any favor, either with God or with luck.

The sun was no ally to the companions on this day, but neither would it offer its allegiance to those from whom they fled. Their pace felt cumbersome, slowed by the tireless heat from above and the unforgiving terrain underfoot. Here the highlands of Judea ran from the northwest to the southeast. These hills alone witnessed three assassins, scrambling across naked rock and wiry grass. The western climbs of the ridges were steep, hot, and painfully slow, but the eastern descents often brought some shade and a return of strength. Increasingly, these slopes were ploughed with gullies, steep ravines, and the welcome sound of gushing waters. During this endless flight from cavalry there was no Egyptian protest at the relentless pace that saw the archer striding uphill, pressing his arms onto his knees as they rose before him and then running down the gentler slopes with a lightness that did not sort well with his age or apparent state of health.

"Look at that," the archer laughed, drawing the brothers' attention to an eagle that circled above them. The glorious sight brought no comfort. Yeshua's exhaustion and paranoia had expelled all reason, and he feared that the eagle might somehow report their whereabouts to the cavalrymen.

Early afternoon had brought them beyond the highest ridge, and the Mediterranean glimmer sank from view. Two hours of progress brought neither sight nor sound of human life, and as the companions descended towards the Jordan valley their pace slowed and their spirits lightened. "You can put those away now," said Amram as he looked at their blades. He did the same with his bow. The brothers stopped under the shade of a palm tree to do as they were told. "You two ready for food?"

"We're Jews!" Theudas grinned. And so the assassins sat in the cool shade of a hot day, drank, and ate. Carrying nothing but fruit, bread and water it was hardly a lavish meal. But after such a pursuit, the satisfaction the brief rest brought was immeasurable.

"Well, I don't suppose you were expecting to have your lunch in Galilee when you got up this morning."

"Where are we going, Amram?" asked Yeshua.

"Arbela," he replied, pointing eastwards down towards the bright glare of the Galilean Sea. Beautiful green hills clothed with fruit trees stretched their way along the distance of around ten miles. A road winding just a few hundred feet below led almost directly to the place to which Amram had pointed.

"I wish we still had those mountain donkeys," said Theudas.

"We'll still be there in time for our next meal."

"Arbela?" Yeshua was groping through his memory. "Do you mean the caves?" He had heard from his father stories of battles between Herod the Great and a group of religious fanatics up in the "caves of Arbela." It was renowned as a hideout for bandits.

Amram relished over-pronouncing his shameless replies. "A veritable den of robbers!" His words fell, followed by a grin and a well-earned belch. "Safe, secure, cool. Good company, and a beautiful sea view."

"We are going to a robbers' cave!" said Yeshua, still trying to absorb Amram's intent. The idea of being a bandit was still struggling to sink its roots into the wealthy Egyptian merchant son of a rabbi. That rabbi's other son reminded Yeshua of the reality.

"Well, you're carrying a purse, I'm carrying a purse, and . . ."

Another over-pronounced declaration intervened, "I'm carrying three!"

". . . and none of it's ours" Theudas continued. "Yeshua! We're all carrying the cash of people we've killed and who still haven't been buried."

"Thieving murderous scum," was Amram's deliberate pronouncement, as though he were about to commence a stoning.

"All I wanted was justice," said Yeshua, devoid of humor.

"If that's what you're after you've come to the wrong place," said Amram. "You can't be on the side of justice without being a thief. At least, that's what Kaleb says. I, on the other hand, take comfort from the fact that not every thief is on the side of justice."

"Amram. How do those Romans seem to know so much about what we're doing?"

The archer made a visible effort to answer with patience. "What would you do, if you were in charge of an occupying army in a hostile land?"

"I wouldn't be in charge of that army unless I knew what to do."

The old soldier rolled his eyes, shook his head and looked at the younger brother. "Theudas, what would you do?" Theudas began to smirk as he drew breath, so Amram rolled his eyes again to caution the Egyptian, ". . . apart from wishing the troops a good morning?"

"I suppose I'd have spies," he stated without a trace of authority, inviting more exasperation. "Er . . . lots of spies." He mimicked the archer by over emphasizing every syllable that followed: "A veritable army of spies," he smiled, as his forehead struggled to contain his inflated eyes.

"Roman eyes are everywhere," Amram lamented. "Watching, waiting, guessing. They see an awful lot." The brothers looked worried, so the archer continued with a grin. "But they don't see everything," he laughed, shaking the coins in his Roman purses. His laughter was interrupted by a belch, which brought Amram's comforting thoughts to a satisfactory conclusion, and he clambered to his feet. "Time to press on, boys."

Within a minute the three travelers were finding their way towards the main route that links the Sea of Galilee with the west of Galilee. Here and there little villages were dotted, and the companions stopped briefly in the late afternoon to replenish their food and water.

The green hills and lush valleys offered Yeshua little in the way of welcome. He was not the kind of person that would fall in with a gang of thieves. "What kind of people are we going to meet this afternoon Amram?" Yeshua had horrible pictures of club-wielding primitive creatures making their living by inflicting terror upon innocent travelers and traders.

"You're one of them! They are people, people just like you."

"Thieving murderous scum," said Theudas through a smile, winning a glare from his elder brother, but some appreciation from the archer. Amram soon exorcised his grin and expressed a fear sufficient to silence the brothers:

"The real worry about those caves is not who's there but who isn't. I'm worried that not everyone from Narbata will make it."

SHADOWS WERE BEGINNING TO lengthen as the hills of Arbela came into view. Yeshua had always imagined them to be a dark and threatening sight. But there was neither darkness nor threat on any skyline, which from these heights stretched at least ten miles in every direction. The hills were silent, even welcoming, scattered with nothing but sheep and bushes. A sheer, sand-colored rock-face of about a hundred feet crowned the terrain on which it sat. These cliffs bestowed their golden dust upon the green of the upper slopes immediately below. This was a colossal natural fortress, divinely crafted by God himself. Yeshua could see why rebel forces had chosen this site to take their stand against Herod the Great a generation earlier. Yet, the beauty of these hills charmed their inhabitants' attention away from the tragic and recent history they concealed. As the companions began their final ascent of the day, the blemishes became apparent: dark pots in the cliff revealed themselves as the caves came into sharper view.

The archer stopped and waved his arms towards the empty cliffs. They answered with an audible voice. "What do you want you thieving, murderous drunkard." The accent was noticeably Galilean. Amram laughed.

"Some of your red juice if you haven't finished it all you dastardly pork-eating vagabond."

"What about your descendants?" the cliffs replied.

Amram looked down towards the Egyptians. "They've brought you some gifts."

With that, a rope ladder appeared from the mouth of a cave and hit the ground forty feet below, still not fully unfurled. Amram climbed and eventually disappeared into the mouth of the cave that was furnished with a carefully crafted archway. Echoes of laughter were heard within the hill, before Amram peered down and invited the brothers to ascend. Yeshua climbed first, his head throbbing with anxiety. Twenty feet below was his brother. Twenty feet above was the man who'd saved his life. But dangling from the flimsy ladder of a bandits' hideout, Yeshua was alone. His fear of the cave's inhabitants was indistinguishable from his fear of Roman soldiers. His veins began to pump icy liquid around his body, amplifying his heartbeat so that it pounded in his ears. The final rung of the ladder appeared all too soon, and then a hand reaching out to grasp his. He was helped to his feet a round, rosy-cheeked face with a warm glow. "Shalom!" said the stranger in a theatrical voice, "My name is Kochba. Welcome to our estate!"

"Shalom!" he replied, "I'm Yeshua." He clambered to his feet as Amram invited Theudas to begin the climb. Kochba had neither the appearance nor the voice of an outlaw, nor did he look as though he lived in a cave. He was older than the brothers but younger than Yudah, stood shorter than all three and his smile came from a shaven face that wore only fresh stubble and a dark moustache. He leaned forward as he spoke, and his eyes bored into Yeshua with intensity but warmth. "We didn't expect to see you this soon. Amram must really have been cracking his whip."

"It's surprising how quickly you can move when you're being hunted by the soldiers of Pilatus."

In an instant every trace of warmth evacuated Kochba's face. "Hunted?" he replied, before looking at Amram for confirmation. The archer closed his eyes for a moment as he nodded. Kochba retreated into himself for a couple of seconds before his smile returned. "Well you're quite safe here. The prefect's soldiers wouldn't cross the hills. We're in Galilee. He has no power here."

With that, Theudas arrived in the cave to be greeted by Kochba's enthusiasm. He then turned towards the back of the cave where a much younger, much skinnier character rose to his feet. Immediately the Egyptians recognized him as the young man who had appeared at Yudah's house in an agitated state. His face was now relaxed, and he too was pleased to welcome new guests.

"Shalom," he said, "I am Eliazar."

"Ah, we've heard all about you!" said Theudas.

"As we've heard of you," Kochba grinned at the boys, raising his eyebrows to extend the meaning of his words. "You've been helping to eliminate the locusts," he smiled.

"Typical farmer . . ." said Eliazar, before Amram lifted his cup of wine to interrupt.

"As long as they don't touch your grapes, Kochba!"

Eliazar put his hand on Kochba's ample belly, "If locusts have taken our crops then no one's told Kochba!"

"I think we've just come from your house," Theudas said to Eliazar.

"And it's a bloody good job you weren't there," added Amram. Silence now filled the cave.

"Go on," said Kochba.

"If you *were* there you'd be entertaining a cavalry platoon."

"What! How could the prefect know anything about Eliazar's house?"

"That's what worries me," said Amram. "Kaleb can fill us in when he arrives, I hope."

"*If* he arrives," Yeshua added.

Eliazar was quietly shocked, and turned from the others to hide his alarm.

"Eliazar!" said Kochba softly, placing his hand on the shepherd's back. "You're here, you're safe, you're with us . . ."

"Whether I like it or not," said the youth, before he gathered himself and turned back. "There's no going back now," he said, suggesting that there existed a course of action to which he and the others were committed. Yeshua looked at Theudas as though his younger brother had spoken these words to him.

Blankets were laid along the mouth of the cave, and its inhabitants sat in a row gazing down upon the Sea of Galilee and the villages that fed off it. The evening air was heavy with the day's events, but as the companions broke bread and drank wine together, Yeshua began to feel that he was home. Here, in a bandit's cave, enjoying the loot of murdered victims, something felt strangely right. The Promised Land for once looked full of promise. They had found safe refuge with fellows who were not the thugs he had imagined to find here. The hope returned that there might be a way back to Egypt after all. Surely there was divine providence in all that had happened over the last two days: the success of their assassination; bumping into Yudah at the right moment; the escape from Narbata, the flight through the hill country under the protection of Amram and now the safety of the caves. It all seemed miraculous. Maybe God was honoring the brothers' quest. Yeshua sat back and exhaled a breath long enough to expel many demons. They made way for him to feel the luxury of tiredness, which was no doubt aided by red wine.

"You're looking relaxed, Yeshua," said Amram with a tone of approval.

"I should think he's ready to relax after the day he's had," said Kochba.

"Never thought I'd feel such bliss in a bandits' cave," he yawned.

"Well there are bandits and bandits," said Kochba. "We are your sophisticated sort! Isn't that right, Amram?"

Amram belched.

"But I have to say, you two don't look like assassins," Kochba puzzled.

"The deadliest sort of assassin," said Amram in a voice that led Yeshua to suspect that the archer might still treasure plans for his Egyptian friends.

For now there were no plans because there was no news. Someone from Narbata would hopefully arrive some time in the next day or so. Until then, the companions would stay in the hills and wait. Yeshua sat back and fumbled through his belongings and food. Again, he stumbled across the figurine of the boy that he could not force himself to dispose of. As he gazed again at the image of this child, the notion that there might just be some divine involvement in the Egyptian's plan disappeared into the sky like warm breath on a cold morning. It was replaced with silent guilt broken only by the return of the young girl's screams. The deeply rooted hopelessness he felt re-asserted itself.

Sleep came easily that night, but it left him just as easily. Dawn had penetrated all but the furthest recesses of the cave, bringing with it the recognition of cold realities from which the Egyptian's dreamless rest had been a refuge. Yeshua rose and walked towards the front of the cave, half expecting to see a detachment of soldiers encamped at the foot of the cliff. All he could see was the lushness of a paradise that appeared too beautiful for any human to inhabit.

"It's our land." Yeshua turned to see who had whispered to him. Eliazar had clearly been awake for some time. "I've lived in these hills all my life," he said, as he threw the ladder to the ground below and a sack over his shoulder.

"Are your family shepherds?" Yeshua asked.

"My family are dead," came the reply as the shepherd began his descent.

As Yeshua arrived at the foot of the cliff, Eliazar had begun to prepare a fire. "So," he continued after a minute or so, "I have nothing to lose."

"And what do you hope to win?"

"I don't want to win anything. All I want . . ." He paused as the sparks became a tentative glow. "All I want . . . is justice . . . for my family."

"What happened to them?"

"My mother and sister died in childbirth. My father and brother were crucified outside Jerusalem." Eliazar spoke with such apparent disinterest in these events that his grief was all too obvious. Yeshua could only shake his head in response, but the shepherd continued. "We couldn't pay our tax!" he said, as though he were talking to himself. "So they sent soldiers to collect it." Eliazar paused. "We gave them all the tax they deserved."

"What do you mean?"

"My brother was better than King David with a slingshot. And my father and I both knew what we were doing. And they only sent two soldiers." Eliazar had begun to cook fish, and his words dissipated with the smoke from his fire. "We killed them both. The prefect said we were rebels."

"They didn't punish you?"

"My father told them I had nothing to do with killing the soldiers." Eliazar paused, drawn back into the events that still haunted him, until released by Yeshua's question.

"No justice then?"

"Not yet," the young shepherd lamented after a sigh. "But justice has to come. Every morning the sun rises and the sun sets, as though nothing had happened. I watch it, out with the flocks. If the sun had seen what happened to my brother, to my dad, why would it still rise? Why would it still set? The world should have crumbled after what happened to my family. And we're not the only ones this happens to. Our blood cries from the ground. But who hears it? Sun rises, sun sets. It's turned a blind eye to what happened here." For the briefest moment the shepherd chanced eye contact with Yeshua, who was riveted to the story from which its teller tried to maintain a safe distance. This young peasant, awkward and immature, had articulated beautifully the grief that Yeshua himself felt. This nervous shepherd—and everyone knew a shepherd couldn't be trusted, a shepherd's word was not valid in court—this young shepherd had brought unspeakable comfort to the Egyptian, and both of them knew it. But the atmosphere was too heavy for Eliazar, who brought his story to a swift conclusion. "We weren't rebels. We were poor."

The aroma was working its magic on the cave's inhabitants, drawing them out one at a time for their breakfast, where they sat and waited for news from Narbata. By the time the fire had cooled and the sun was high, there was still no word. The frenzied paranoia that had followed Yeshua for over two days began to reassert itself upon the Egyptian's imagination. If the Romans knew about Eliazar's house, then they must also have known about Yudah and probably Kaleb. But how could they have known? By now they must have learnt about the companions hiding in these caves, and would probably send troops, regardless of whose jurisdiction Galilee came under.

The ladder from the cave rattled as Eliazar climbed to retrieve his slingshot for a demonstration of his proficiency. As he disappeared from sight a voice echoed from the valley below.

"Friends!" It was Kaleb, and he was not alone.

"Miriam," said Theudas to himself. "I knew she couldn't bear to live without me!"

Few words or even glances were exchanged until the Narbatans arrived to embrace their friends. The greetings carried little welcome or warmth. Kaleb looked mostly toward the ground, and seemed to have left his charisma in Narbata. For the first time he appeared speechless. "Well?" asked Kochba anxiously.

"They've taken Yudah," said Kaleb.

"Who has? Taken him where?" Only in its absence did Yeshua notice that the eyes of the Pharisee usually had a reach far beyond his conversation partners. The gaze that had seen a hope just beyond some horizon, the power of his eyes to awaken courage in others, had abandoned him.

"Who do you think? The Romans . . ." Bereft of the composure he had demonstrated at the synagogue, the Pharisee struggled to finish his sentence. "The Romans . . . they've taken him to Caesarea."

"What? How do you know that?" Kochba pushed.

"Because I saw it," Miriam snarled. Silence gripped the companions and fastened their attention on Yudah's daughter. "I knew something was wrong. You can see the twisted pleasure in their empty faces. I didn't have to follow them to see where the soldiers were going." She closed her eyes for a moment. "I saw them go to *my* home, enter through *my* gates and take *my* father!"

A nameless chasm entered Yeshua's stomach. He had known Yudah for as long as he could remember. And now he was as good as dead. Because of me, he thought, this woman has lost her father.

The anger in Miriam's voice gave way to exhaustion. "I went straight to the Pharisee, because I knew he could bring me somewhere safe." With that she slumped to take a seat beside the charcoal.

"What. What are we supposed to do now?" asked Eliazar, looking at Amram and Kochba, both of whom ignored him.

"Well, it explains how they knew about Eliazar's house. Yudah knew that's where we'd be heading," said Amram. "When was this?"

"About the third hour," Miriam replied, trying not to weep. "Yesterday," she added.

"How could they possibly have known about Yudah? Even if they saw us at his house." For once, Amram was surprised at the Roman efficiency in tracking criminals.

"Miriam came straight to me and we left almost immediately," Kaleb announced.

"They must have spies everywhere," Kochba declared in astonishment. "What do you think they'll do now?" he asked, looking at Amram.

"Well, that will be an end to it for now," the archer declared. "They won't follow us from Judea to Galilee. There's too much hostility between Pilatus and Herod for him to come marching into Herod's territory."

"After all the trouble they've gone to so far?" said an unconvinced Yeshua.

"He might seem like a god, but even the prefect has limits to what he can do." An intense emotion, a mix of frustration and anger, seized Yeshua as he heard Amram compare the prefect with a god.

"But he'll know exactly where we are," said Kaleb, siding with Yeshua.

"You know as well as anyone" said Amram, "that the prefect does not care about getting the right people. He just needs an excuse to butcher Jews. We all know how he works."

"So you think this will be an end to it?" Kochba asked suspiciously.

"I didn't say that," Amram cautioned. "Most likely he'll find another way of taking revenge, but it won't be on us." He looked at Miriam who glared at him in disgust. "Not directly anyway," he added.

"This will give the prefect an excuse for more slaughter. He'll find a way of doing it, he always does, " said Kaleb, now in agreement with the archer. "Any ideas?"

"What about my father?" Miram asked no one in particular. "We haven't all disowned our fathers as quickly as the Pharisee disowned his. What will happen to my father?" Amram again was left to answer.

"They definitely took him from the house?"

Miriam nodded.

"Then that's a good sign. We should be grateful they didn't kill him on the spot."

"Grateful?"

"If they've arrested him, he'll be processed according to their laws. And believe me, Miriam, that's a good thing." Yudah's daughter looked far from convinced. "They're proud of their legal system. They won't dish out punishment without evidence. And really, what has Yudah done that's illegal? He has committed no crime that there's a shred of proof for."

"His only crime was the company he keeps," Miriam said defiantly as she addressed the hillside.

"And if that's the conclusion they come to, we should be grateful." Amram turned to Kaleb. "You should pray . . ." Miriam stormed away, closely followed by Theudas. Amram lowered his voice. "You should pray that he says little, that his sentence is short, or that he's killed quickly."

Kaleb did as the godless archer requested, and spoke his prayer. All bowed their heads in silence, as Kaleb launched into thanksgiving for the life and courage of their companion. The image of the boy in Yeshua's hand was exacting his revenge. This figurine was a curse, but Yeshua still was unable to rid himself of it. He returned it to the purse as Kaleb's prayer concluded.

The Egyptian knew only too well to keep his mouth shut, given that his actions had been the catalyst for the disaster that was now unfolding in Israel. By now he understood well enough that this had long been a disaster waiting to happen, and that sooner or later these catastrophes would be faced by those present, with or without the Egyptian assassinations. But such an objective view is beyond the reach of those held captive by the shock of grief. The Egyptian kept his silence.

After murmurs of praise for Yudah had subsided, Eliazar left a respectful pause and repeated his question. "So what are we going to do now?"

"Home!" said Kochba in panic.

"It won't be long before none of us have any homes to go to, that's for sure," grumbled Eliazar, but not without some relief that his companions now shared his fate.

Another wave of horror spread through the cave. Resistance to Rome had been theoretical and passive until the Egyptians had arrived. Like it or not, everyone present in the cave was now a fugitive.

"Except for me," said Kochba.

Amram justified his optimism. "Kochba. Even if they've got your name from Yudah—and there is absolutely no reason they would—they won't be going to your house. You're a foreigner to the prefect. You live in another region. He might report your name to Herod some day, but you've committed no crime and neither has Yudah. No need to panic."

"That's easy for you to say . . . I've got a wife . . . I've got a family. What if they've changed their policy? Look at what they've done in the last few days. You're probably right, but I want to be on the safe side. I want my family here for a few days at least." Amram raised his eyebrows. "Anyway. We're best off staying here while the dust settles. We'll need food and drink to do that, and I have it all on my farm."

"Have you got any wine?"

"Only the best."

"Well that's good enough for me."

The possibility of a short-term plan offered a welcome focus for a group under the spell of shock. Kochba owned an estate just three miles away where he had a wife, two sons and three servants. They could be there and back before sunset, bringing with them the resources that would be needed to sustain twelve rebels in the caves while they made their plans.

Miriam and Theudas were to stay in the cave, and both seemed quite happy with their role. The rest would go with Kochba. Yeshua looked about him, the hillside alive with a hurricane of emotion and an immediate purpose. Now it felt like a bandits' hideout. Yeshua loved it. An opportunity to save life rather than take it filled him with hope. His departure from the cliffs was far happier than his arrival. He no longer felt alone. He was without his brother, but he trusted his companions. The journey to Kochba's farmland began. Eliazar had been ignored a second time, but his question had been answered.

ഏ

Kochba's farm stretched across the flatlands to the west of the Galilean Sea. Theudas and Miriam sat at the mouth of the cave, watching the small company shrink into the distance and out of sight. Any attempt to offer words of comfort or assurance to Miriam would be greeted with the hostility it deserved. But Theudas was sufficiently acquainted with grief to know that the awkwardness he felt could not help but be shared, and that his wordless presence might bring some form of comfort to Miriam. And so for half an hour, he endured the discomfort of silence before Yudah's daughter broke it.

"Why did you come here?" she asked, without looking at him. "Kaleb says you came to avenge your brothers. Is that right, Theudas?"

"I came here because if I hadn't, my brother would have come alone."

"So you don't agree with his little quest for vengeance? You came here against your will? Or at least against your better judgment! Why did you come here and bring all this misery with you?"

"This land has enough misery of its own. Misery is what we found here. We didn't bring it with us."

"And what does your father think about you coming here, for no other reason than vengeance?"

A pause. "He didn't want us to come," Theudas confessed. "He thought it would bring more misery."

"Well perhaps you should have listened to him." She hadn't verbalized it. Her silence had spoken for her.

Theudas remained quiet for a moment. "Miriam?" he said, looking at her, with the intention of offering some form of apology. She turned to face him. But on seeing the depths of grief that spilled over her brown eyes, Theudas was paralyzed.

"What?" she asked, still looking at him.

After another moment he managed to summon up a whisper. "I don't know." He mouthed the words and averted his eyes. The silence that followed brought a different calm. Theudas was not sure what he had said, but felt that he had done something important. Another pause followed. Its length was immeasurable, but it ended as the daughter of Yudah lifted her hands to sob into them. Now it was time for Theudas' awkwardness to feel awkward. He put his hand on her forearm to offer he knew not what. It was a gesture that opened the floodgate for a torrent of emotion, and Theudas embraced her until its force was spent.

৯

Returning from Kochba's residence, the companions were considerably slower and more numerous, laden with a dozen donkeys and carts carrying wine, bread and fruit. Amira, the farmer's wife, was encumbered by her displeasure alone, cursing, weeping, inflicting upon her idealistic husband as much torture as a broken woman could. Only one of Kochba's servants joined them but his sons, Nathan and Sol, both of similar in age to the shepherd, trudged wearily along in the company of their parents, some distance behind the rest of the group. This was not accidental. Amram had pointed out that Kochba's household should not be seen traveling with a gang of bandits. Amram, Yeshua, Kaleb, and Eliazar accompanied a cart several hundred yards ahead of Kochba's family. This wagon, laden mostly with wine, was also a mobile armory.

"God help anyone who touches wine destined for Amram's lips!" Eliazar laughed as he lifted the skins on the cart to reach for a piece of bread to chew as he walked.

"God help anyone who interferes with our quest for justice," the Pharisee frowned. "What do you say, Yeshua?"

"What's that up ahead?" Yeshua replied.

"Just kids," said Eliazar, straining his eyes to see two small dots several hundred paces ahead.

"Well?" asked Kaleb.

"Well what?"

"Do you think God will bless our cause as he has blessed yours?"

"How do I know if God has blessed our cause? I'm beginning to think that the quest for justice is best left in the hands of God."

"But we *are* the hands of God, Yeshua," he grinned. "How does God act in this world if not through his people?"

"I used to think justice and revenge were the same thing." Yeshua sighed. "But now that I have tasted revenge, I still haven't tasted justice." The Egyptian looked down at his hands, and over at the Pharisee. "These hands have brought revenge, but not justice . . ." Yeshua shook his head and looked back at his grubby palms. "These are not the hands of God," he declared, but there was a question buried somewhere in his tone.

"Revenge is not the same as justice, you're right," the Pharisee mused, "but do you think you can have justice without vengeance?"

"Listen!" Yeshua replied, pointing at the two small boys who approached, the sound of a child's screaming becoming clearer.

"It's just kids, Yeshua!"

The Egyptian felt unusually sensitive to the distress of a child. The boys ahead were moving quickly northwards towards them on the track that skirted the western shore of the Galilean Sea. "I wonder what they've been up to."

The boys were coming into clearer view. The younger, about five years of age was screaming at the heavens, his nose pouring with blood. The other, about five years older, also had blood streaming down his mouth and off his chin. His face was a boiling cocktail of anger and distress, as his skinny left arm embraced his younger brother. Yeshua saw in this older brother a mirror of himself, and taking a jar of water from the cart ran to meet them.

"Bloody soldiers!" the elder boy shouted, pointing south along the road as Yeshua stooped to wipe the blood from the younger boy. He handed the elder brother a wet cloth and gestured for him to apply it to his little brother's nose.

"My name is Yeshua. It's okay now, fellows. Just tell me what happened."

The older brother shook with rage, livid at his inability to protect his little brother from soldiers. His anger made him shameless of the tears he shed as he spoke. "Those soldiers back there," he pointed again, "said that Simeon was laughing at them when he came past, and one of them hit him across his face!" The boy shouted at Yeshua as though the Egyptian were the criminal. "He's not even five years old!"

"And what about your face?"

"Well I wasn't just going to stand there was I?" And with that, he began breathing heavily to prevent himself from sobbing out loud.

Eliazar, Amram and Kaleb arrived on the scene just as the younger brother had ceased his crying. "What's going on?" Amram demanded, with a face vacated by every trace of emotion.

"These young men are like King David's 'mighty men!'" Yeshua smiled, as he placed a hand on each of their shoulders with gentle admiration. "They've been in a fight with soldiers!"

"How many?" Amram asked, apparently disinterested in whatever answer followed.

Yeshua repeated the question to the brothers. "Two!" said the elder, still breathing heavily, but smiling involuntarily through his tears at the compliments he had just received.

"You're sure now, no more than two?"

"I'm sure," the boy nodded, "two bloody soldiers, and they were both full of wine."

Eliazar appeared from the back of the cart, handing bread, figs and water to the brothers—whose faces were now lighting up as they were cleaned up. "You must be very brave!" he said with a tenderness Yeshua had not yet heard from the shepherd. "But do you know—this man is a real soldier," he pointed at Amram whose spirit was elsewhere, "not like Herod's ruffians!" The boys were now smiling from ear to ear as the archer disappeared to the rear of the cart. He reappeared, not with his weapons, but with a jar of wine.

"Take this to your father!" he ordered, still emotionless. "Tell him that his sons have been avenged . . ."

"And tell him . . ." Eliazar added, "tell him to be proud of his two strong sons!"

Kaleb rolled his eyes and shook his head.

"Run straight home now with that wine," said Yeshua, "Go! Now. You get yourself home, as fast as you can." The older brother almost dragged the smiling infant at high pace, their laughter slowly disappearing into the distance.

"Well?" Kaleb looked at the archer.

"We say nothing of those boys to these soldiers. Do I make myself clear? Nothing! Not a word. Otherwise they will suffer for what we do here." The others nodded. "We just walk by, smiling. But have your weapons ready to hand."

A few hundred yards brought the road south under the shade of a sycamore tree. Two figures gradually came into view. One reclined beneath the tree while the other leaned his back upon its trunk. Both wore the black leather amour of the Herodian Guard with a sword about their waste, and as the cart neared they stood to greet the travelers.

"What are you carrying here, brothers?" asked one.

"The fruit of Israel's finest vine," Amram smiled.

"Well, all who travel this road must pay a tax!" the other grinned.

"Thought you might say that . . . Would you like to taste our cargo?" asked the archer. The soldiers grinned at one another as Amram walked to the back of the cart. He retrieved a medium-sized jug and returned briskly to the first soldier, exchanging a large smile with him. Amram's composure was so measured, his manner so compliant, that the first soldier fell to the ground with blood streaming from his temple before he realized that the jug had been used as a weapon. The second soldier's right hand had drawn only an inch of naked steel before the archer's right hand connected with its next target. Amram's entire bodyweight was instantaneously channeled along his arm, through his two largest knuckles and deep into the soldier's left jaw, sending him to join his companion on the ground. Eliazar and Yeshua ensured that both soldiers had a sword to their throat as they lay on their back. Amram held his tongue.

"Who . . ." the first soldier touched his head and inspected his own blood-covered hand before looking back to the bandits. "Who are you?" he frowned, trying to disguise his fear.

"We . . ." Kaleb replied, ". . .we are the hands of God!" he said, and smiled at Yeshua. He drew breath to continue, but Amram jumped in.

"Your swords, please," said the archer, helping himself to the soldiers' weapons. Amram's entire demeanor was terrifyingly cold and efficient. Producing his bow from the place where he deposited their blades, he gestured towards his friends to step back from the guards. "Now, on your feet." The soldiers complied. "I want to see you wash your greedy filth in the lake," he demanded quietly, nodding towards the nearby Sea of Galilee. The soldiers remained silent, and hurried towards the shore, grateful for their lives.

"Do you feel justice has been done here, Yeshua?" the Pharisee smirked as the humiliated soldiers, now fifty paces away, began to remove their amour. "Justice *and* vengeance!"

"And no loss of life," the Egyptian muttered.

The company of bandits reappeared soon before the sun was baptized into the Mediterranean. They arrived at the rock face looking tired and miserable, and one at a time climbed wearily up the rope ladder and into the safety of the cave. Kochba's family and servant remained on the slopes below, while Amram and Eliazar disappeared around to the southern side of the hill carrying a bundle of rope each. Yeshua was still waiting his turn on the ladder when a rope fell from above about twenty feet over to his right. It hadn't quite hit the ground but it didn't need to. Eliazar was lowering himself down it and disappeared into a cave slightly lower than halfway down. He was followed soon after by Amram. The humid evening sky was full of anguish, the air sticky with the anger of Kochba's refugee family.

By nightfall the donkeys were tethered, the western cave was housing Kochba's family, and a mountain of provisions had been successfully delivered to both caves. A watch system was set up and the companions settled down. To what, none of them knew, but for now they had agreed to try and sleep so that any decisions they made would be the result of careful thought rather than tired panic.

Yeshua bedded down beside Theudas, who fell asleep before the mood of the cave evolved from relief at completing this mission to anxiety about what would be their next. Anguish opened up an unbridgeable chasm between Yeshua and his much needed rest. How can the death toll still continue to climb, he thought, trying desperately not to count the victims of his quest for justice? And now an entire family was living in a cave, all because of his desire to avenge the death of his brothers. In fact, an entire but reluctant community had been established, the fruit of the Egyptians' actions. He began to feel the weight of this responsibility, and had he thought it possible to escape the cave with his brother he would have done so in an instant. He began to wonder whether this was why one had been chosen to stay and the other appointed to go with Kochba to the farm. He shifted his eyes toward the Pharisee who was scribbling onto a parchment using only the light of the moon. The deep, indigo sky that drew its color from the moonlight was distinct from the *gevil*, the lightly tanned goat hide across which Kaleb carried his hand freely from right to left. The crisp, golden texture of this parchment reflected, or was reflected in, the features of the scribe at work upon it. It remained unclear to Yeshua which was the source of the golden warmth that rested somewhere between the Pharisee and his parchment.

"What are your writing?" Yeshua gestured with a slight lift of his chin. Nothing. "Kaleb?"

"A prayer."

"What are you, a Pharisee or a Psalm-writer?" Amram grunted from the back of the cave.

The Pharisee offered no response.

"What have you written?" Yeshua asked again.

"A prayer," Kaleb frowned after a pause, although he appeared unaware of anything beyond the dynamic between his eyes and his parchment.

"What kind of prayer, what does it say?"

Kaleb sighed, pulled himself from the world of his musings and lifted up the unfinished petition.

"*Father,*

You have delivered us from the mouth of the lion, from the soldiers who would tear us to shreds. You have brought us to the safety of your fortress, and granted us food and drink, company and shelter, freedom and hope.

We are here to be your hands, to do your will.

I am here to be your servant. And from here I bring my petition for justice. Do not forget your people . . ."

THE CAVE FELT LIKE a bandits' hideout, with all the danger and fear
that this brought. Yeshua knew how futile it had become to hope
that somehow, he and Theudas could make it home. And yet the hope
lingered, a disease too deeply rooted to be easily shaken, bringing shallow
calm, but deeper convulsions in his spirit. He sat at the cave entrance,
awake, yet somehow unconscious of the world. Surveying the land below, he saw none of it, his sight deactivated by the conflict that tortured
his thoughts. Shame at where this quest had led him, pride at what they
had done for those young boys, relief at not killing the Jewish soldiers,
remorse at the grief he had caused in others. But above all, fear. Fear of
expressing his desire to flee to Alexandria.

"Do you understand what's going on here, Yeshua of Alexandria?"
His vacant spirit was dragged back into his body by Kaleb.

Yeshua turned to see the sympathetic face of the Pharisee, and began
speaking before his consciousness had fully returned. "Does anybody?"

The Pharisee nodded in tacit agreement. "At some level, you understand as well as anybody. You've done what few would dare to do. You
have attacked professional soldiers, you've done it for the sake of justice,
and by doing it you've caused a landslide in Israel."

"And we're all sliding with you," Eliazar grunted from the darkness.

Yeshua returned to consciousness. "Kaleb. We didn't know what we
were doing. And now look. That poor man in the market place. Those innocent people in the other towns. And now Yudah." Yeshua stopped, still
unable to comprehend the reality that someone he knew so well could
have been taken and tortured. The conversation hosted an uneasy silence
as the companions recalled the fate of their friend. Yeshua continued. "I
thought I'd been so careful choosing Caesarea as the place to make the hit.

It's the capital, it's a seaport, it's a garrison. What we did could have been done by anyone from anywhere and mean anything."

The ladder to the cave began to rattle with tension from below. "Kochba," Amram smiled as he peered over the edge. The farmer's face had lost his friendly glow, carrying the scars of his family's anger at their current predicament.

Kaleb continued the conversation as the farmer found his seat. "Well you know the prefect a little better now."

"Look. We came here to do a simple job . . ." On looking around the cave Yeshua realized that he had better not finish the sentence by claiming "It's done." Instead he sighed and thought of his brothers. "My family was drawn into what happened here. We didn't choose this."

"But it is happening," said Kaleb, "your fate has chosen you, as it has chosen us all," he announced, looking with some concern at Kochba.

"To do what? What do you want from us?" The silence that greeted his question prevented Yeshua from asking other questions: Why did you follow us from Narbata? How did you know what would happen? How do the Romans know so much about what's happening now? The Egyptian restrained himself, growing ever more conscious of his own naiveté in the group's eyes, while at the same time, and for this very reason, ever more curious about why they were so keen to recruit him.

Theudas took the opportunity to ask a question of his own. "Er— how do you know you can trust us?"

"Yudah suspected everyone," said Amram, "but he trusted you."

"And, I have to say, what you boys have done says more than you know." Kochba's tone was unusually serious.

A single confusion spread across the brothers' faces.

"Nobody does what you have done without being driven by justice," Kaleb explained. "But none of us are thinking only about our family. We are thinking about our people."

"Oh come on, Rabbi! Just say it," Miriam snarled as she buried her eyes into Yeshua's. "Running away now is self-centered, it's not justice!"

Yeshua waited for someone to correct her, but even Kochba and Amram simply looked at the Egyptian, endorsing Miriam's comment with their quiet.

"Self-centered!" Yeshua tempered his indignation with a soft, cautious tone. "We gave up our lives for our brothers. How can that be selfish?"

"Wealthy Jews, thinking about no one but their wealthy brothers, then running away back to the comfort of their wealthy home." The grief emitted by Miriam's expression put the force of a sledgehammer behind her words. "That's what you wanted isn't it, Yeshua? Is that the limit of your justice?"

The words that battered the Egyptian expressed not so much an argument to be countered as a passion impossible to withstand. Again they were backed up by the obvious agreement bursting through the silence that seeped out of the cave whose very walls seemed to consider Miriam's words well chosen. Yeshua looked at his brother, and for the first time Theudas looked like one of them.

Kochba attempted to frame the criticisms inside a wider affirmation of Yeshua's quest. "We want for our people what you want for your family. And your actions have shown that you know what commitment and sacrifice are. We'd like you to join us."

Yeshua stood and walked to the mouth of the cave to gaze again on the Promised Land and look down from the mountain upon its people. His brother carried on for him.

"To do what?"

Kaleb glanced quizzically at Amram who shrugged his shoulders in reply. "We want to hit the Romans," he said, looking at the archer, "and we want to hit them hard."

"Where?" Theudas asked, in full knowledge of the answer.

"Jerusalem!" said Eliazar, before anyone else could. Yeshua turned so that he could hear the rest of the cave express its discomfort, but saw nothing other than composure.

"How often has that been tried?" Yeshua asked in astonishment. "And how many times has it worked?"

"No one has had such courage for a generation."

"And it didn't work a generation ago, because?"

"Bad planning, semi-commitment, poor timing. It was not God's purpose."

The seriousness with which such a scheme seemed to be taken by apparently sane people left the Egyptian speechless.

"At the Feast of Tabernacles," Kaleb continued. "That is the time to start a revolution. The road will be full of people entering Jerusalem anyway—every pilgrim is a potential warrior . . ."

"Whether they like it or not!" Miriam scoffed.

"Well, if they reject their calling as a Jew . . ."

Yeshua's horror at Kaleb's pronouncement, while unspoken was not unnoticed. Kochba interrupted the Pharisee to present the case in more gentle terms.

"When I was a child, I remember several gangs of armed bandits who attacked Roman soldiers, as well as Herod's guard. Once or twice they even tried to march on Jerusalem to liberate the nation. Every time, it was a bloodbath. Every would-be Messiah killed in battle or captured and crucified."

"And why was that?" Theudas asked.

"Swamped by numbers. Betrayed by spies . . ."

"Led by monkeys," Amram interrupted.

"Disobedient to God's holy law!" Kaleb added.

"The fact is," Kochba explained, "we stay small in number. And we do not try to rally support until we are upon Jerusalem. Now. . . this is where you come in . . ."

Yeshua froze. For the first time, a moment of revelation, his questions answered. What great gift could he possibly bring to a band of rebels destined for a sticky end? All eyes fell upon Amram.

The archer sighed, and continued with the history lesson. "There've always been too many factions in Jerusalem: too many competing for power; too many with their own veiled motives; every cell of bandits and rebels, competing with every other. The lower classes, the people of the land, can easily be united—they are fighting for their daily bread. But many of their leaders are from the upper classes, the educated, the wealthy, those with power. We need them. This plan will fail if they cannot be recruited, united with . . ."

"And you think the plan will work if they *can* be recruited, united with God knows who?" Amram did not answer, so Yeshua continued. "Here's a history lesson: when the Greeks took this land, Judas Maccabeus gathered an army fought them off. He managed it because . . ."

"Because he was a divine instrument, blessed by God," Kaleb moaned, wearied by the frequent necessity to state the obvious.

"He managed it because the Greek Empire was not the Roman Empire. What do you think will happen here, even if you do capture Jerusalem? Do you think you could hold it for any length of time? How long do you think you'll have before an army is encamped around the walls of Zion? How long, before history repeats itself in another mass slaughter? How long before God has to find himself another Pagan instrument to bless, because his own people were too busy baying for blood?" The Egyptian had not been conscious of his rising anger until he entered the silence that followed it.

The stillness was broken by Kaleb. "Yeshua," he whispered audibly, "why did you come to this land? You wanted justice—and rightly so. You wanted justice for your brothers, for your family. And you have won that justice with Roman blood. Now you ask us about the consequences of *our* quest for justice, *our* drawing of Roman blood? You were happy to leave the consequences of *your* quest in the hands of God, an act of faith. And here we all are—the fruit of your quest for justice."

The Pharisee needed say no more. The Egyptians' little quest was identical to the one being planned under his nose by these cave-dwelling rebels. The only difference was the scale, and the Egyptians had been recruited to widen that scale still further. Unlike anyone else from the group, the Egyptians could move with ease amongst the upper echelons of Jerusalem society. Some of the rebel cells were led by privileged members of the aristocracy—who would not be easily swayed, even by the rhetorical genius of a charismatic Pharisee. Kaleb, although relatively comfortable, simply did not have the social status required to gain a hearing with Judea's elite. What is more, as sons of a Rabbi, few—of any social class—would match their knowledge of the Scriptures. And, perhaps most important of all, they had already achieved for themselves the goal of countless thousands living in the Promised Land: justice, by the flow of Roman blood. Yeshua could find no reply, unlike his younger brother.

"Have you ever killed a man, Rabbi?" asked Theudas as his eyes buried themselves in the Pharisee's. Kaleb was as stunned as Yeshua. "I killed someone, and I thought it would make me feel better. I thought I'd be able to say I was glad I did it." Theudas paused to regain control of his emotion. "I thought I could return to my father with my head held high. I thought it would honor my brothers. Have you ever killed a man, Rabbi? . . . I thought my cause was just, that their deaths would be pleasing to God."

The only movement in the cave was Amram reaching for a jar of wine.

"That man that I killed waits for me in Sheol," he said as he dropped his head, indifferent to the presence of others. "At night he wakes me by tugging my shoulder, but he only half wakes me. And then I open my eyes see him in the dark, across the valley. He beckons me to join him across the abyss. He's trying to hurry me to my grave. He's haunting me, just watching me, all the time, without a word."

Amram did not pour a drop. Theudas lifted his head toward the Pharisee.

"Have you ever killed a man, Kaleb?" Theudas asked a third time. "If you had then you'd know in your bones that it is not pleasing to God. You don't need Moses and the Prophets to tell you that."

Amram poured.

The Pharisee looked towards the floor, nodding silently before he spoke up. "I know the Scriptures, and I know the voice of God, and I know the cost of sacrifice." Kaleb sighed. "But you remind us, brother, that today is for mourning. Tomorrow we make our plans."

The shadows of the Galilean hills were reaching for the sea as the brothers walked a little distance and stood side by side in the evening humidity. Theudas drew deep breaths as he felt the hand of his brother upon his shoulder. Yeshua had missed the effect that the last few days had inflicted upon Theudas. "I'm sorry," he said, "I hadn't . . ."

"I don't know where that came from," the younger brother puffed apologetically.

"You'll never get over it," said Amram, rubbing the back of Theudas' neck before refilling his cup, "but hopefully you will get used to it."

Yeshua said nothing, but transferred his support through the shoulder he was touching. Theudas then felt a gentle squeeze on his other arm as Kochba smiled at him and clambered down the ladder. "Think we need some more wine, boys."

ə❧

"Well you can do it without me!" A woman's voice echoed from the western cave above. It was followed by an uneasy peace that lasted until Kochba emerged.

There was no pretending he hadn't heard. "You alright?" asked Yeshua.

"We'll be alright—it's not an easy situation—not for any of us. But none of my family chose to come here."

"I know how that feels," Yeshua laughed sympathetically, forcing a smile from Kochba. "Gave up waiting for you to refill our cups so thought I'd come and do it!"

"Amira doesn't want to be here. And I have to say I can't blame her. I've given up trying to make her see reason. Reason may well be on her side anyway."

"Anything I can do?"

"Give her a wide berth!" Kochba grinned and tried to shake himself out of his misery.

"Your sons don't seem to share your enthusiasm for rebellion either."

"Of course they don't! They've always had it easy. What possible reason could they have for risking all that?

"Well, what reason do *you* have for jeopardizing all that, Kochba?"

"Justice. I want justice for my people."

"And you've brought your children up *without* a hunger for justice?" Yeshua looked up towards the cave where Kochba's family rested. Kochba's younger son, Sol, withdrew from the archway to hide in the darkness of the mountain.

"My sons have had it easy. Of course they want things in our land to be fair. Of course they don't want t o be crippled by taxes. But they don't remember a time when this wasn't normal. Herod is all they can remember."

"At the very least you might expect them to sympathize," said the Egyptian before pausing. "Don't tell me," he continued after a pause, "wealthy boys, concerned about their wealthy lifestyle and going back to their wealthy home."

Kochba laughed reluctantly. "Sound familiar, Yeshua? What does your father think of you being here?"

"I guess he just wants us home. But here we are, ensnared in Kaleb's plans . . . Where is Kaleb's father, Kochba?"

Kochba whistled as he drew breath. "Now that's a long story," he sighed, shaking his head.

"Well so is mine, but everyone knows it. It's not like we're pressed for time up here."

"Kaleb will tell you he has no Father. And that's partly true. His father . . . you won't believe this . . . Kaleb's father is a Sadducee."

Yeshua laughed.

"I'm serious. A wealthy, aristocratic, Jerusalemite . . . a Sadducee. A follower of Moses . . . a collaborator with Rome."

"How does a wealthy Sadducee end up with a son who's a rebel, a Pharisee, a . . . well, a Kaleb!"

"Told you it was a long story!" Kochba uncorked the vat of wine that lay on the back of the cart, as Yeshua held a smaller vessel beneath it for the farmer to pour. "The short version is that Kaleb is a bastard!"

"Has he ever met his father?"

Kochba shrugged. "His father supported him financially growing up, to stop his mother blabbing, I suppose. Kaleb didn't know, of course. He thought his mother was a widow, and that his Father was a trader from Cyprus. He found out when he was about twelve. Can you imagine what that did to him?"

Yeshua remained in a state of disbelief. "Is his father still alive?"

"Not according to the Pharisee! As far as he's concerned, his only father is the God of Abraham, Isaac and Jacob."

"So that's why every Jew is his brother . . ."

"His plan is exactly the same as yours was. He just has more brothers to avenge."

Yeshua shook his head. "How can you honor Abraham if you cannot honor your own father?"

"Perhaps you should go and ask my sons." Kochba tugged at the rope, signalling for the wine to be hoisted up to the cave. His face carried a trace of the fear Yeshua had witnessed when he first arrived at the cave, but it was gone in an instant. "You'll honor your Father, Yeshua, I don't doubt that."

"Which one?" Yeshua smiled.

Birdsong and daylight invaded the cave and began to prize its inhabitants from their rest. The evening's wine and the battle to find sleep had kept Yeshua from his usual early awakening. Only the tug on his sleeve brought him to the reality of the cave. The yawning Egyptian's eyes settled straight into those of Miriam. The morning suited her, he concluded, delaying his awareness of what was happening outside.

Miriam sat straining her eyes towards the sight that had captivated Kaleb and Theudas. A man of about thirty, walking slowly along the valley between this and the hill opposite. It was nothing remarkable in itself, although there was something about him that was thoroughly at home in the paradise of the Promised Land. What was he doing up here at this time? He was no shepherd and no traveler. He did not look once toward the cliffs, but he radiated the fact that he was aware of the outlaws. Who was this man? Why did he carry no hint of fear if he knew there were bandits watching him? What had he been doing up on the hills at night? The questions were a mere curiosity to Yeshua who returned to his horse blanket and his dream. For Kaleb the man's identity was an intrigue, and his fascination was contagious to those who were awake. The mystery figure edged his way carefully down the slope for half an hour until he became a tiny dot on the distant plain. But there he met a group of other tiny dots who had obviously been waiting for him.

Kaleb turned to shake Yeshua. "Are you ready for a walk?" He threw a piece of bread at the dazed Egyptian, lowered the ladder and disappeared. Yeshua consumed the bread and followed the Pharisee down the ladder, still chewing as he went.

"I think I know who that is," said the Pharisee. Yeshua yawned in response, still not fully aware of where he was going. "I've been looking forward to this."

"Kaleb," said the Egyptian as he began to wake up, "I still have no idea what you're talking about . . . or where we're going. Who is that guy?"

"He," Kaleb enjoyed pronouncing that first word so much that he repeated it. "He, is Israel . . . apparently." Yeshua looked confused, so the Pharisee elaborated. "The Messiah . . . Israel in person. This is Yeshua of Nazareth, the Galilean Prophet."

"Oh, and the last thing you want is a Messiah to bring justice to these people," Yeshua sniggered, "that's our job after all."

Kaleb laughed. "I'm intrigued, that's all." He bit into an apple and spoke on with his mouth full. "What makes these people think they are Messiahs? Who appoints them as kings over Israel? Aren't you even curious?"

"Why should I be curious? Even our greatest kings were just Caesars with Jewish names." The Pharisee's crunching left room for Yeshua to continue. "Every one of them claims to be the son of God." He put his hand inside the Roman purse of his victim as Kaleb continued. He knew well enough that the coins were inscribed with the phrase "Caesar is the Son of God." But as usual, his fingers found their way onto the figurine he assumed was his victim's son.

"Instruments of God, so they claim," Kaleb chuckled, "but they are wrong. Israel is the Son of God, all Israel, all our people, as one. We are God's Son . . ." He took another bite. "So how has this peasant from a flee-infested, Galilean slum-dwelling convinced everyone he is God's own son?" He stretched his eyes into the distance. "And I bet you thought *I* was obnoxious," he grinned as he spat out an apple seed.

Kaleb and Yeshua had seen growing numbers moving toward this figure on the plain, but the path had then taken him out of sight. As the companions crossed the final and gentle ridge that would bring them down onto the levels near the lake, they saw that the crowds had swollen up to at least several hundred.

"Why has he got such a following?" asked Yeshua.

"That's what I want to find out. There are stories of him healing people, driving out demons and promising that the Kingdom of God has come. But I'd like to know what kind of kingdom he's promising us."

"What kind of kingdom would you like to see, Kaleb?" The Pharisee enjoyed the question too much to be capable of any answer before the next question came. "A kingdom of anger?"

Kaleb's pleasure gave way to defensiveness. "A kingdom of justice," he said. Yeshua knew that he had hit a raw nerve.

"So why are you so angry?"

"Angry?" he replied, as though the Egyptian had mistaken him for someone else.

"Do you want a kingdom that just reflects your character?"

"Would you say I'm an angry character?"

"I wouldn't dare!" Both grinned silently, before Yeshua continued. "Anger can be righteous. But what is it that drives you?"

"Justice!" he frowned, cramming his entire personality into his eyebrows.

"Where is your family?" Yeshua inquired, as though the question had long since been building.

For a moment the Pharisee eyed his companion, scanning Yeshua's spirit to identify the source of such a question. "Out there on the plain," he declared eventually, as though he were now interrogating the Egyptian. "These people are my family, and I desire justice for all of them," he concluded, showing with the light behind his eye that he knew well enough this was no answer to Yeshua's question.

"You know what I'm asking. Where is your family?"

The Pharisee paused, and then frowned. "Dead!" he answered, as though they deserved to be.

"Well, I'm sorry to hear that. But where were they?"

Kaleb grunted as though forced to confess a crime. "My mother was from Caesarea, and was moved to Narbata by the man she loved. He bought her a house, gave her a living, paid for her son to be clothed and fed. But he never once saw her after she conceived. He's in Jerusalem. He wants nothing to do with his son, nor his son with him."

"Why not?"

As they approached the crowds the Pharisee and the Egyptian found their paths converging with others. Two men, probably father and son, appeared beside them, having traveled from the South.

"Rabbi," the elder called to Kaleb. "Is this him? Is this Yeshua of Nazareth?"

"I believe it is," said Kaleb. "And you don't sound like Galileans. How far have you traveled to hear this man?"

"Two days' journey, from Jerusalem."

"What news from the holy city?" asked Yeshua of Alexandria.

"Bad news for Galilee," the old man answered gravely.

Kaleb and Yeshua braced themselves for what would follow. "The prefect is in Jerusalem at the moment. And before we left two days ago, while there was a group from Galilee offering their sacrifices in the temple, he sent his troops in."

"To the temple?" Kaleb asked in Disbelief. "To do what?"

"Bloody murder," answered the younger man, who looked as though he'd witnessed the event. "Sword and spear. While the Galileans were making their sacrifice. A godless cocktail of human and animal blood."

"Why?" asked Yeshua, fearing that he already knew the answer.

"He said he was trying to stop a rebellion that had started in Caesarea and was working its way east," said the older man. "He said that rebels were plotting against him, rebels from Galilee . . ."

"How many did he kill?" asked Kaleb.

"Twenty," answered the son.

Yeshua moved to the side of the road and vomited.

T HE PHARISEE FOLLOWED THE Egyptian who had wondered aimlessly from the road. "Yeshua, stop," he called. Taking a seat beside one another, they set their gaze across the Sea of Galilee. "There it is: the prefect's revenge," Kaleb growled, "the murder of worshippers from Galilee because he knows we're here."

"So Amram was right," muttered Yeshua. "How much blood has been spilt on my account?"

"Brother," said Kaleb softly, "you did not kill them." The Egyptian looked at the Pharisee, who touched his arm gently before continuing. "You are part of this—but you're not responsible for prefect's actions. It is he, not you, who will be judged by those actions. You cannot control whose blood is spilt."

"I wish it had been mine," said Yeshua, devoid of all conviction.

"And why do you think it wasn't?" Kaleb's words brought an unexpected depth of comfort. "He isn't finished with you yet."

"But those Galileans were innocent. Was he finished with them?"

"No one is innocent, not a single human. But if God has chosen to take the lives of those Galileans, even by the Roman sword, all we can do is live as best we can and entrust ourselves his mercy." The Egyptian's attention began to drift. "Yeshua! You are not God. You have no power over life and death. But God has a purpose for you."

The Egyptian shook his head and then turned it to the South. "He has to be stopped," he said, too lost in his thoughts to speak with an ounce of conviction.

"Who?"

"The prefect!" His mouth uttered the words but the Egyptian was distracted by his imagination. Kaleb looked at him and seeing only an empty shell held his tongue. Unlike those of Theudas, Yeshua's inner thoughts were not about to be flushed out by silence and Kaleb knew it. Nearing the fringes of the crowds that swelled about the Galilean prophet, the Egyptian sighed but uttered no word.

Rumors had circulated that the Messiah and his followers were working their way towards Jerusalem where eventually he expected to carry a cross to his death. He had warned his followers that they must share his fate, the destiny of every failed rebel against Rome. Such expectations seemed too defeatist to account for the enormous crowds that he pulled, but he was a figure of such charisma, his followers must have assumed that talk of his own downfall was some dark picture language they hadn't yet grasped.

The companions came within hearing distance of the Galilean prophet and found a seat on the grass of a slope forming part of a natural amphitheatre. The preacher had chosen his platform well, and his words echoed clearly and deliberately around the seated crowds. He would say just a few at a time to make sure he could be heard, but the frequent pauses as the prophet unburdened himself added weight to all he said. The companions from the caves had joined the spectacle at the right moment.

"Today we hear twenty of our countrymen in Galilee have been murdered by the prefect's soldiers as they offered their sacrifices in the temple." He allowed the ripple of horror to dissipate before continuing. "The prefect says they were rebels!" The mention of the senior Roman in the province of Judea was enough to evoke various and widespread expressions of ridicule and disgust from his listeners.

"Others say that rebels or not, their death is God's punishment." Yeshua glanced at Kaleb, who was one of these 'others'. The Pharisee had begun to frown. "Do you honestly think that these poor Galileans were worse sinners than all other Galileans because they suffered this way?" Yeshua of Galilee lifted his palms and allowed the crowd to answer the question in silence. Yeshua smiled at the number of listeners who could not resist the temptation to answer his rhetorical question out loud. The prophet continued. "Well if you do not turn your life around you too will die by the Roman sword."

What was he talking about? The crowds simply looked confused, some with disapproval, others with genuine curiosity.

"On the other hand, what about the eighteen from Jerusalem, looking for healing at the pool of Siloam, crushed to death when the tower collapsed on them? Was God angry with them?" The Egyptian knew of this incident only through Kaleb, who had drawn precisely this "angry God" conclusion. He could feel the expression on the Pharisee's face without looking at him. "Do you think they were more guilty than everyone else living in Jerusalem?" This time no one verbalized an answer. "Well if you don't turn away from violent resistance, you will die the same way."

As disapproval intensified for some and confusion grew for others, the prophet unburdened himself:

"Whether by Roman sword or falling rubble, violent resistance will lead to a violent death." Yeshua guessed he was talking about Jerusalem falling to a Roman army, but dared not ask Kaleb for confirmation. "But when vengeance comes, it will come upon all. Roman swords are no more choosy than falling masonry about their victims." There was his answer.

Over to Yeshua's left a man of about fifty, surrounded by his own miniature group of disciples, challenged the prophet. "Look at what those Roman swords have done to our people. Those who carry them are our enemies."

The prophet looked him in the eye and issued a command: "Do not take up arms against them." His gentle voice spoke with an unidentifiable authority. But not enough to stay Kaleb's anger.

"An eye for an eye, a tooth for a tooth," Kaleb shouted, using the word of Moses against the word of this Messiah. The groundswell of murmured expressions suggested that Kaleb had voiced a conviction treasured by many present.

The prophet's gaze fell with full force upon Kaleb, who looked away. Yeshua of Galilee addressed the crowd. "You heard someone say 'an eye for an eye, and tooth for tooth.'" He gestured towards the angry Pharisee from Narbata. "But I tell you, do not buy into violent resistance against evil."

A voice erupted from elsewhere in the crowd. "How else do we resist our enemies if not by force?"

The Galilean was passionate but not perturbed, and seemed to have prepared himself in advance for the specific objections thrown at him. "You cannot arm yourself against this enemy, but you can disarm your enemy."

His challenger was not convinced "And how do we do that?"

"By loving him," he said, and cast his eyes from right to left. "Yes, love this enemy."

Half the crowd laughed at him, but the prophet laughed with them. It was obvious to many that the prophet's answer was already loaded on his bowstring, leaving him at ease to share the amusement of those who ridiculed him. His laughter soon ended theirs.

"Love your enemies," he said again, "Love them. Pray for them. Pray for these persecutors of yours. If he slaps you across the right cheek, don't be tempted to slap him back."

"Sorry to hit your hand with my face!" said an angry voice that gained a few chuckles. "Some pig-scoffing foreigner steals our pride and we apologize for it?"

"If you sacrifice your pride you can rob him of his," said the prophet. "Instead of hitting him back, let him slap your left cheek as well—he'd have to hit you with the palm of his hand, and he can't do that without considering you an equal. Who loses their pride then?" A broader laugh came with the recognition that Roman customs and Roman authority were being undermined without violence or lawbreaking.

"And if someone wants to commandeer your tunic, let him have your cloak as well." The chuckles of ridicule had ceased. "If one of these soldiers forces you to carry his pack for a mile, don't break the law by re-fusing, but don't honor the law by complying. You can undermine their law by exceeding it: go with him two miles instead of one."

The subversive logic of the prophet from Nazareth was growing on the Egyptian. This would-be Messiah was showing that refusing violent resistance was by no means cowardly. But the message was too late for Yeshua, fumbling with the figurine in his pocket, thinking of the violence he had already set in motion. Too many people had been killed because of Yeshua's desire for revenge. The prophet's words could be admired, but seemed too idealistic to bring about change in the harsh realities of Israel. Still, as he spoke them, the prophet's conclusion wielded power. "Love this enemy."

Another member of the crowd was unable to contain himself. "Love your neighbor and hate your enemy," he shouted with a hint of satisfaction. Again it was not without the crowds' approval that he threw his objection at the prophet. Again the prophet made eye contact with the heckler. Again the heckler averted his glare. "You have heard it said, 'love your neighbor and hate your enemy.'" He scanned the crowds. "But I tell you, love your enemies and pray for those who persecute you, that you may be sons of your father in heaven."

"What kind of father is that? . . . A father who loves his enemies and prays for his persecutors is a collaborator." Kaleb retracted his lips in anger. "This man is whitewashing over the filth of injustice, and they are all being sucked in. Who wants to worship a collaborator?"

For Yeshua, however, the Galilean's message had more authenticity than that of Kaleb. This Messiah did not seek the approval of the multitude, but seemed to gain much of it regardless. He thought back to the synagogue at Narbata, where the entire crowd had felt almost as one in their approval of Kaleb's message. He thought back to that fateful day in Jerusalem, as the prefect had addressed the people. Again, the masses responded as one, but on that occasion they were one in their disdain at what they heard. Within the small groups scattered around, opinion was clearly divided, right down to brother against brother. Some were stamping their feet in anger; others were overjoyed at what they heard. Yeshua of Nazareth had shaped the crowd's reaction in a way that he never seen before.

"Violence will only lead to a violent death!" The prophet continued in his exhortation to abandon murderous resistance. "Not because your enemy is great, but because Yahweh has appointed you to be a light to the Gentiles, not an enemy to them. Does the kingdom of God bring healing and peace, or does it bring violence and death?"

He could see that, regardless of whether they agreed, the confusion had lifted from the crowd and they grasped at least something of what Yeshua of Nazareth was saying. He paused for a moment and looked at the multitude. He seemed to be assessing a dimension of the crowd's spirit invisible to all but him.

Unlike any preacher Yeshua had heard, this man seemed to proceed by asking questions. Instead of quoting from Scripture as though he were standing above it, the Scriptures themselves seemed to flow through his words in a way that carried immense credibility. It spilled out through every breath, gesture and glance. Too many of those glances were directed at the Egyptian, or so he felt. The entire message of this prophet seemed to have been crafted with the assassin in mind. Having completed his survey of the crowd, the Galilean plotted his course and continued.

"There was a man who had a fig-tree planted in his vineyard." He nodded south along the river Jordan towards Jerusalem. The nod was unnecessary as Jeremiah, the ancient prophet of doom, had used fig tree and vineyard language in his infamous warnings about the fall of the city and its temple all those centuries ago, when his prophecies—hated though they were—had proven themselves true. The Galilean prophet continued. "This man went to look for fruit on his fig tree, but couldn't find any."

This was a blatant warning that destruction was imminent, and that rebellion was futile. If the people of the Promised Land do not bear the fruit of righteousness and peace, that land will be taken from them and given to others. Yeshua of Nazareth followed in the footsteps of his prophetic ancestor. "So the owner said to the man who took care of the vineyard, 'For three years now I've been waiting for this tree to bear fruit, and so far it's given me nothing. Cut it down—soil here is too precious to waste on a pointless tree.'" Even as far North as Galilee, describing Jerusalem, the city of David, the holy city, as a pointless tree was a dangerous move. But the prophet continued the story to suggest that hope was not lost, and that there was still time to repent, still time for Israel to abandon its futile attempts at armed resistance. "'Sir', the man said 'leave it just one more year and I'll dig around and compost it. If it bears fruit next year, fine. If not, I'll cut it down then.'"

With that, Yeshua of Nazareth disappeared. Probably a good thing to disappear after making that kind of threat, thought the Egyptian. It seemed to take a few minutes for those who were angry to grasp the significance of what the prophet had just said. But by the time their anger had risen those whose opposition to this prophet looked like it might escalate beyond verbal debate were unable to find him.

"No wonder he's told his followers to carry a cross: If he tries that in Jerusalem he won't get away so easily . . ."

"You didn't agree with the Galilean then?" asked Yeshua mischievously.

The Pharisee forced a smile, which was promptly displaced by an eyebrow raised at Yeshua in feigned curiosity.

"You agree with him then?"

"This time last week I might have," Yeshua conceded, "but I can't see how he's going to solve the problems the Romans are creating."

"Exactly. Murders won't cease. Taxes won't be dropped, farmers will still lose their lands, tax collectors will still get rich, peasants will still get poor . . . But that man . . . he makes the people of the land be happy with their plight . . . That's what makes me angry," said Kaleb, frown and all. "The God of Israel is not a God who tolerates this injustice. The father of us all is no collaborator." Yeshua turned to face Kaleb. The Pharisee would usually issue such declarations with the full force of his distant gaze, but the strength of his eyes again had petered out even before it left his own head, depriving his strongly spoken words of any conviction. "Tolerating evil makes us sons of our Father in heaven? What kind of father is that?"

Though Kaleb and Yeshua walked alongside one another back to the caves, they traveled separately. The fiercest whirlpool drew Yeshua in on himself: Swirling recollections mesmerized, disorientated him: the news of Galilean deaths, the words of the prophet, the frustration of the crowds, the reaction of Kaleb. The Pharisee remained ensnared by the sermon he had heard, now and again regurgitating a sentence or phrase as if to exorcise it from his mind. If either spoke, the other would not hear them.

The Sun had passed its zenith by the time Kaleb and Yeshua arrived back at the caves, carrying with them some freshly laid eggs and a basket of prunes they had collected from a village en route. Amram, Eliazar and Kochba were sitting in the afternoon sun enjoying a jug of wine.

"You were right," Yeshua said to the archer.

"Of course I was right," Amram answered. "Right about what?"

"The prefect," Kaleb declared. "He's slaughtered twenty Galileans in Jerusalem."

"What?" Kochba choked up his drink.

"In the temple, while they were offering their sacrifice," Kaleb's righteous anger mounted as he relayed the news. "He must have relished that thought. Killing them as they were worshipping. It's a metaphor of who that man is."

"Twenty men!" said Kochba, still in disbelief.

"Do you think he'll stop there?" asked Eliazar.

"It certainly won't have won him any friends in Herod's household," Amram grunted. "I believe we may have forced a conflict between our great leaders," Amram smiled, before expressing his satisfaction in the usual manner. "Still, at least your family can go home safely now," he continued, earning pensive nod from Kochba.

"Do I think he'll stop there?" Yeshua said to Eliazar. "I know we won't."

FROM THE HEIGHTS OF Galilee, the Promised Land below was all at peace. Shades of deep green had defied the law of seasons and survived into late summer, suggesting plentiful harvest and the absence of hunger or thirst. In all directions this was a land that flowed with milk and honey. The Jordan river, feeding the quiet Sea of Galilee, which in turn invited towns and villages to cling to its banks and suckle from all it contained. A light rain was carried along a light breeze, which even on the hilltops brought comfort as it brought the skies to life. Compared to the dry wastelands around Alexandria, the land below was a picture of beauty as the Egyptian brothers gazed across it.

"Do you think this is how Adonai sees the Promised Land?" Yeshua asked his brother.

"When he ventures out of his cave you mean?"

"Well that's just it. Does he sit above it as we do now? Does he watch it from a safe distance? Does he enjoy the beauty of all that he has created, without caring about the horrors of the people who live in that beautiful land?"

Theudas looked at his brother. "Er—why are you talking like this?"

"I can't get Miriam's words out of my head. I swear that woman can read my spirit." He waited for Theudas to disagree, but received no answer. "I can't get Kaleb's words out of my head either."

"Well, there are too many of those for that to be healthy!"

"He said we're here in Israel for a purpose."

Theudas shrugged his shoulders.

"I could go along with Kaleb, but that prophet . . ."

"Not more words rattling round your head? You need some more wine to help you think straight." He refilled Yeshua's cup.

"He spoke about us being sons of our Father in heaven." Theudas offered a confused frown. "I swear he was looking straight at me. . . The God I rejected was nothing like the father described by that prophet."

"Will you please drink up!" said Theudas, only half in jest.

"If that's true. If God is our Father—then who are our brothers?"

"If my memory serves me, all Israel is the Son of God. Moses said it, the prophets said it, and—correct me if I'm wrong—but I'm pretty sure Yeshua of Alexandria said it!"

"Down on the plain today. . . those are our brothers," the Egyptian pointed with a tremble in his voice. Theudas lost his grin and sat up. "We came here to seek justice for our brothers. But our brothers are right here, suffering because of that pompous cowardly pig-turd from Caesarea." Yeshua turned to face his brother. "We can do something about that."

"So you're not still obsessed with getting home?"

"We're children of Abraham and we're in Israel," said Yeshua. "This land is in our blood."

"This land will swallow our blood, just like every other piece of land under heaven," replied the younger brother, earning an exasperated glare from the elder. "Okay, okay. You know I'm with you, brother. And I hope I still am your brother now that you have multitudes of them!" sniggered Theudas.

Their conversation was interrupted by the complaints of a donkey in the valley below as it was loaded up by Kochba's servant.

With the slaughter of Galileans visiting Judea, tension between Pilatus, the prefect of Judea and Herod, the Tetrarch of Galilee would be running high. Collaboration between the two rulers was near impossible. Kochba's family could get back to the farmstead without fear of Herod exacting revenge for crimes committed in the territory of Pilatus. The brothers hurried down to see them off.

Amira and her two sons had lost no time in their preparations to return to comfort, while Kochba himself made no attempt to dissuade them. Bitterness at their confinement within the caves was tempered by relief at the prospect of returning home, and allowed Kochba's family to part with the others on good terms. No one looked more relieved than the farmer, released as he was from the guilt of dragging them into the dangers that arose from his own actions.

"Do you think he'll be back?" asked Theudas as the family trundled downhill.

"Sooner than he plans if the look on her face is anything to go by," Amram squirmed.

The crack of a burning log thrust orange sparks searching for the sky, each one a passionate prayer destined to burn out long before it reached the heavens. The faces gathered around the fire reflected its glow, especially the face of Kochba, newly returned, hugely relieved, and looking forward to tasting the stew Amram was busy preparing. Yeshua waited for a lull in the conversation about Kochba's journey before rising to his feet purposefully enough to command quiet. The fire cracked again as it bestowed its blessing on Yeshua, illuminating him against the darkness.

"Kaleb and I listened to a prophet this morning," he said, while Kaleb puffed out in his bewilderment at the Galilean. "He told us that God disapproves of rebellion against Rome, that it was doomed to failure." So far he had told them nothing they hadn't already heard. "I think he was right," he said, while the rest of the group sighed in frustration.

"I thought you said he was a dreamer," Kaleb frowned, but in confusion more than anger.

"He was. But I think he was right to say that violence was wrong." Kaleb began to shake his head but the Egyptian continued. "I also think that what I'm about to suggest is wrong." A rapid exchange of brief stares rebounded around the group, all eyes channeling a hidden energy that fuelled the flames before them.

"I think we should kill the prefect."

After a moment's silence, the group responded with laughter. Theudas himself coughed out his wine in shock and was wiping his mouth as Amram answered.

"That's what I like to hear. Simple, straightforward. . . ridiculous," he declared, emphasizing his final word with relish. "Have you got any further in your planning?"

"He'll be in Jerusalem next month for the Feast of Tabernacles, addressing the people from his usual place."

"From the high walls of his garrison. How do you plan to get in there?" asked Kochba.

"I don't." Yeshua left the thread dangling. After a few seconds, all eyes moved towards Amram who smiled at the audacity but apparently not at the potential effectiveness of the plan.

"You think we can just leave Amram to shoot him?" asked Eliazar.

"How can we get his bow into the city?" asked Kochba.

"We don't have to." Again, he left his comment hanging, for Amram to answer.

"They say there's quite an armory in the temple," the archer conceded, his voice suggesting that a more promising brand of grin was imminent.

"In the temple?" asked Kochba.

"It's the perfect hiding place," Kaleb explained. "The Romans aren't allowed in there. But I know how to access it."

"The beating heart of Israel," said Yeshua sarcastically.

"I can get whatever weapons we need from our temple," said Kaleb regardless.

"So we just leave it all to Amram?" Eliazar said. "There's at least fifty guards posted around the colonnade when the prefect gives his speech."

"More like two hundred," Yeshua smiled.

"And they'd be on him before he could string his bow." Eliazar had identified the real problem, but it was clear from the Egyptian's confidence that he was a step ahead.

"If the prefect gives his speech from the same place at every festival . . ."

"Which he does," Kaleb interrupted.

". . . then there are buildings on the far side of the colonnade where you can take all the time in the world to string a bow and take aim," the Egyptian explained. "You'd be indoors and invisible."

"What are those buildings?" asked Kochba.

"Private dwellings aren't they? Some are store rooms for animal food," said Kaleb warming to the idea that was taking shape.

"Won't they be guarded if the prefect's exposing himself to the people he's persecuting?" asked Kochba.

"And that's why—in answer to Eliazar's question—we do need more than just Amram," said Yeshua. "Let Kaleb lead his riot. If the riot works, can you imagine the effect that killing the prefect would have? If Kaleb's plan doesn't work, it would still set up a diversion to help us hit the prefect. If the prefect dies, there'll be a riot anyway—and if that riot is planned in advance, think of what Kaleb could do. At the very least, we would rid ourselves of the tyrant that's crushing our brothers. But that's as far as I've got. Do you think it could work?"

"Amram?" said Kaleb, whistling as he inhaled.

Amram launched into a string of highly relished, over-pronounced observations. "Half a dozen amateurs, attacking a Roman prefect, while he's in his fortress? It's pure unfermented cow dung." He winked at Yeshua, "Of course it will work."

"What made you change your mind, Yeshua?" Eliazar asked. "You didn't want to kill anyone, now you want to kill the prefect."

"One more life. If we invest all of our energy in taking just one life, the man who most deserves to die, it will have a far greater effect than just attacking random soldiers. Less bloodshed, greater chance of success. I'm still not sure about the riot beyond its job as a diversion. This is an assassination not a massacre. Massacres are what Romans do."

"It's got to be a hundred paces from those buildings to the fort," said Kochba with an eyebrow raised towards Amram. "Are you really that good?"

"Well, best we find out!" Amram replied. "I'll go and get my bow, you walk a hundred paces uphill!"

"In the dark?" the farmer contorted his face in confusion. Amram chose not to hear. "Right you are," Kochba laughed. He grabbed a horse blanket and marched up the hill. "Behold the prefect of Judea!" he called to the mountain, waving the blanket behind him as he marched.

Amram returned with his bow and a small bundle of arrows. The bow was made of Mediterranean Cypress wood, its length about a foot shorter than Amram's height, the horns at either end curving away from the archer and towards their target. Tipped with steel, the arrows were furnished with goose feathers to keep them true. Kochba tied the blanket around the trunk of a small bush just over a hundred paces up hill, and hurried back to the others.

The bow voiced its complaint as Amram's powerful right arm drew the feathers to his cheekbone. The archer's fingers gently loosed, and drew immediately for their next shot. A crack was followed by a thump. His first arrow had sunk itself deep into the prefectorial bush. He loosed the second. Again there was a crack but this time it was followed by a muttered curse rather than a distant thump. He loosed his third. The crack and thump found each other again. And then a third time. And then a fourth.

"Not bad," laughed Kochba, who was not alone in his involuntary amusement at Amram's proficiency.

"Have you been an archer all your life?" Theudas asked.

"Not yet," the archer grinned as he set off to collect his arrows. Amram winked at Yeshua, a gesture that was witnessed only by the Egyptian and Kaleb. Yeshua knew well enough that this display, unnecessary though it was, would seal the group's approval of the project as a whole and came as a silent but invaluable endorsement.

"And Kaleb has contacts in Jerusalem?" Yeshua asked.

"Places to lodge, access to weapons and help to plan an escape," he replied, indicating his support of the plan.

"You think we'll be able to escape this time, from a Roman fortress that's just lost its prefect?" asked Theudas. Yeshua noticed Miriam's eyeballs shift briefly towards his younger brother. Her eyes were a strange mix of optimism and hopelessness, but as she shifted her gaze towards Kaleb it was unclear which emotion had the upper hand.

"We may as well plan for it," said Kaleb, once again, without the full strength of his usual energy.

"We'll need to be in Jerusalem a good week beforehand," Yeshua insisted.

"So we'll need more money," said Kaleb.

"I think we should use Roman money." Yeshua removed the figurine, which had lost its voice, from his purse, and threw his remaining coins to the sandy earth around which all were sat. Theudas threw his, and Amram, having rolled his eyes, also threw a purse.

"Er—I thought you had three?" Theudas smiled.

"What do you think you're drinking?" Amram grumbled, before descending into more guttural convulsions.

"We need to feed ourselves for another month," said Kaleb with some concern. "We'll need money for lodging and food in Jerusalem, and we'll need plenty of coinage while we're there."

"How much do we have?" Yeshua asked.

"Not enough!" Kaleb replied, ignorant of how much money lay on the ground before them.

Amram shuffled with the coins. "Thirty, thirty five denarii," he said.

"Enough to get us through a couple of weeks here, but we'll need as much again for Jerusalem," Kaleb declared. "I think we'll need to take some more," he concluded.

"From where?" asked Theudas.

"From Rome," Yeshua answered.

"I'd like another drink on Rome," Amram smirked.

"Then we take it from tax collectors," said Kaleb. "They get rich off the people of the land, stealing their money and passing it to Roman pockets." Pointing down towards the assassins' loot, the Pharisee continued, "That money belongs to this land. And all of it's traveled through tax collectors. There's a tax station on the road from Capernaum." He turned his head north. "It has four guards. I say we hit them."

"But they're Jewish. They're our brothers. We can't . . ."

"They are collaborators," Kaleb interrupted, "and they draw their profit from the poverty of our people."

"Those tax collectors are Jewish civilians. Even the soldiers guarding them are Jewish." Yeshua repeated himself to address the Pharisee. "If we start on civilian targets, on Jewish targets then we have become the very thing we oppose."

On seeing the rising emotional state of the Egyptian, Kaleb answered in such a way as to invite the rest of the group to share his cynical smile. "Come on, Yeshua. It's not that simple and you know it." But the Pharisee was the only one smiling.

"Justice is always simple," Yeshua replied, with seriousness if not composure.

"Things here are never simple, you know that. Rome is more than Roman soldiers. Every tax collector, every Sadducee, every collaborator is . . ." his voice slowed to synchronize several syllables with his rhythmic pointing at the ground, "al-ready com-promised."

"And where then do we draw the line, Kaleb? Prostitutes used by soldiers? Builders working on their garrison? Slaves in their household, farmers in their fields? Yeshua paused to restrain his voice from raising any further. "It was Rome that made collaborators out of our brothers."

"Collaborators *are* no longer our brothers . . ." The calm of Kaleb's voice reveled itself as artificial.

"Well, I thank the God of Scripture that he is more merciful than you, Kaleb!" said the son of the rabbi.

"Mercy without justice is not the God of the prophets or of Moses. God's mercy is for those who love him; his wrath is for those who dishonor him. Those collaborators dishonor our God."

The argument between the Pharisee and the Egyptian was interrupted by Kochba, whose input pulled the rug from beneath Kaleb's feet. "I have to say, I think Yeshua's right," he pronounced. "I'm not spilling any of the blood of Abraham."

"Me neither," Amram grunted, inviting the group's attention. "Not because I'm merciful! And not because I'm angry. I just want to hit Romans." On seeing that the conversation left him room for further comment, he continued, "Every Roman soldier has sworn an oath. Their lives are no longer their own. They are ready to die."

"We need funds to see this through," Kaleb declared with a restored pretence of calm. "We do that by hitting soldiers here in Galilee where we know the land and the routines. Why take pointless risk by hitting Roman soldiers in a different province?"

Kochba stared at the ground as he shook his head. "No more Jewish blood. No more death for Abraham's descendants," he insisted.

"What is everyone's problem?" asked Kaleb with an expression that combined confusion and understanding. "The Galilean prophet was right about one thing: It's not our blood that makes us Jewish. Abraham was chosen by God because of his courage. His readiness to take risk because of his faithfulness to God. That is what makes a true descendant of Abraham. Our faith, not our blood alone. Herod's soldiers are not faithful to Adonai. Tax collectors are not faithful to Adonai. They are not Jewish, and neither is their blood.

Eliazar, who had been nodding his head, now spoke up. "My slingshot, Amram's bow. There is no risk here in Galilee. Kochba's house is within a few miles of the tax station. We could do it tomorrow."

"The only valid target is a Roman target," Yeshua maintained, without separating his teeth.

"Our ultimate target remains a Roman target," Kaleb said, before addressing the rest of the group. "Don't you see? All else is to serve that main objective. We shouldn't jeopardize our plans in Jerusalem by taking such risks."

"Didn't you just say that these risks demonstrate our faith and make us good Jews, descendants of Abraham," Yeshua snarled. "If we trust in the God of Abraham, he will honor our faithfulness."

Kaleb's frustration at failing to change anyone's mind had kindled a fire beneath the words he spoke. "God has already given us all we need, right there—on a plate." The Pharisee pointed in the direction of the distant tax station. "Turning down that gift to try and keep our consciences clear is godless insanity. If you all want to go and attack Roman soldiers, go ahead, but I will have no part in it." When Kaleb saw that his threat met with no objection, he continued. "Fine," he grumbled, as though the decision were his. "But while you do that, I will go ahead to Jerusalem to prepare things there and to pray that God blesses this insanity with success. You stick to your Roman targets so that Yeshua can be the Son of his Father in heaven. Is that what you are, Yeshua? The Son of the Father?"

"We need to call him something to stop us confusing him with the Galilean prophet," Kochba laughed. "Son of the Father—*Bar-Abbas*, seems to suit the son of a rabbi—*Bar-Rabbas*."

"Especially if Bar-Abbas is pushing these morals at us," muttered Eliazar, in quiet support of the Pharisee.

Yeshua screwed up his face in confusion.

"It's a clever word play, Yeshua . . ." Amram explained, delighting in his sarcastic over-pronunciation, ". . . it's amusing and it's humorous . . . You are both the son of a Rabbi, *Bar-Rabbas*, and you're a holy man, *Bar-Abbas* ."

Yeshua's expression remained.

Kaleb sank his head and lifted his eyes out of sight to observe the inner workings of his forehead. "Bar-Abbas, or Bar-Rabbas? Either way it suits. We can't keep calling you Yeshua anyway, we have too many Messiahs already."

"You can call me what you like, but where are we going to find Roman targets in Galilee?"

"We're not." Amram declared. "We either have to go on the road to Jerusalem, or back across the hills to Caesarea."

"Why not make for Jerusalem in two weeks' time, and find our targets when we get there?" Kochba suggested. "I certainly don't want to try anything else in Caesarea."

"What do you think, Bar-Abbas ? Any words from your father in heaven?" It was unclear how playful Kaleb's questions were. "This is *your* plan after all."

"I think Kochba's right," he replied. "We can start our planning from here. Practice with our weapons. When the money starts to run low we can get to Jerusalem before the festival begins." Bar-Abbas looked at his brother, but Theudas was lost in his thoughts.

"I will need to go ahead and work on some of my friends," said Kaleb. "You know I'm not happy with unnecessary risks. But at last, we are going to hit Rome where it hurts." The Pharisee's excitement was measured, restrained, but obvious. "It's going to take some work to make the weapons in the temple available for the uprising. But we can work on that in Jerusalem. Liberation is coming to the Holy City. I'll send word ahead of me."

From that moment, Yeshua Bar-Abbas set his face resolutely toward Jerusalem. Like the prophet from Galilee, he knew that his life would probably end there, as would the lives of his companions. But it was now purpose-driven, pleasing to God and liberated from the hopes of returning home.

Miriam brought another jug of wine and replenished everyone's cup. "At this rate, your money's not going to last another week," she smiled, touching the arm of Theudas to bring him back from wherever his imagination had carried him. Kaleb too was increasingly lost in thought, the strength of his gaze again had forsaken him. He shook his head to wake himself as Miriam offered him wine. "I can't get my head around all this," he announced. "I need to go and pray." With that he withdrew to his holy parchment and poured his confusion into a new composition.

> *Father,*
>
> *Today, the so-called prophet spoke. He spoke of our Father in heaven. So I closed my eyes and pictured you. In your white robes, in the comfort of your estate, far away, blind to the suffering of your people, indifferent to the fate of your son.*
>
> *But my ancestry comes from you, my bloodline from you, my heritage amongst this people, my share in this Promised Land: it all comes from you.*
>
> *Why then, have you remained so distant? Why so disinterested in the suffering of your own people? And why do you turn your face*

from me? Why, for my whole life, must I have striven, struggled, fought, simply to exist, to survive, to live?

But now, I am to coming to Jerusalem, to your city. I am coming to do what is right. I am coming to seek you. I will become the son of my father. There, in the holy city, I will see you face to face.

The brothers also withdrew from the conversation and sat together. Bar-Abbas found himself caressing the figurine in his hand, which still quietly asserted a corrective but barely noticeable doubt amidst the Egyptian's growing confidence.

"Are you sure about this Jerusalem thing?" Theudas asked, now that his tongue had been well lubricated with wine.

"Not sure. I have no certainty. Just conviction. Deep conviction. A conviction I can feel in my bones, even if I can't reconcile it with what I really think. I still don't believe it pleases God to go looking for blood. But Kaleb's right. If we sit here and wait for God to put things right it will never happen. The prefect needs to be stopped."

"Do you feel anything yet about those we killed?" asked Theudas, a veiled statement that contained his own answer to the question.

"Still having nightmares?" the elder brother asked as he looked at the figurine in his own hands.

"It felt good at first. *I* felt good. But I don't feel justice has been done. If our brothers could return to us now, Yeshua, they wouldn't thank us for what we did. And I don't think God's particularly grateful, wherever he is."

"What do you want to do?"

Theudas looked his brother in the eye. "I want to go home," he said. "I doubt it will happen. But that's all I want now."

"What about seeing this through?" asked Bar-Abbas. "What about the people here?"

"Do you really think killing the prefect is going to help them? They'll just get a new prefect. None of them will ever know any differ- ence. There is no 'seeing this through.' It's a never-ending cycle, and we can't stop it. But that's not my biggest worry." Theudas looked again at his older brother. "What bothers me is that you're digging a hole for yourself. You don't feel avenged by killing those soldiers, any more than I do. But you think that if you kill the prefect then everything will be alright and you'll feel better. And where will it stop? Yeshua, we are not killers. I've had enough of all this . . . It seems to me that your talk of justice or about God might just be a smokescreen to hide your desire for revenge. And that you're hiding it even from yourself. That's what's rekindled your faith. However you dress it up, it's revenge, and we both know it doesn't work."

"But I don't care about revenge any more. I don't care how we got into this mess, or how it started. All I know is that we are here, and there is something we can do that might make a difference. I don't expect to feel good about it even if it works. We'll only have succeeded in doing what we know to be wrong."

Theudas smiled and shook his head warmly. Bar-Abbas shook his head too, but the red wine had slowed his eyes and he waited for them to find their natural position in his head before he continued. "It's time you went to bed, Theudas," he grinned, "your face is looking blurred."

10

WINE HAD CARRIED BAR-ABBAS into his deepest sleep since arriving in Israel. But his deep sleep was not welcome. It only made his dreams more believable and less escapable. And since the day he had avenged his brothers, a recurring set of images returned with growing frequency and clarity. The feelings of comfort came first. Memories of meal times he had once shared with his older brothers, thoughts of meals he would one day share with his younger brother and his father, and occasionally the blurred glimmer of a distant future when somehow the entire family would be reunited. But the moment the Egyptian found himself happy in their company, a snake would emerge from somewhere and sink its teeth into his wrist. The venom would cause his arm to shake and then thrust him from the comfort of repose and back into the nightmare of reality, turning the sleep he so desperately needed into an enemy.

Yeshua had, until now, understood his dreams as nothing more than a reflection of what had passed. The wealth and comfort and family that made him secure had been stolen from him. As time went by and it became increasingly clear that his return to that comfort would be impossible, so the snake's venom seemed to lose its potency. He was becoming immune to his enemy's attempts to destroy him as the old soldier's slogan sunk its roots into the Egyptian's inner being. "No safe path to victory." The transformation Bar-Abbas felt came with the growing realization that he was abandoning his safety. And yet it was in abandoning his desire for safety that he had begun to feel more secure. No longer was it the kind of security he had felt in the comfort of his wealth and his family, a security he had always taken for granted. This was a security that could be felt sleeping in a bandits' cave, as a wanted criminal, as a man with no resources and no future. Like any wealthy man talking of justice, he might once have spoken of his comfortable life as though he would be just as happy without it. He might have spoken about the virtues of living a simple life, and admired those who did. But however genuinely he might have spoken about wealth being unimportant, his pronouncements had been those of a wealthy man who had always known comfort. Now that comfort had been lost. Not virtuously abandoned, but reluctantly and regretfully lost. And in its place he had discovered a deeper source of comfort, affecting the way he walked and breathed and spoke. The venom of the snake had no power to threaten this newfound security. Until last night.

Last night the comfort felt by the Egyptian was to be found not in the company of his brothers or his family, but with near strangers in a bandit's cave. Here, Bar-Abbas felt at home. But when the snake bit him last night, this newfound comfort was threatened, his present reality shaken, his security undermined. The venom forced him out of his sleep, and into the restless wastes of his thought as he tried to interpret his dream. If this snake was no longer a reflection on reality, was it a warning of what was to come? Had the God that he had so long ignored begun to speak to Bar-Abbas? And if this were true, what precisely was he being warned about? The last two weeks had taught the Egyptian the futility of attempting to return to his sleep. With this newly developed interpretation of his dreams, with the possibility that there was more reality in his dreams than what had already taken place in his life, he got up and went outside. Was God speaking to him? He would find out.

Bar-Rabbas, the son of the Rabbi, who desired to be Bar-Abbas, the son of his Father in heaven, walked up the hillside to pray. It was a time of day that had become all too familiar to the sleep-deprived Egyptian. The sun was preparing to assault the darkness, but not quite ready. Its position just below the Eastern horizon had brought enough light for the land below to appear in its humid anticipation of what the day would bring. Bar-Abbas was not sure where his prayers would take him. He found himself asking no questions, seeking no guidance, making no requests. He simply allowed the images that flickered through his mind to spill out into the presence of Israel's God.

The sun was summoning up the energy to rise as Eliazar's words returned to Yeshua. The sun was rising, the sun was setting. The course of days, weeks, months would not allow itself to be interrupted by the cry for justice. Eliazar was right. The Egyptian lifted his head towards the skies, marveling at their indifference to the pain of the earth that stretched out below them. He returned from the upper heights to the valley where a dark column of smoke was trying to assault the dispassionate heavens. Miriam was preparing a breakfast of broiled fish, but she was alone, and for a moment afraid as she became aware of the lone figure descending the hill. On recognizing him, she returned to the fire.

"Are you not sleeping either?" he asked her.

"I've had enough sleep," she said, without lifting her eyes. Bar-Abbas sat himself on a convenient rock and felt the discomfort of Miriam as she prepared food.

"Are you worried about your father?" he asked.

"Are *you* worried about my father?" she replied abruptly.

"Of course I am." The air was filled only by the sound of distant gulls beginning their hunt for breakfast. Miriam's anger, though she denied it, was seeping through every pore of her skin. After a long pause Bar-Abbas asked again.

"Do you blame me for what's happened to your father?"

Only the gulls spoke, but the glance she gave the Egyptian was all the answer he needed. Bar-Abbas dreaded the outcome, but he was determined to access Miriam's thought.

"Miriam. What are you doing here?"

"Cooking your breakfast." Another long pause ensued.

"Why? What's keeping you here?"

"Where else can I go? If I go home I'll share my father's fate."

Bar-Abbas watched her as she continued her charade of indifference. Every motion, every sound, every ounce of her being betrayed her dislike of the wealthy Egyptian.

"Miriam. You can speak plainly with me."

Miriam's brown eyes had a language of their own and uttered a silent curse.

"Listen. Would you do something for me?" Yeshua knew well enough that waiting for an answer would be pointless, so he paused only a second to leave room for a response, which to his surprise came quickly.

"Look at me, Egyptian. I am from Narbata and here I am in Galilee, because of you. I had a home, and now I live in a cave, because of you. I had a family and now I am alone, because of you. And now you ask me to do something for you." She paused, toyed with her hair and unveiled her face to deliver her judgment with full force. "I have lost everything because of you."

Bar-Abbas was impervious to the rebuke. He had been expecting to hear it from somewhere sooner or later. He had felt it himself for long enough, and a few days ago would have felt it bite. But his growing convictions made him as immune to the woman's accusations as to the snake's venom. Although he knew that her accusations were just.

"Miriam!" She brought her busyness to what seemed like a natural pause, walked towards the Egyptian and with folded arms she attached her eyes to his. Yeshua was stunned by the sight, and found himself clutching for an automatic response as he tried to re-take the composure she had stolen. "Hear me out," he said, "I have a suggestion."

"You want me to kill someone?"

"I want you to carry a message to someone." It was enough to temper Miriam's aggression with a hint of curiosity, and allowed him to gather his nerves. "To my father," he said.

"To your father in heaven? I'll be meeting him soon enough thanks to you, Bar-Abbas."

"To my father in Alexandria," he replied, as though it were necessary. "I want to let him know what has happened here. I will also explain how I want him to look after you. He'll provide you with work and home and . . ." Bar-Abbas paused. He was going to say comfort, but ran short of the word. Miriam, however, had abandoned her earlier penchant for silence.

"You think you can click your wealthy fingers and make everything alright? Have you learned nothing?"

"I'm not trying to make everything alright." The Egyptian turned to escape her penetrating glare. "I know I can't do that." He stared at the ground beneath him before lifting his eyes to look at her, "I'm just trying to do what I can."

"You are not the answer to my problems." Miriam returned to the fish that were ready. She bent towards the fire and pulled the tight curls of her long hair behind her ear. Placing some fish in a bowl, she added some herbs and handed it to Yeshua. "You are only the cause of them."

"What did Yudah think of all this? Did your father want nothing to do with armed resistance? With rebellion?" Miriam served up her own breakfast silently. She answered before taking her first mouthful.

"It was nothing but talk before you arrived. It was nothing but a harmless dream before you came. My father wasn't really interested in rebellion, he was too . . ."

"Too Comfortable?"

"Your hands are drenched in blood, Bar-Abbas. You're in no position to criticize anyone from our land."

"You're not the only one who feels his loss." Miriam accepted the remark. "It's no criticism to say that a man is comfortable. And it's my land as much as it is yours."

The two continued to eat in silence, gazing down the slope towards the shimmers of the Galilean Sea that had granted them their breakfast. "How's the fish?" Miriam asked, with a glimmer of humor hidden somewhere within her hostility.

Yeshua closed his eyes, shook his head and allowed a smile free reign over his expression.

Rattling from the cliff told them that someone was coming to share their breakfast. Looking behind them at the same time, Yeshua and Miriam noticed Theudas half way through his descent. Miriam stood and, as if against her will, a smile reserved only for him transformed her entire demeanor and blew away the air of hostility that had lingered around the fire. Theudas seated himself.

"Miriam, finish your breakfast, woman!" said Theudas as he read the situation through his yawning body. "You're not a servant."

"I will be if your brother has anything to do with it," she mumbled, returning to the flames.

Theudas lowered his eyebrows at his brother. "I asked her to go to Alexandria, to our house." Theudas' face showed that he thought it a reasonable offer, whilst not looking particularly happy about it.

"And . . ." he asked, looking at Miriam.

"It's not going to solve much is it!" Yeshua could feel the relief of Theudas, followed immediately by the unspoken traces of previous conversations exchanged between his brother and this woman. He finished his fish in silence, and left them to continue the conversation that Yeshua's presence was clearly preventing.

ॐ

"The temple precincts, at the hour of sacrifice, two Sabbaths from now," said the Pharisee as he gathered his belongings and prepared to lead his donkey down towards the road to Jerusalem.

"We'll miss you at the party," Amram smiled. "Don't worry Kaleb, we'll look after the dirty work."

"Be safe, Amram—and make sure you get them all to Jerusalem in one piece," said the Pharisee, whose face hosted a smile and a frown simultaneously. "May Yahweh bless and protect you all," he declared as he withdrew. Calls of shalom followed Kaleb and his donkey down the hillside.

"Hard to believe he's carrying our fate with him!" said Yeshua, shaking his head.

"Don't worry," said Amram, "he's being led by a Pharisee. That might just improve our chances."

Yeshua grinned. "What are our chances, Amram?" he asked as he lost his grin and turned to face him.

Amram answered with a belch but Bar-Abbas held his gaze. Eventually the over-pronounced answer came. "The main problem with attacking a soldier? Is that you're attacking a *soldier*." Amram's humor evaporated.

"Not a soldier, an auxiliary! Surely there's a difference."

The archer closed his eyes and shook his head. "Not for us," he said. "If you were a general overlooking a battlefield, then maybe . . . *maybe* . . . you'd have a point." There was no avoiding it. Bar-Abbas was about to have his treasured myth demolished. "We have four civilians going up against professionals. These troops have been well trained, and they stay well trained."

"Shouldn't *we* train somehow?" Bar-Abbas asked. "With those swords . . ."

"To do what? If you find yourself in close combat with a soldier, then training all week might extend your life by five seconds . . . if you're lucky."

"But those five seconds might be enough for your bow or Eliazar's slingshot to intervene." Amram's quiet encouraged Bar-Abbas to continue. "Even just a couple of seconds might make the difference between failure and success."

Amram thought for a moment. "Go and get the swords," he sighed. "We'll begin after noon."

The brothers withdrew to the small armory within the cave. A breeze had gathered force as though sent by Caesar himself to sift through the hills in search of the rebels. The rope ladder clattered unnervingly against rock as the Egyptians prepared to climb. As he entered the cave, Yeshua was all too conscious that his destiny would bring down upon them all the full might of Roman fury.

"It feels different in your hand when you have a plan for it," Bar-Abbas muttered as he looked in wonder at his short sword. Theudas held his with disinterest, gazing out towards the East. Kaleb and his donkey had not yet been swallowed by the distance, and below them Kochba and Amram laughed together. The warm breeze lifted Miriam's hair, forcing her to draw it from her face as she went in search of fruit from the cart. Theudas was transfixed.

"Miriam is quite a woman. Does she have anything to do with your new desire to get home?"

"It's a more beautiful desire than any other in these caves."

"And will she still look beautiful once you're away from these caves, and female company is not so scarce?" The younger brother chose not to answer. "Is she as angry with you as she is with me?" Yeshua continued.

"Probably not."

"But she does have something to do with you wanting to return to Alexandria?"

"You can see in those people who went to hear the prophet speak, you can see the real plight of our people in those faces?" Yeshua nodded. "Well I see exactly the same thing in Miriam. But in Miriam I see it close at hand. I see the effects of our work in a real life." Bar-Abbas looked at the crisp, clean steel of his sword, caught a glimpse of his own eyes staring back at him and looked quickly away. "Yeshua! We can't help these people," Theudas continued. "We're just making things worse for them so that we can feel better about ourselves."

"What about all your noise about not getting home?"

"Well, maybe we can find a different way home. We can could travel North to Tyre or Sidon and take a ship from there. What's to stop us, Yeshua, we could leave now."

"No!" Yeshua said with calm conviction. "Perhaps if we can pull this off, we can go home. But we cannot abandon our brothers. We are alive only because of Amram, because of Yudah. We are in their debt, and I will not return to Egypt as a debtor."

"Er—I don't feel good about this," said Theudas.

"What has that woman done to you?"

The younger brother still spoke with a tone of distraction. He thought for a moment, digesting the scenery afforded from the height of Mount Arbel. "When I spend time with Miriam, the whole world looks different. People look different. When I look at her, I don't just see her. This world becomes a different place and I start to see it as she does."

"Do you have that same effect on her? Or are you the over-privileged naïve son of a rabbi?"

৵

The sword sat as naturally as a cup of wine in Amram's hand. "Two thirds of your weight on the front leg, one third on the back . . . spine straight, chin pulled in, eyes straight forward. . ." He paused to correct the posture of the students gathered around him. "Before you even hold a sword— it's your feet that will keep you alive."

"Archer, swordsman, *and* dancer!" Kochba laughed.

"Heads up—looking your opponent in the eye. Now—the tip of your blade should touch the line between your eyes and your enemy's." He paused again to check on his students. "And whatever happens, for God's sake—keep that blade between you and him—do *not* expose yourself. If you have to use these swords, then just stay alive long enough for my arrow or Eliazar's stone." The shepherd could not conceal his pride. "Blocking only for today," he said. "Theudas?" The merchant stepped forward. "I want you to swing from the left, and then from the right." Theudas displayed an excited grin and swung his blade slowly towards the archer, who rebuked him for his caution. "Properly!" he said.

Theudas stepped back, winked at the others, shook himself down, and swept his blade with full force towards the archer's left. Amram's blade barely moved, staying precisely vertical. His arms, packed tightly into his side, the metallic ring greeting Theudas' powerful strike forced a smile from each student. "Now swing to the left." Theudas flared his eyes at the spectators before repeating the move, sounding a second chime. "Now you try it on one another, using the flat of your blade until you're confident."

৵

The days that followed were punctuated by the amateur swordplay Bar-Abbas insisted was necessary. If nothing else, it brought welcome distraction to the caves' inhabitants as they prepared to abandon Arbela for good. The Egyptian brothers had scaled the upper heights of Mount Arbel to conduct their practice with a clear view of the land for which they would fight.

"I don't know . . ." Theudas gasped as his blade circled towards his brother's, "how she feels about me . . ." The clang echoed through the valley below. "Anyway," he panted stepping back, "that's irrelevant until we're out of this mess. All I know is that she carries the scars of wounds that we are inflicting upon this place."

"We didn't bring it . . ." Yeshua said as he forced Theudas to block a swing.

"And those eyes. They show me who I am." Theudas thrust his sword upright into the turf to take a breath. "And they hold back a whole ocean of compassion. Have you seen nothing of that?" Yeshua put up his own blade. "Whenever she comes near me, I can't breathe properly . . . Sometimes I pretend I haven't seen her so that I can catch up with myself before trying to speak. Yeshua. She's been forced into this mess. I don't want her to be sucked in any further, and I don't want to be part of what happens in Jerusalem."

Bar-Abbas retrieved his sword, unable to hide his alarm. "But we need you."

"You'll need me for the next job on the Romans," said Theudas gripping his hilt. "And I'll be ready," he snarled, thrusting once, twice, and swinging a third blow. He lowered his blade. "But after that you'll have everything you need. I'll come to Jerusalem and I'll be there when this happens. But I don't want to be part of any more bloodshed."

"Neither do I," Yeshua now swinging his blade twice from the left, "but we are in this mess," once from the right, ". . . we have to see it through," he concluded as he lunged.

"Er—hold on!" Theudas sidestepped, his parry unnecessary. "Didn't we have this conversation the other way round a few days ago? You were all for going home."

"Well, I've got a sense of what's happening here now," he said, clutching his blade in close to block another swing.

"That's why I changed my mind too!" Theudas grinned, lowering his blade. Yeshua noticed that as his younger brother spoke, he had aged and his words were no longer lightly spoken and carefree. They carried a disturbing weight, all the more because Theudas was not interested in winning a debate, and offered his unqualified commitment to Yeshua. The older brother was thus bereft of his usual ability to dismiss those with whom he disagreed. "You're letting Rome shape you," Theudas continued. "You give Rome too much power over you. You're letting Rome shape what you become," he raised his voice to warn of another imminent strike.

"No. You're wrong," Yeshua accompanied the clash with a growl. "It was these people who are making me who I become. These people of Abraham," he pleaded, waving his blade towards Galilee. "I don't want to kill anyone, not even Romans. But our people, our brothers are suffering now, and we can make a difference for them. I think that's why God brought us here." He lifted his blade as though he had carried it since childhood, but with an expression betraying not even a remnant of self-doubt.

❯❮11❯❮

"BETHSHE'AN!" SAID AMRAM. "IF you want to hit Roman soldiers but avoid Judean troops, then we travel over the border into Decapolis. They have a different prefect. Bethshe'an is the perfect city for an attack. The river is one side of it, the hills on the other. It should be quite escapable."

"Is it on the way to Jerusalem?" Yeshua asked.

"Near the west bank of the Jordan, directly en route," said Kochba.

"And they'll definitely have soldiers there?" asked Theudas.

"We'll find a tax collector! They're always going to be nicely guarded," Kochba smiled.

"What does 'nicely' guarded mean?" Theudas stretched his words to express suspicion.

"Five or six soldiers, but only two at a time would usually be ready for action," Amram explained.

"And you think we can attack five soldiers . . ." Eliazar's sentiment was more excitement than fear, but Bar-Abbas interrupted.

"If we plan carefully we can. We'll need to get ourselves into Bethshe'an a couple of days beforehand." The others concurred. "How much money will a tax collector hold?"

Kochba laughed. "Far more than we'll need."

"Well," the archer yawned with apparent disinterest, "the big advantage is that it's a different region. Before the prefects get together, one of them will be snugly settled in his tomb."

"And even if Pilatus does hear about it beforehand, it won't be up to him to take revenge," said Eliazar.

"I can't see that stopping him," Miriam's input enforced a brief silence, broken eventually by Yeshua.

"Well he won't even know it's us. This will look like a basic robbery."

"Which it is!" Theudas chipped in. "But not too basic I hope. . . What will we do with all that money?"

"We put it into the temple funds . . ." The silence that followed was not the sound of approval. "Well most of it . . ." There were no nods of agreement. "Come on," Yeshua reasoned, "Jerusalem is the ultimate goal. Whatever happens after that there'd be more than enough to get us free of Jerusalem. And if we give half of it to the temple funds, it will show our allies there how serious we are, and what our motivation is."

Amram didn't look convinced, even though Bar-Abbas had quietly dropped the quantity from 'most' to 'half'. Neither did Kochba. Although both could see the wisdom of Yeshua's suggestion and did not voice their disapproval.

"And you really think we can kill five soldiers?" Eliazar asked.

"We don't have to kill them all," said Theudas.

Amram belched.

"We can do this if we prepare properly," Yeshua announced. "We need to watch for the vulnerable moments in the changeover of soldiers . . . and to find out how many soldiers are in the city as a whole."

"It's a big place," Amram said. "There'll be no shortage of soldiers, and they'll be ready for the chase."

"In that case, we set up a decoy." All eyes fell on Yeshua. "Have someone ready to run for the hills and to make noise as they go. Draw their attention away from everyone else."

Kochba looked at Eliazar. "There's your hill runner. Even without amour they'd never catch him."

Eliazar enjoyed the compliment, but deflected attention by asking another question. "Which way would the rest of you go?"

"To the river," said Yeshua, as if the answer were obvious.

"And sail straight back towards here after taking their money?" asked Miriam.

"We would paddle south," said Yeshua with a daring look in his eye.

"And paddle right round the town carrying its money bags in the boat?" Kochba asked. "I have to say, I think that's ridiculous!"

"You're right, it is ridiculous," the archer admitted. "But no more so than any other plan to escape a provincial capital with several bags of Roman money." Kochba grinned and raised his eyebrows in concession.

"And since no one in their right mind would try to escape along the river, no one in their right mind will think to watch the river . . . It may sound daring, but it may also be the safest option." On seeing agreement from the others, his gap tooth appeared as he pronounced his conclusion. "We'd be in Judea in less than three hours, job done, chase finished, cash in hand."

The conversation determined how their final week at the caves would be spent. Kochba returned to his estate to gather supplies and transports. The others began to practice the roles they were to perform when they brought their terror to Bethshe'an.

"How good are you with that thing?" Theudas asked, as Eliazar examined his slingshot in the light of the early sun.

"Good enough," grunted the shepherd, slightly embarrassed by the attention of Miriam.

"Have you killed anything with it?" she asked.

"Of course I have," he replied, still caressing the leather. "I'm a shepherd. It's what we do. We do it to protect the sheep, we do it for our meals."

"So could you catch us a meal?"

"Catch it, cook it, serve it," he grinned. "You want a shepherd's meal?"

"Why not?"

Eliazar picked up three stones and led Miriam and Theudas around the hillside, where a dozen rabbits were scattered on the southern slopes.

"You can really hit a rabbit?" Theudas whispered.

"Usually," he replied, dropping a small, smooth stone into the leather cup of his slingshot. Holding the weapon in his right hand, he pointed his left towards the nearest unsuspecting rabbit. Flicking his wrists, he spun the shot in a circle three times, the speed gradually increasing until he thrust his entire upper body towards where his left hand had pointed. There was little sound as the woolen cord whistled faintly about his head, but thirty paces away his rabbit lay dead. Instantly the other animals lifted their heads, watched for a moment and darted. Theudas had not seen Eliazar swinging a second time, noticing him only as he thrust his body forward again, releasing a second stone down the slope. Again, it found its target, this time a fleeing rabbit hit the ground silently. The third stone had begun its revolutions as Theudas looked back toward the shepherd, but it bounced harmlessly down the slope and its target found a safer place to nibble grass.

"You're as deadly as Amram," Theudas gasped.

"I don't have the range or the power of an archer. But my weapon's easier to carry and my missiles are easier to come by!"

"So is your breakfast," Miriam laughed.

"You haven't tasted it yet," the shepherd replied, walking briskly towards the rabbit meat that he was about to prepare. The shepherd basked in the attention that he rarely received, but was not quite comfortable in it. He hurried, chattered, fidgeted and yet delighted in the activities of skinning and stewing the rabbit. He explained the process as he went, seeping with pride at the skills his father had taught him. These skills, second nature to a shepherd, were deeply admired by well-to-do Jews unaccustomed to living so directly off the land.

For Eliazar, shooting and cooking rabbits was an activity that came far more easily than debating Holy Scripture or plotting assassinations. The busyness of the shepherd's familiar environment put him at an ease that neither Theudas nor even Miriam had witnessed before, not having been on the road from Kochba's farm. But with that boy's relaxed manner, something of his vulnerability surfaced.

"Your father taught you how to do all this?" Miriam asked, sipping at the stew and raising her eyebrows in appreciation.

"If you think this is good, you should have tasted his."

Miriam smiled as she watched Eliazar relax into his memory. For once it seemed that recollections of his father brought him peace rather than turmoil. Performing physical acts, killing the rabbit, preparing a meal, evokes memories of a different kind to those brought about by sleepless grief or vengeful rhetoric, she thought.

"Two years he's been gone . . ." The shepherd continued. "He was just a normal man. He was no bandit. He was a great father. He didn't deserve what happened to him. He didn't deserve to die."

"Killing Romans isn't like killing rabbits," said Theudas, inviting a glare from Miriam. "I'm sorry," he added quickly. "I understand why you want to avenge them . . . But it doesn't work. It doesn't give you anything. It won't give your family anything."

"Nothing will ever make me feel better about that."

"So why are you desperate to kill Romans?"

"Because they deserve it. Because that's justice."

"That sounds more like Kaleb than Eliazar," Theudas winced. "What do you think your father would advise if he were here in the hills with us?"

"He *is* here with us. He's in my dreams every night. Every morning I wake up expecting him to be there, along with my brother." The shepherd looked at Theudas, in the knowledge that the Egyptian was familiar with the experience.

"And what does he say to you?" Theudas could see immediately that he had asked the wrong question, but it was too late.

The shepherd retreated into a few moments of uncomfortable silence. "Why are you asking me all this?" Eliazar frowned. "You're not going to talk me out of anything."

"Er—No, I wouldn't try that," said Theudas. "It's just that—if you're wanting to kill Romans to relieve you of grief, it doesn't work." Eliazar had begun to take hold of his usual discomfort. "No, I know that you've already worked that out for yourself."

"There's no place for me in a world without my father and my brother. I don't want to be in a world that can stay the same while these injustices go unpunished. I don't care about anything more than that."

Theudas nodded his head, realizing how deeply the boy remained trapped in grief. "I'd love to be able to do what you've done this morning, Eliazar. You are deadly with that slingshot. I've got no doubt you'll be deadly with it when Romans are your prey."

At the end of a long day's journey south from Mount Arbel, the brothers found a place in the hills looking down towards the quiet shimmer of the Jordan River adorning the city of Bethshe'an as a silver necklace. This was a fine vantage point from which to begin surveillance of their next victims. A small, stone toll house greeted travelers from the north as they approached the outer boundaries of the city. The tax collector sitting at his wooden table was of less interest to the brothers than the soldiers who guarded his takings.

"That makes it six," Bar-Abbas grunted as two figures from the house joined their comrades at the roadside.

"Yeshua! Do you really think we can do this?" Theudas' voice carried a baseline of fear as he looked at his brother. "I know," he continued in answer to the argument contained in Yeshua's expression. "No safe path to victory. But five of us, six of them. These are not good odds."

"Kochba, Eliazar with his slingshot, Amram the soldier, Theudas the assassin, and Bar-Abbas. We have done this before."

"But the biggest city of Decapolis? Six professional soldiers? Against a farmer, a shepherd, two merchants and a drunkard? The odds are not good."

"This time we know what we're doing. And this time we have Amram." Bar-Abbas placed his hand on his brother's shoulder. "Theudas, we can do this."

Theudas turned towards the blood-red sun surrendering itself to the horizon, and sighed in resignation.

"We can do this," his brother repeated through gritted teeth. Yeshua waited a moment. "Can you do this?"

"You'll find out soon enough!" he replied with a face betraying more confidence than his words suggested.

৯

"*When I consider your heavens,*" said Yeshua, lifting his eyes towards the stars now forcing their way into view, "*the moon and the stars that you have set in place . . . what is man, that you are mindful of him?*"

"Don't start quoting psalms at me," Theudas scoffed. "You sound like Kaleb."

"King David wrote that hymn, and he knew more about killing men than any Pharisee."

"So you think God is bothered about our little quest to spill blood?" Theudas pushed.

"He was bothered about David's," Yeshua reflected. "And David spilt more blood than any Roman god."

"Er—why was it that God would not let David build a temple?"

"I know," Yeshua conceded, "he'd seen too much violence."

"And don't you think it ironic that our temple is now full of weapons, ready to spill blood that is not worthy of the temple."

"David was part of God's plan" Yeshua concluded. "And you know he was reluctant to spill blood, as am I."

"Well," Theudas sighed, "I know how important it is for you to believe that."

Yeshua puffed out a breath, closed his eyes and shook his head.

Two of Kochba's donkeys pulled a cart carrying grain, the fruit of the year's final harvest from the farmer's estate. The farmer was accompanied by a merchant and a shepherd, and in the afternoon warmth of autumn, they made their way towards the tax station on the northern borders of Bethshe'an. A tax collector sat at his desk positioned under a canopy outside the small stone house. As the cart crunched its way slowly towards his desk, two soldiers emerged from the house to join him. One carried a spear but neither had a shield, nor an unsheathed blade.

Eliazar's expression was identical to the one Yeshua had seen him wearing back at Yudah's house in Narbata. A state of anxiety emanated from the shepherd's entire body. "Relax," Yeshua whispered, "if not for your sake then for ours." Kochba's was the only speaking role, and for the attack to work he had to conceal its imminence for as long as possible. His footsteps along with his face, bore the hallmarks of calm, resolute concentration.

The only sign of the Egyptian's fear was the icy cold he now expected to fill his hands, one of which gripped the side of the cart as it crunched to a halt. "Good afternoon!" the tax collector grinned, as he contemplated the toll he was about to receive.

"And a good afternoon to you," Kochba smiled as he approached the tax booth with open arms in an attempt to draw attention away from what was happening behind him. "I suppose you'd like our payment?" Before his sentence had finished, the merchant had sprinted past him, carrying the unsheathed Roman short-sword that had lain concealed in the cart. The Egyptian sped with fury towards their unsuspecting and unprepared Roman targets.

As Bar-Abbas ran, the two soldiers came to symbolize more than their present threat, more even than Rome herself. For Bar-Abbas, these Roman hands were bloodied with every atrocity inflicted upon his whole race. From the prefect of Judea right back to the Pharaoh of Egypt, every godless tyrant to oppress his people was embodied in these unwitting scapegoats. Every death from Abel, son of Adam to the grey-haired market trader of Narbata, was about to be avenged. If the Egyptian could have exchanged all the remaining breath of his natural life for a hurricane, he would have swept his targets to Sheol.

An almighty thud filled the space over to the right of Bar-Abbas. Eliazar's slingshot had sent its first victim to the ground. The second soldier turned to his fallen comrade, stunned in disbelief. Bar-Abbas was upon him in an instant, and executed the move that he had rehearsed countless times in the cliffs of Arbela. His right arm was bent with the short sword facing towards the Roman's stomach. His cold right hand was joined by his left as he thrust the entire weight of his body, carrying a force that was multiplied by the speed of his attack, behind the lunge at the chain mail that protected his target's belly. As Amram had promised, the blade penetrated both the armor and the leather beneath, and slid into the stomach of its victim. The expression of the soldier had not changed from the moment the Egyptian began his run to the moment he yanked his blade from Roman flesh.

Dark Gentile blood dripped from the Egyptian's sword as a giant of a soldier hurried out to investigate the uproar. On seeing that his companions were down, he called to the others inside the house. This enormous guardsman threw his upright spear instantly to its horizontal position, but Eliazar's slingshot had begun a second set of revolutions.

Eliazar was back in his natural environment, preparing to loose a deadly stone at his next target. Triumphant after his first kill, his anxiety was rapidly displaced by measured aggression as he prepared to exact further revenge for his family. Unintimidated by the man who towered above him, he swung his slingshot as though he were King David himself.

As Bar-Abbas edged towards this Roman Goliath, a crunch and squelch sounded simultaneously. Eliazar stumbled, crossed in front of Yeshua and fell to the ground. Something had forced the shepherd to the gravel and left him on his back staring at the sky. His legs lifted towards his stomach. His arms gripped the arrow that had penetrated his neck. Time had slowed down, and as the shepherd writhed at the merchant's feet, Goliath moved in on Bar-Abbas.

The Egyptian adopted a defensive stance and prepared to parry the giant's thrust. As the next of his two companions in the house emerged, Goliath's arms were loading the spear's first lunge. They moved behind his towering frame, which was side on to Bar-Abbas, gripping the six-foot shaft ready to strike. Then came the metallic hammer blow that Yeshua had heard before in the hills outside Narbata. The horizontal spear fell harmlessly, along with the man who carried it.

A Roman short sword unsheathed, as a newly emerged soldier moved towards the Egyptian. Kochba arrived at the fallen giant and commandeered his weapon. But before either farmer or merchant moved within striking distance of this fourth target, the hammer blow sounded again, sending its victim to the ground.

Eliazar made no sound above his short breaths as his heels lifted his lower back and pushed sand away from his body. Theudas was now visible beside the hut, dagger in hand, ready to move behind the next soldier to emerge from the doorway. He was too slow. The hammer struck again, cutting down the soldier the moment he stepped into daylight. For a moment all was quiet, apart from the short heavy breaths of exhilaration or injury, until the hammer spoke its final word, this time from within the house. After a momentary pause it was followed by a rattle and clatter. An impossible shot had found its mark. The archer had shot into the darkness of the house and pierced the soldier's chest. Amram's bow had accounted for six deaths, but only five of them Gentile.

Eliazar's arms had left his neck, his short breaths had ceased and his muscles had twitched and jerked every trace of life from his body. The sun had risen upon the shepherd for the last time, and would set without him. His killer appeared from across the track, ran straight to the fallen youth and dropped to his knees to confirm what needed no confirmation. Amram took the shepherd's hand within his own and looked blankly into his eyes, in time for the boy's lungs to release their final breath. All was quiet. Silently Kochba placed a hand on the archer's shoulder. Yeshua did likewise. The gestures were unacknowledged. Amram stood, and looking at no one he retrieved a short sword and worked his way around the fallen Romans.

"Is that payment enough?" Kochba asked the tax collector who had spent the last twenty seconds glued to his desk by shivers of trauma. Kochba received no reply.

"Pray that we take no more," said Theudas as he removed a bag of coins from the desk. There was little jubilation as five bags of coins were collected from inside the house. Quietly the money from the house, the weapons from the Romans and the body of Eliazar were loaded onto the cart, which turned and headed back in the direction from which it had arrived a minute earlier.

"You're free to go!" Yeshua declared to the tax collector.

"Free?" he said with a stutter.

"Well, brother," said Kochba as he busied himself with loading the donkeys, "if you'd like to go and tell your inspectors their money has been stolen, six of their soldiers have been killed, and the only survivor was a Jewish collaborator, then—I have to say—God be with you."

"Or do you think we spared your life out of mercy?" Theudas added.

Theudas took Eliazar's role as decoy, moving up into the hills to draw whatever retaliation the town might offer. But this was not Caesarea. It had no cavalry, and little in the way of guards ready for a rapid response. The towns of Decapolis were more favorably disposed towards their Roman occupants and, in comparison to the towns of Judea, needed little in the way of policing. Nevertheless in Bethshe'an six Roman soldiers lay dead, and the companions needed to escape.

As Theudas disappeared eastward into the hills to watch the town from safety, Kochba, Amram, and Yeshua drove their cart westwards towards the river. As the Jordan twisted half a mile north of the town, a miniature beach harbored two boats that awaited the companions under Miriam's care.

"Where is Theudas?" she called as the cart rattled hurriedly toward her. Bar-Abbas shook his head and looked at the ground. "Where is your brother?" she asked with more alarm.

"Theudas has taken Eliazar's place up in the hills," Kochba sighed.

"Eliazar?" Nothing. "Where is Eliazar?" Kochba gestured towards the cart that carried the shepherd's body, shrouded in a blanket. Miriam's hand met her mouth. "What happened?" No answer. "Tell me what happened."

Kochba held Miriam by her shoulders and revealed his bloodshot eye. "Miriam, please, not now." She hurried to the back of the cart and unveiled Eliazar's face. She stared for a moment, closed her eyes and kissed his forehead.

੨ও

Theudas had scaled the heights with some speed, although not as much ease as a shepherd might have. He looked below, seeing how his companions had made their way unmolested to the safety of the boats. As they paddled gently downstream, no relief emerged from the town. The tax house contained nothing but the bodies of soldiers. Occasionally a traveler would leave the town and glance back towards the tax house, but its deathly quiet aroused little suspicion with passers by, only bland curiosity.

Once they had paddled beyond the open plain in which Bethshe'an sat and were back under the shadow of the hills, the boats were pushed ashore on the west bank. Over an hour's paddling brought nothing in the way of conversation. Amram's own silence commanded the same from all others, as his remorse imposed itself on the bandits.

Eliazar's body was taken ceremoniously from the boat to a secluded patch of rich soil, watered by the river and shaded by the trees. Here, in the shadow of the mountain, on the banks of the river Jordan, Eliazar the shepherd was buried. Theudas arrived, out of breath, as the final stones from the river were laid over the makeshift grave of their fallen brother. Once it was complete, Kochba broke the silence with a short prayer of thanks. With that, the companions returned to the boats, too distraught at the loss of Eliazar to feel relief at their escape.

Silence returned to the boats, as Bar-Abbas dismissed questions that his mind briefly posed, questions of whether God had cursed their quest. I have endured three Roman attacks. I have survived three Roman attacks. Eleven soldiers lie dead. I am unscathed. The voice of Kaleb rung in his ears as though the Pharisee sat in the boat behind him. "Maybe God is not finished with you yet." But God had finished with Eliazar, and no one dared to count the five small sacks of coins and the six Roman purses that were carried south against the stream—whoever dared to announce the total of their contents would be declaring the value of Eliazar's life.

✦❮12❯✦

"WAKE UP . . . wake up!" Theudas tugged at Yeshua, who was becoming accustomed to the recent phenomenon of being woken by his younger brother. Jerusalem was a two-day journey from Bethshe'an, and the weary travelers were less than half way. They had chosen to spend the night in the company of one another and the stars rather than finding lodgings in one of the towns they hurried through on the road.

The previous evening had passed awkwardly but quietly and the absence of belching had been conspicuous. The distance between Amram and his grave had never seemed great, but the last day had reduced it still further. Conversation was slowly returning to the companions, but it was minimal, functional. Not even Kochba could lighten the atmosphere, nor did he try. "It would be nice to have our lunch within view of Jericho," he said. The ancient city was six hours away, but the day was young enough for Kochba's hope to be realistic. "We want to be in Jerusalem before sundown," he added.

The sore-footed brothers, new to traveling such distances by foot, walked side by side with Miriam to their left. Amram and Kochba walked some distance behind, but the hurried pace they shared showed to all they passed that the group traveled as one.

"Are you happy with your loot, Bar-Abbas?" asked Miriam provocatively. Bar-Abbas had been cursing the sun, rising as it was without an ounce of grief over the fallen shepherd.

"Do I look happy?"

"Happiness is easily concealed when you know it's wrong," she said calmly. "Remorse is easily faked when you know it's required." Nothing was said for a minute or more, so Miriam continued her attack. "Are you remorseful or are you happy, Yeshua Bar-Abbas?"

"Miriam!" Theudas frowned.

"No!" said Yeshua, "Let her speak. She can say what she likes. She can imagine what she likes. She can draw whatever conclusions she likes. Who knows where her imagination will lead her."

"Unless you loosen your tongue, O son of your Father in heaven, imagination is my only guide," she snarled. "Speak, Bar-Abbas!"

"If I felt nothing do you think we would be going to Jerusalem? We are going to make sure that Eliazar's death was not in vain."

"So you did feel something yesterday," she said. "Well that's a relief. And tell me, Bar-Abbas," she pronounced the name with enough scorn to declare him unworthy of it, "tell me, did you feel anything as you killed that soldier? Will he haunt you as the soldier from Caesarea haunts your brother?"

Bar-Abbas was impervious to Miriam's verbal onslaught. She was clearly not the snake of which his dreams had warned him. Perhaps he was still numbed by yesterday's experience, he thought, as this angel of criticism continued her assault. "Because if your victims haunt you, if they trouble you and harass you, then you sleep surprisingly well."

"Their ghosts have no power over my convictions," he said with artificial indifference.

"Does your 'Father in heaven' have any power over your convictions?"

Bar-Abbas stopped in his tracks and faced the young woman, whose feet and tongue had also stopped. Their eyes met, and although hers matched his in resolution, they did not contain the ferocity of her tongue. "Why are you still traveling with us?" he asked. "You are free to go anywhere, do anything. Yesterday you became a wealthy woman." The coins had not been counted, but five bags of money and five soldier's purses had been evenly distributed among the five who now traveled together. "Your fortune is restored."

"I have my own convictions," she said. The three resumed their march.

"And your own money. But your convictions are driving you. Why are they driving you with us, Miriam?"

"That's what I'm trying to find out," she answered. She still looked like an angel, but no angel of criticism. "I want to know who I'm following."

"My convictions won't fit into words."

"Neither will his ego," Theudas muttered, before raising his hand with a smile to deflect the glare with which his elder brother had responded.

"Jerusalem will not leave you as you are," Miriam continued. "The holy city will bring out the worst of you as well as the best. I've seen it." She paused, retreating into her thoughts for a moment, before piercing Yeshua's spirit with her brown eyes. "And I will not follow an Egyptian Kaleb into that city."

"I don't share Kaleb's convictions. I don't have his certainties. I don't . . ."

"Er—you do have a clever answer for everything," Theudas spoke into the sky. His brother took it as no compliment.

"Well, I am not Kaleb," said Yeshua. "My convictions rest on circumstances beyond my control."

"That's true for every human being that ever lived or ever will," said Miriam with a smile. Yeshua took a few moments to fathom her observation.

"You know what I mean," Yeshua continued, "We've started something here that we can't stop. It *is* beyond our control."

"And does your God approve of you as Kaleb's does of him?" she asked.

"You already know the answer to that," he replied. "Yes I believe this task is God-given. I've tried not to. But my spirit is defeated. I have lost the battle to deny it. I think God approves of this plan. I think God brought us here to fulfill it. But I can't help thinking that He is wrong. So where does that leave me?"

"By tomorrow it will leave you in the same place as Kaleb," Miriam concluded. "In the holy city with money, assassins and murderous intentions."

"Kaleb and I follow different paths. Kaleb is a leader, a revolutionary, a man of influence. I am no leader. I have no desire to lead anyone or anything. I have a task, one task, one target." Yeshua could feel a glimmer of approval from his female companion, and since he also felt this might well be short-lived he decided to hush himself before he lost it again.

"Well, Yeshua, I'm not gonna kill anyone else," said Theudas. "When we get to Jerusalem, I'll be watching your back, but that's all I'll be doing. I'll stay ten paces behind you. I'll have a dagger in my hand. I'll be ready to use it. But I won't go looking for any more blood."

"Watch my back!" Yeshua snorted. "Why would you want to watch my back? No one in Jerusalem knows I exist. I don't need a bodyguard."

"For someone who plans so carefully, there's a lot you don't see," Miriam laughed in fake surprise. "You obviously don't know the holy city that well. I will walk with Theudas as his guide." The hostility had evaporated from the angel's voice as the road brought them in plain view of the Jericho.

Yeshua gazed in wonder at the legendary city for the first time. "It's twelve centuries since the bloodthirsty Joshua neared this city with the armies of Israel," said Bar-Abbas. "What do you know of this city Miriam?"

"That its walls fell because the God of Moses ordained it," she replied.

"Joshua led a mass slaughter in this place. Every woman of this city, along with every child was butchered because God had ordained it. At least, that's how our Scriptures tell the story. And God didn't just allow it. He demanded it." As the city loomed near, its dark history imposed itself further on the Egyptian.

"So you think you're right to obey God," Miriam frowned in confusion, "but you also think God is wrong?"

Theudas smirked.

"I know how this sounds," Bar-Abbas conceded. "But remember what Kaleb said, remember what Yeshua of Galilee said. . . It's not our blood that makes us children of Abraham, it's our readiness to obey God.

"Well, anyone can put words in God's mouth and then pretend to obey them. You don't have to be a child of Abraham to play that game."

"But think of Abraham himself," Bar-Abbas replied. "God tells him to sacrifice his only son. What does he do? God told him to do it! But God was clearly wrong!" A pause. "Abraham was ready to do it. It was only the angel of Yahweh that stopped him."

"Do you think an angel of Yahweh will stay your hand when you go to Jerusalem?" Miriam smiled.

"I don't know what will happen in Jerusalem. All I know is that God will not abandon us."

The money weighed heavily on the back of each traveler as they approached the gates of the city that had once been declared "holy ground." Every companion coming from the caves of Arbela was now well acquainted with grief, and as Yeshua crossed the streets of the city, he pictured every inhabitant as a besieged victim of the ancient and merciless Israelite army. Every white-haired elder, every hurried woman, every laughing child was seen as a potential victim of God's butchering army. The Egyptian did not feel proud of his bloodline or its heritage.

Kochba and Amram remained outside the walls of the city with a hidden pile of weapons and money. The others had passed through the gates of new walls to gather food and transport, but Bar-Abbas had no desire to linger. The wonder he had felt on seeing the city evaporated as he rushed through its busy streets, desperate to escape the ancient city, built upon the mass murder that surpassed even the atrocities of a Roman prefect. Struggling to exorcise such thoughts from his minds, Bar-Abbas and his companions left Jericho as hurriedly as they had entered it. The five resumed their journey, with a new cart and fresh donkey, but they carried with them the absence of the shepherd boy.

The road from Jericho was a long and tiring uphill climb, and they watched their shadows dance further ahead as the afternoon progressed. Evening would be upon them before they arrived at their destination, and not one member of the party looked ready to purge the city where heaven and earth met. Wearied and miserable, the travelers trod through the afternoon.

"Halt!" The cry echoed from the road ahead. Out of nowhere, a tall man with a drawn sword had appeared. Flanked by the rocks that filled the bottom of the valley, he stepped onto the otherwise deserted road. Was this the angel of Yahweh? Was he intervening to prevent catastrophe in Jerusalem? Was this how God's divine messengers appeared? This angel looked as though he were about to demand a toll, but did not possess the happy face with which the tax collector from Bethshe'an had greeted them. He raised his hand. "We want your packs, your cart and your donkey," he shouted, still thirty paces ahead of the travelers. He was flanked by a man from either side of the road, both carrying a large club.

Yeshua looked behind to see three more men emerge from the rocks to the road. "I don't believe this," said Theudas to himself, as though he were surrounded by children threatening to call him names. All, including the donkey, stood motionless as the sword-carrying angel spoke again. "All your possessions are now property of the Lestai."

"Lestai?" said Theudas.

"Bandits," sighed Yeshua.

"Isn't that *our* job?" Theudas whispered with a grin that brought comfort to his older brother.

As the Egyptians stepped back towards the hidden armory and treasury of the cart, they seemed to their assailants to be backing down. As Yeshua walked, he shouted so that all six members of the Lestai could hear.

"We have no quarrel with you, brothers, but all you'll be taking from us today is punishment."

Chuckles were heard from in front and behind, as six men began to close in. Bar-Abbas was not shaking, nor short of breath, nor excited in any way. Even his hands were not cold as they reached into the cart. All five travellers did the same. Each retrieved a Roman sword, apart from Amram whose deadly bow suddenly became visible to all, though the arrow that already sat on the string was as yet pointing towards the ground without stressing the cypress wood.

Yeshua had no idea whether the six on the road would be joined by more from the rocks. The fear of the assailants suggested not, but the arrogance of the sword-carrying bandit was undaunted. "Roman swords," he smiled, as he continued his approach.

"With fresh Roman blood," said Yeshua as he advanced. "But I have no desire to spill any of Abraham's blood," he declared, while his body suggested that such a desire could be conjured up any second. Both men smiled at each other as they stopped just beyond the reach of the other's blade.

"What is your business in Jerusalem?"

"We have come to rid you of foreigners," Bar-Abbas replied.

The bandit laughed and addressed his companions, turning his head but not his eyes from Yeshua. "An Egyptian has come to Israel to rid us of foreigners." He turned again to address Yeshua. "Have you come to start a rebellion? All five of you?" He made a sarcastic gesture to his companions. "Or are you joining the resistance?"

Yeshua was surprised to hear the resistance described as though it were a single movement. "Something like that," he replied, allowing the disturbing calm of his companions and the impressive array of weapons they wielded to speak for themselves.

"We're not interested in resistance," the bandit said. "We're interested in eating. In feeding our families and ourselves."

Yeshua reached for his purse and threw it at the feet of a club-carrying bandit, who picked it up to inspect its contents. "Have a meal on us," said Yeshua, with ferocious composure.

The bandit peering into the newly acquired purse shouted back. "He means a week of meals."

"What is your name, Egyptian?" asked the leader, looking slightly less aggressive.

"Bar-Abbas," he replied, almost as though it were a name he was happy with. Immediately a boy of about ten years of age darted from the rocks to their leader, who for the first time looked disturbed as he moved backwards towards the boy. The expression reserved for that boy was one of anger, as he bent down to hear his whispers. He smiled as he stood up again, and the boy returned to his refuge.

"Bar-Abbas," he said, moving to the side of the road, followed by his companions. "Bar-Abbas, the liberator! Thank you for your gift. Be sure to convey to Kaleb the Pharisee the greeting of Simon the Zealot."

ﻉﻭ

The company continued on their way unhindered, but walked more closely with one another, and with greater caution.

Yeshua dropped back towards Amram and tried for the first time since leaving Bethshe'an to engage him in conversation. "I've lost count of the number of times I should be dead by now but for your presence." Amram said nothing. "Without you we would have lost more than one man from our company." Amram looked at Yeshua, but still held his tongue. The Egyptian resorted to forcing words out of the man he still feared. "How long before we arrive in Jerusalem?"

"Two hours."

"Amram, once we enter its gates, I have no idea what to do, where to go."

The archer walked several more paces before answering. He spoke as he had always spoken. "I can find us a place to stay. It'll be expensive but I think we can afford it."

"Will they have much wine?"

"Would I take you anywhere that didn't?" the archer said. No words passed between them for two minutes. But the Egyptian's fear of the holy city was rising above his fear of Amram.

"How did those people know who I was?" he asked.

"Kaleb is well connected."

"But why would he give them my name? Why did those people react like that?"

"Because God is guiding you here. You have come to fulfill his purpose!"

"*His* purpose? What—Kaleb's or God's"

"Is there a difference?" Amram smirked.

"Will they know our plan to hit the prefect?"

"No," said the archer, who was easing into his role as comforter. "But this is a city full of squabbling groups. Kaleb knows of them all. And he knows which ones to feed. There'll be plenty in Jerusalem awaiting your arrival. And you won't find many opposed to your plan."

Yeshua drew a long breath and as he exhaled its quiet tremble betrayed the terror that had seized his spirit and covered his body with the shiver of goose bumps. It was answer enough for Amram.

"Yeshua" he said, with more seriousness than his voice had ever carried. "You're not coming to Jerusalem as a pilgrim this time. You're coming as a popular figure. You're expected."

"But all I want is this job done."

"That's why you're popular. And if you want the job done, then best you get used to being popular."

⚜13⚜

THE HILLS BECAME STEEPER and their shadows longer as Mount Zion came into view. Enthroned upon it was the holy city, a living monument to the God of Abraham, Isaac and Jacob. Situated near to the city's great eastern gate, was the Temple. For a thousand years, this had been the meeting point of *ha shamaim* and *ha'aretz*, the heavens and the earth, the sky and the land. Its walls were not golden colored stone, but real gold, gold that gathered any light that struck it, intensified it, multiplied it, and shared it with the world. This after all, was the function of the temple and its people: a light to the nations.

But one nation dominated it. Towering over was the gentile garrison that silently mocked it from above. Every mortal walking the high walls of the Antonine fortress could do what, in the past, only God himself had been able to do: to look down upon the Jewish temple. And every mortal to walk the high walls of the garrison was a pagan. The temple of God was dwarfed by the might of Rome, and its pagan audacity was designed to put every Jew in his place. All who came to the city, all who entered the temple to worship the Lord of heaven and earth, faced the unspoken ridicule of the Roman stonework.

The Romans allowed worship in the temple to go ahead almost unimpeded. But this tolerance was no act of grace. The descendants of Abraham were carefully kept in their place as the stonework of the Roman propaganda machine reminded all who walked the streets of the holy city, that it belonged to Rome. The Roman gods looked down upon Yahweh, the Holy One of Israel. The fortress declared to the city's inhabitants that resistance to Rome could have only one result, the manner of execution reserved for rebels against the empire: crucifixion. Those who walked the streets of Jerusalem were reminded constantly that failure and death were the only possible outcome of any attempt at rebellion. And yet, in the depths of the holy city, countless hearts and blades were scribed through with an eager readiness for insurrection. Israel's God had delivered them before. Why should He not do it again? Even the anti-violent prophet from Galilee had warned his followers that they must reject the empire's dictates, that they must risk a sentence of death, that they must carry the cross-piece of their crucifixion stake every day.

Had this been any other city, the dictates of the empire would have been easier to swallow. Living in the Jewish quarter of an ancient Greek colony, Bar-Abbas had never registered the hidden message of Roman architecture. Alexandria was happily Roman, as were the Jewish merchants like Yeshua's family who lived there. They had never tasted injustice. They had never seen the God of Israel taunted by pagans. They were Diaspora, scattered but Jewish. They would gather together in their synagogues to hear stories and scriptures of the Promised Land and the people of Abraham. Some would even travel to Jerusalem for the city's great festivals. But those who lived in the holy city would see the filthy shadow of the fortress crawl slowly and daily around the beauty of the temple and its precincts. How could they react? Loss of faith in Israel's god? Resignation to the might of Rome? Some would feel no hint of tension, just as Yeshua had felt none on his previous visit. But this time Bar-Abbas had traveled from Galilee rather than Egypt. This time he entered Jerusalem not as trader but as assassin.

His merchant's mentality could only exacerbate his anger. Rome had taken the land, its people and its capital, and turned them into a giant storehouse of merchandise. The fruits of a land flowing with milk and honey were taken from those who worked the land and produced the fruit, and were diverted to distant, invisible, privileged gentiles. The fruits of the Promised Land were now mere resources for Rome. The animals grazing on the land were no longer creatures, they were "live stock." The people, whose destiny had always been deeply intertwined with that land, found themselves sharing its fate. If the Promised Land was a Roman resource, then so too was its people, unwitting slaves deprived of their humanness, two legged livestock.

All that relieved Caesar of his humanness was the divinity accorded to him by his provincial subjects. But the emperor himself would feel all-too-human when he heard the fate soon to befall his prefect in Jerusalem. Still, for now that future was too distant and the potential repercussions too enormous for Yeshua to entertain anything but the vaguest thoughts of what orders might echo around the marble hallways of imperial Rome. For now, the Egyptian simply had a job to do. He knew well enough about similar quests in the history of this city. He knew of the enormous consequences that lay ahead if he were successful. But Yeshua Bar-Abbas was not aware that this entry into Jerusalem would transform him into a historical figure. He entered the city unaware he was fulfilling not only his destiny but hers, oblivious to how future generations would hear of his exploits. He had a job to do, and every split second, every breath of his lungs and every beat of his heart were bent towards achieving his end. All else was secondary.

Bar-Abbas walked alongside Amram as the track widened and the shadow of Solomon's Portico cast its dark welcome upon the travelers. A surge of pride animated the Egyptian's entire body and pushed an excess of salt water behind his eyeballs, which overflowed with quiet tears, unseen by any but the God of Israel.

Walking alone a few paces behind his brother, Theudas had already adopted his role as bodyguard. In the centre, donkey, Kochba and Miriam moved together. The cart had been emptied of weapons, an event deliberately conducted in plain view of the child who had followed them from the valley of the Lestai.

For the second time in his life, Yeshua entered the city of Jerusalem. Not this time as pilgrim, tourist or trader, but as rebel. The contrast with his previous visit could not have been greater. Its streets, its shadows, its people, its noises and its smells, were those of a new Jerusalem. Every corner, every dark recess, every narrow alley was a hiding place, a safe refuge, an escape route. Each roof was scanned to see whether someone running along its top could access places that were inaccessible for any who might be in pursuit along the road. Every wall, every roof, every grain of dust was his ally. They had spent their existence awaiting his arrival.

"Can we just go straight to the garrison for a quick look before we find a place to stay?" Yeshua asked Amram, his guide who replied only with gestures. Two minutes' walking brought them under the shadow of the platform where the prefect would address the crowds.

This evening there were no crowds. Several suns would pass over the temple before faithful Jews arrived from around the empire to celebrate their birth as a nation at the week-long Festival of Ingathering. For now the square below the fortress was open, uncluttered. The row of buildings kept at bay by the Roman pavement stretched along a shallow descent towards the southern wall of the city. Yeshua imagined Amram's bow, concealed within the safe darkness of stone walls, sending its deadly missile up towards the speaker's podium. It would take place in the morning when the sun would shine in the prefect's face, and make Amram's aim that much easier. Nevertheless, the distance was a formidable hundred paces. Still reeling from the shock of the archer's recent mishap, Yeshua looked at his companion. Amram's mental calculations were almost visible and brought reassurance that the bowman knew exactly what he was doing.

"Time we find our beds for the night!" said the archer. After three weeks in the caves of Arbela, three adjacent rooms in a rough corner of Jerusalem brought a luxury that felt excessive, even if the rooms were small and dark. The smells spoke of crowded and unsanitary conditions, and the nearby animal compounds carried the complaints of livestock as overcrowded as the people. The anonymity was more welcome than the aroma, but the companions would not abandon the wealth hidden within their rooms for the scent of olives that the evening breeze carried from the adjacent hills. They remained indoors.

Amram was slowly returning to conversation, even his usual humor at times. The belches had not returned, although no wine had been touched since yesterday's loss at Bethshe-an. Despite his words, his smiles and his laughter, Amram looked like a condemned man. Condemned by no one other than himself, and condemned by more than yesterday's actions. Filling his purse from his sack of money, he turned to Yeshua.

"What does that proverb say, Bar-Rabbas?" Yeshua looked puzzled. "Give wine to the needy and beer to the oppressed," he continued, "my favorite Scripture."

"And which are you," smiled Kochba, "needy or oppressed?"

"I am both" he grinned, "but no more than the rest of you." For the first time in two days, he spoke with over-pronounced relish. "I will return with the necessary supplies for us to fulfill this Scripture together."

Theudas and Miriam left soon after Amram, too tired for an evening of awkward or difficult conversation, fuelled as it would be, by whatever strong drink the archer could find.

Amram's temporary absence had left Bar-Abbas and Kochba to fill an atmospheric vacuum.

"Is he going to be alright?" asked Bar-Abbas.

"You don't have to worry about Amram," came the reply, to which the Egyptian lifted an eyebrow, forcing Kochba to correct himself.

"Well no, that's not quite true. You *always* have to worry about Amram, but in the end you realize there was no need."

"I don't even want to think about the state he'll be in later. Doesn't that bother you? Everything we do here revolves around Amram. He has to be ready." It was now Kochba's turn to speak with his eyebrow, forcing Bar-Abbas to clarify himself.

"Yes, I'm concerned about Amram for his own sake," he said. "And there's no reason we can't delay this, give him time to sort himself out."

Kochba breathed more easily. "Like I said, there is no need to worry about Amram."

"I know he likes his drink, but this evening he is going to get utterly bladdered . . . This is more than anyone could cope with." The companions were silent for a minute, but it was a pregnant silence. "Kochba. Why did Amram miss that shot?"

"No one can be precise all the time," Kochba shrugged, wholly unconvinced by himself.

"Is he likely to miss again?"

"I have to say, Bar-Abbas, I've known Amram a long time, and I can tell you, he'll be fine. This job will distract him from himself. When it's over and done, then we can attend to his wellbeing. But for now the best thing we can do for him is trust him to do his job."

"Do you think it will work?" The Egyptian's question threw Kochba off balance.

"What—killing the prefect?"

"Yes."

"Do you mean, 'will we manage it' or do you mean, if we do manage it, 'will it have the effect we want?'"

"I'm not sure," Bar-Abbas smiled.

"I have little doubt we can kill the prefect. Kaleb will fill us in tomorrow. But whatever news he brings, it will only affect our planning, not our success. There is no reason why this can't work."

"Ah, that's all I wanted to hear."

"It's an inspired plan, Yeshua." Kochba's ready praise of the task in hand betrayed his doubts over its long-term effectiveness, and the Egyptian realized that he had no desire to hear those doubts. He was committed to this task, and the cost had been too high to entertain any misgivings about the outcome. He jumped in before Kochba could express any concern about the consequences of assassinating a Roman prefect.

"We're in an inspired place." Yeshua grinned as he finished the sentence. He had Jerusalem in mind as he had begun it, but then realized that he was making conversation in a noisy, smelly chamber of dust and growing darkness. Kochba laughed in response, but his humor quickly disappeared as the day's events caught up with him. "This shouldn't have happened. This shouldn't happen. Adonai should not have allowed this to happen . . ."

"This is happening every day in Israel," said Yeshua, as though he had witnessed widespread injustices at close hand. "It happens outside the gates of your farm." Kochba remained expressionless. "I still can't work out what's drawn you to this desperate group of rebels."

"I thought we'd already had that conversation," the farmer grunted.

As he would have done with his brother, Bar-Abbas enforced quiet upon Kochba in the hope that it would evoke further confession.

"That life, my comfy life . . ." the farmer whispered, "it doesn't bring what it promises. I have my family and farm, my comfort and my wealth . . ."

"But?"

"Well, that's it. After those things, there shouldn't be a 'but.'"

"You're bored. Is that it? Is that why you're really here?"

"Look, I thought we were talking about Eliazar. In case you didn't notice, he . . ."

Yeshua continued his assault and spoke over the top of his friend until he had forced him into submission. "Why are you . . . why are you . . . why are you, Kochba the Successful, sat in a crappy Jerusalem hovel, listening to a naïve foreigner a decade younger than yourself? . . . Why?"

"I'm not having that . . .

"No. You are, Kochba, you are having exactly that, and the question is why? And don't give me all the virtues about justice for your people. Why are you here—really—why are you here?"

The farmer said nothing, but for once did not attempt to have the final word, leaving Yeshua's question to intensify as it echoed around the chamber. Eventually he spoke.

"Most people of Israel envy me. And it's only right that they should. I'm not over wealthy, but I am comfortable. It was Amram's friendship that brought me to Arbela. But when we sat in those caves, for the first time, I envied these people who had nothing but a purpose. What does the proverb say? 'Without vision the people perish.' Yeshua, I had no vision." Kochba's spirit had lightened and his voice calmed. "Who, in my position, who at my age, is going to bring vision and bring purpose? Those things arise from desperation, not comfort." The farmer looked straight at the merchant. "You're as wealthy as I am. You know in your bones what I'm talking about." Kochba's voice was showing signs of giving way, so he paused to regain composure while Bar-Abbas nodded. "The only difference between us was that you had been bereaved. You had your crisis that made you desperate. My grievance only came yesterday. When that peasant boy was shot through the neck I lost a member of my family."

"What about your family in Galilee?" Yeshua muttered. "Every day my mind wanders back to Alexandria. I want my father's approval. I want to go home with something that will force him to admit we were right to be here. But the more I see, the more I doubt that he will ever approve of this. Much as I want him to. And you can see the danger we are in. You don't have the support of your family, any more than do I! Don't you just want to go home?"

"It's too late for me to teach my family. At least with words alone. Action, sacrifice, my neck on the line is the only way to teach my family anything worthy of remembrance. I want my sons to remember their father as a righteous man, a man of justice, not a man who provided them with comfort. You asked me why I am here? I am here for my sons, Bar-Abbas."

An hour had proven Amram true to his word. "Tonight we relax," Amram declared, "because tomorrow we meet with Kaleb the Pharisee."

The archer's jovial habits seemed to be returning to him gradually, but there was something absent about the apparent normality he brought along with the beer, the wine and the boy who helped to carry them. For all the archer's presence, an entire dimension of his inner self remained trapped at the dusty tax house of yesterday's Bethshe'an.

As a former Roman soldier, certain emotional outlets were unavailable to him. He had unlearned them permanently, and the range and type of his natural reactions to difficulty remained forever limited by the requirements of the empire's military machines. Should a soldier like Amram be party to or even witness to human atrocities, his emotional responses were severely restricted in scope. Amram had always coped by means of the legitimate outlets that military convention had conceded and left intact: laughter and bitterness; secrecy and anger; wine and bear. The shorthand term for this cocktail was "honor." And since completing his military service Amram had, regretfully and helplessly, remained an honorable man. But the edifice that had long caused such emotional constipation was beginning to crack. The storms that had gathered inside him for years and yet never surfaced were already fierce. With the death of Eliazar the ferocity was building. The external, superficial return to normal behavior was no reflection of the hurricane spinning inside Amram. Although he could not explain why, for Bar-Abbas, an eruption looked inevitable and imminent. The atmosphere created by Kochba's confession, as inescapable as the evening humidity, besieged the archer's spirit.

Cups were filled and drinks consumed. "So," the archer growled as he wiped his mouth, "it feels like I'm interrupting a private conversation." Bar-Abbas glanced at Kochba and back at Amram.

The dimly lit room concealed whatever truth may have been spoken by facial expression, so Yeshua broke the silence. "Can you make the shot?" he asked in gentle provocation.

"You mean, will I accidentally put an arrow through your neck?" He grinned. But in a moment the grin subsided. Through the half-light, Yeshua saw the veteran's appearance become that of a child in distress. The transformation was all the more noticeable on the face of one whose natural comportment had always seemed secure, impervious. The archer contorted his lips in a last desperate effort to hold his composure. Like the setting sun, fighting off its nearing reflection on the sea, the futile battle was soon lost. A whooping noise echoed from Amram's corner as he dropped his head into cupped hands.

That didn't take much, Yeshua thought to himself. But the storm had broken. The whooping continued and got louder. Kochba joined his old friend. And still the noise continued. It didn't sound much like weeping to the Egyptian, but then Amram was a novice.

Jerusalem brings out the best and the worst of you. Miriam's words were dancing in Yeshua's mind. He was unsure whether he was witnessing the best or the worst of Amram. Whichever it was, it flowed at full force and yet did not feel out of place, even if it was out of character with all that Bar-Abbas knew of the archer.

"We are at war Amram," whispered a tearful Kochba. "These things happen, you know that better than anyone." And still the wailing continued, even as Amram rose to his feet and walked aimlessly around a room that could not contain his grief. Eventually, a different noise began to interrupt the whooping rhythm. The soldier was trying to speak, but needed several attempts before managing a comprehensible sentence.

"Yesterday wasn't the first time," he sobbed. "It's not the first time I've hit the wrong man." Having won the small victory of a complete sentence, the archer returned to his seat.

"Germania?" asked Kochba.

Amram nodded. "In a village. The men had left to defend their lands. Their village was defenseless. My section moved in." The whooping resumed, but was curtailed much sooner than the first round. "My commander, Flavius, took one of their women, while her children watched." Deep breaths rather than whooping now intervened. "They were sub-human. Little more than animals. Merciless savages, hell bent on mindless destruction. That's why we were fighting them. Nothing to do with enlarging the empire and stealing their lands. They were evil. That's why we fought them. That's what we were told."

Having heard none of this, and yet having known Amram so long, Kochba felt at liberty to push his friend. "What happened?"

"A man from the village had returned, and rushed at Flavius, with a sword. Flavius had no chance if I didn't act. He was less than fifty paces from me. I raised my bow." Again, Amram was interrupted only by his own deep breaths. "I aimed at the villager, and sunk an arrow into my commander's back."

"That would make you a dead man!" frowned Kochba.

"It should have done. But that man who had come back to his village was at the head of a war party. They killed the rest of my section. I survived because they all saw it and believed I had acted justly." Another brief pause ensued. "Hitting the wrong man saved my life."

"What about the war party?"

"I don't know what they said. All I know is that they put a drink in my hand. I guess they thought I had a conscience." Amram's head sank as he shook it. "They weren't the savages. Flavius deserved to die." The deeper breaths returned. "Eliazar did not deserve to die." The sentence had barely ended before the whooping returned.

Yeshua reclined, looking around this dirty, stinking back street of a tired city, in peasant's accommodation, confronted with the undignified wailing of a man he hardly knew. Unexpectedly and utterly out of context, he was seized by peace that warmed his bones. He was witnessing a miracle, and for a time revelled in the privilege of the event.

"I never wanted to be this," Amram confessed. "I have drawn too much blood. And I don't care what the Pharisee says, God turns his face from those who draw blood so easily." Yeshua had the feeling that Amram was explaining something of his affection for the Egyptian brothers. The archer then addressed him directly.

"The Persian kings kept a walled garden, where they would take their honored guests. Do you think the God of Israel has a garden like that, Bar-Rabbas?" Bar-Abbas shrugged his shoulders. "Because I think he does. I've started to see it in my dreams. Since you arrived at Narbata, I have seen that garden in my dreams. And the God of our fathers beckons me to join him." Amram paused to laugh through a nose blocked due to this excessive use of his newly functioning emotional valve. "Can you imagine that? Yahweh beckoning Amram to be his privileged guest?"

"Is that what you want?" Yeshua asked tentatively.

"It's what I dream." Amram was recovering his composure. "And a dream is all it is. I have killed men and enjoyed it. Not even Kochba has the livestock to provide enough blood for my atonement!"

Yeshua lifted his hands to express what he felt but could not name. He was ready to abandon the assassination plot for the sake of Amram, and that readiness could be heard in his voice as he addressed the archer. "Do you want to go ahead with this?"

"I'm with you, Bar-Rabbas. I don't condone this. But we are compelled." Again, Amram rose to his feet and his walk communicated his undiminished resolve. Although even the darkness could not conceal his bloodshot eyes, they only added weight to what he was about to say. "You asked me if I could make the shot. The answer is 'yes.' I will send the prefect ahead of me to Sheol."

❧ 14 ❧

THE NEARBY SHEEP, GOATS and oxen did not observe the day of rest and fought to make the loudest noise on the quietest day. The competition would have prized the companions from their sleep, had it not been a sleep with the strength of the empty jugs, pots and jars that decorated a room not even Sabbath daylight could penetrate. Eventually Bar-Abbas emerged from the darkness into the streets of Jerusalem.

He paced through Jerusalem as through a dream. Walking towards the temple, the stench and the noise of the animals were slowly displaced by the scent of summer flowers and the song of larks, doves and sandgrouse. But for Yeshua, these contrasts, familiar to the city's inhabitants, now seemed alien. He moved in a separate world, albeit one that would soon enough engulf theirs. The early mist had refused to lift, and as the Egyptian went to remind himself why he was there, the uppermost battlements of the Antonine Fortress were just visible behind its morning veil. He drew a deep breath, trying to inhale the image so it would remain inside him throughout the day that lay ahead.

Bar-Abbas returned to the lodgings where his companions still slept. "Has anyone seen Theudas?" he said, with some alarm. "Or Miriam! Where are they?"

"They've probably gone to find breakfast," said Kochba, reaching for some water but barely awake.

"It's the Sabbath! They won't find anything."

"Well, maybe they've gone for a walk."

Kochba rolled back into his sleep while Amram's grunting snore showed how he had never left his. Bar-Abbas climbed into his bed and tried to sleep away the time that stretched before him as a yawning chasm while he waited for the afternoon rendezvous with Kaleb. The figurine had returned to his hand. After hearing Amram's confessions the icon of the young boy had a different texture, and would have spoken with a different voice. But Yeshua refused to hear it, just as he refused to hear Kochba's opinions on the potential consequences of murdering a Roman prefect.

&

The cacophony of animals being slaughtered told the time to all within earshot of the temple. From the hour of sacrifice, of animal cries and blood, Kaleb the Pharisee emerged with a joy impossible to conceal. "Shalom," he laughed embracing each of them.

"You came through Bethshe'an I take it?"

"Then you've . . ." Kochba's eyes sunk beneath his words. ". . . You've heard."

Kaleb nodded. "I heard one of your number was wounded." Nothing. "Where is Eliazar?" Kochba, Yeshua and Amram looked at the ground. "Theudas?" Still no answer. "Miriam?"

"We haven't seen Theudas and Miriam since we arrived yesterday evening," said Kochba. "They're somewhere in the city."

"I hope," added Yeshua.

"Eliazar?"

"Eliazar is dead," said Amram. "I missed the target, and put an arrow through his neck."

"We buried him on the banks of the Jordan," Kochba explained, "in the shadow of his beloved hills . . . I'm sorry"

Kaleb was silent as he greeted the news he had half expected. Turning from his companions, he leaned towards the ground, placing his hands on his knees. Amram moved his gaze towards the sun, as Yeshua grasped the Pharisee's shoulder. This is what Kaleb had warned against, the cost of pointless risk against a Roman target, when an attack on Jewish soldiers in Galilee would have risked less. The Pharisee had no hint of "told you so" in his voice, but his expression was sufficient the fill the air around him with the angry sentiment. Bar-Abbas, however, was in no state of mind to notice. Nothing in heaven or earth could now distract him from the task in hand. The dull white robes hung motionless around Kaleb, whose entire frame had been rapidly transformed into a Greek statue. No smooth marble cut with pride to honor a glorious leader. Here stood a disheveled, pathetic figure, stooped in shock.

After a few moments of silence, he raised himself to full height. "Come," he said, unaware for once of his audience, "I have better news for you here in Jerusalem. Wait here a moment." Kaleb excused himself from their company, disappearing back into the temple. Within seconds he had reappeared, his hand on the shoulder of another Pharisee, whispering to him news of Bethshe'an.

"This is Ehud," Kaleb announced in a pragmatic tone, devoid of his usual charisma. "Ehud is a friend, and he's found us a place to stay." His friend smiled vaguely, an expression at odds with the general gloom that weighed upon his face. His entire bearing, clumsy and heavy, was at odds with that of Kaleb, whose manner was precise and deliberate, but his penetrating gaze seemed no less inflammable, looking poised to conjure up divine energy at any moment. His admiration as each of the names was spoken in Kaleb's introductions was impossible to hide, but his eyes were fixed mainly on Bar-Abbas .

Ehud the Pharisee simply nodded his head towards the companions. "We'll speak more where it's quieter," he whispered, hurrying away assuming they would follow. The animal cries faded into the distance behind as the group made their way through the quieter northern reaches of the city. They were led to a light, spacious house with its own courtyard, not dissimilar in layout to the house of Yudah in Narbata, although much smaller. Bar-Abbas wondered whether a similar fate would befall this home. There were no servants, no drinks, no food. This was, after all, the home of a Pharisee, and it was Sabbath. Ehud, like his friend Kaleb, was fasting.

"Ehud has found us not only this place to stay," Kaleb declared.

"I have accessed all that you need from the temple," said Ehud, looking directly at Amram.

"Well let's have a look," the archer demanded. Ehud disappeared to collect the tools for the task. "You've collected the weapons already, Kaleb?"

Yeshua was relieved at the thought of one dangerous task already accomplished. "Should we ask how you managed that?" he smiled.

"We've done it. That's all that matters."

Ehud reappeared, his arms furnished with weapons that never looked so out of place upon the one carrying them. The Pharisee, who could barely carry himself, had a bundle of about twenty arrows, along with three bows, none of them strung but with the lines of hemp and animal intestine ready. "None of us know about bows," he announced, as though it were necessary, "so we thought we should give you a choice."

Amram began to inspect the weapons. An expression of the child-like abandon seized his features again, no longer in helpless despair but in excited pleasure. He discarded the first, but examined the second with delight. "This is a good Jewish bow!" he said with surprise, although his gratitude was directed towards the bow rather than the Pharisee who delivered it.

"*With Jewish archers I conquered Persia!*" Ehud gloated.

"Alexander the Great," Amram replied, knowing the quotation well enough, but still not raising his eyes from their fascination with the bow "This is quite a gift."

"We brought a gift of our own," said Yeshua as he unburdened himself of his pack. "Is it lawful to accept a gift on the Sabbath?" he asked, unloading a large bag of coins onto the paved ground. "We thought to make it a donation to the temple. It is money that has come from our people."

"The temple has enough money," Kaleb snarled. "But there are plenty of godly causes that do not," he smiled, turning his head toward Ehud.

"Of course it is lawful to accept a gift," said Ehud. "And this feels like quite a gift."

"So does this," Amram muttered. He had strung his new bow and was playing with its tension.

"It will do the job alright?" asked Yeshua.

"In the right hands," the archer winked.

"And, Yeshua," Ehud paused and flared his eyes towards him. "We have also arranged for you to address a synagogue this afternoon." Kaleb prepared himself for the inevitable Egyptian protest.

"Were you talking to me?"

"Yes I was," Ehud nodded smugly. "The last of my gifts."

"And the greatest gift I can offer in return is my refusal," Yeshua replied.

"This is an enormous privilege," said Kaleb, curling his eyebrows into an impossible shape. "And you have plenty to say."

"But far less than you, Kaleb. I bestow this privilege upon you. You're the preacher. Take this opportunity yourself, enjoy this privilege!"

"I have enjoyed that privilege already, on three occasions in the last week."

"We're bored of him now," Ehud laughed. "We'd like a change of voice."

Kochba interrupted. "Is that how Simon the Zealot knows who we are? Has our pharisaic friend been name-dropping from his pulpit?"

"All part of the plan," said Kaleb. "We'll need the people behind us." The only person Yeshua wanted behind him was his brother. The atmosphere now confirmed the wisdom of having someone to watch his back, but Theudas was nowhere to be seen.

"And the people will be behind you, Bar-Abbas," said Ehud, concerned this might not be enough.

"I am no preacher," Yeshua objected in a tone intended to finish the conversation.

"Well, don't think of it as a sermon." Amram's input was, for once, unwelcome.

"And what else should I deliver from the platform of a synagogue?"

"Just do what most rabbis do," laughed Kochba. "Read the Scripture, then ramble on with some unrelated moral rant!"

"About what?"

"Don't tell me that Yeshua Bar-Abbas has nothing to say when he comes to liberate Jerusalem," Kaleb chuckled, whilst looking at Kochba and Amram.

"I came here to kill a Roman, not preach a sermon," he replied in bemusement.

"It won't be a sermon," Amram said. "It will be a speech. And that speech might make the difference between achieving our goal or not."

"How?"

Ehud took up the argument. "Because to do what you're going to do you will need the greatest diversion possible." Everyone nodded. "You can inspire people to be part of that."

"I don't doubt that. But Kaleb can do it better. He's made for this."

"It's true, you and I have different motives, different backgrounds, different experiences," pondered Kaleb artificially. "But we speak for a single cause. Your voice will strengthen our chance of success."

"Especially as yours is the voice of an assassin." Ehud flared his eyes as he spoke.

"I just don't see this." Yeshua wished that Theudas were present, and allowed his thoughts to wonder the streets of Jerusalem and beyond in search of his brother. Where was he?

"Can you trust us enough to see it for you?" asked Kochba. Yeshua looked at Amram. The archer's expression betrayed his total agreement with the farmer.

The Egyptian voiced a concern that had not previously occurred, but now he was in Jerusalem seemed obvious. "Are you sure we should be seeking this kind of publicity when we still have ten days to go?" He asked. "We'll arouse suspicion. The Romans will be onto us. Why not leave the sermon until the festival itself? Why not next week?"

"Because, Bar-Abbas, next week there *will* be reason to fear doing it." Kaleb showed less than his usual frustration when stating the obvious. "Next week there will be strangers in the crowd and soldiers in the midst of them, listening out for any sign of trouble."

"It's the same at every festival," Ehud added. "That is why now is the perfect time. If we reach the right people, news will spread when pilgrims start to arrive for the festival."

"Now is our chance," Amram spoke in the whisper of excitement, "Now."

Yeshua sighed and sat down. He said nothing, but his resolve had been broken in plain view of all. "What is the Scripture to be read?" he asked with as little enthusiasm as could be squeezed through a genuine question.

"Whatever you want it to be!" said Ehud, excited at the possibility of hearing an accomplished assassin preach to his congregation.

"You might not like what you hear!" Yeshua warned them.

"At least there's a chance we might! Which is more than can be said for most Pharisees," Amram laughed.

Bar-Abbas sat back and resigned himself to a commitment he had hoped unnecessary. Becoming a public figure, even without his real name, was hardly a relished prospect. "Well," he said, "I'm off back to our lodging to see if I can find Theudas. I need some space, and I need to learn my way around this city." A flurry of glances ricocheted around the group. "Don't worry. I'll be back in time for the synagogue, and I'll have something to say."

"Do you need parchment?" the Pharisee asked.

Yeshua raised his eyebrows to decline the offer. Kaleb shrugged, withdrew and began to make use of his rejected parchment.

> *Father,*
>
> *Here, I have seen you with my own eyes. I feel your embrace and receive your kiss. I have tasted more than hope. I am reconciled, restored and honored. The honored guest at your banqueting table, in the city of our fathers, of my father. You have said to me, "You are my Son, today I have become your Father." I am here to serve your will, to fulfill your purpose, to be your son.*
>
> *I can only pray for my companions. I commit them to your hands. For righteousness' sake, I hand them to you, I present their task to you, I entrust their destiny to you. And at last they will taste for themselves the justice of the LORD.*
>
> *I will wait patiently for the LORD, who alone brings peace. Who alone reconciles the father with his son. I will watch, and I will wait, and I will present myself before you. I will do all that you have required of me, and be your son in truth.*

"Are you sure we're doing the right thing?" Theudas asked, as though Miriam were his elder brother.

"It's you who wanted to protect Yeshua," she replied, "and you can't do that if he knows we're here."

Theudas hung his mouth agape, and frowned slightly, leading Miriam to marvel that the younger brother was as naïve as the elder.

"He'll trust everyone he's going to meet over the next few days. And who knows who that will be when Jerusalem is brewing for a festival?" Theudas was beginning to grasp something that made sense, but couldn't quite make the connections. "He'd tell everyone he's got someone watching his back. And then we'd need someone to watch our back."

"We could have quite a procession at this festival then?" he smiled. Miriam suppressed a smirk and shook her head.

"How on earth you boys manage to do what you've done and plan what you've planned is beyond me."

"Perhaps we have divine protection?" grinned Theudas.

"If you do, then I'm it!" she frowned, with mock superiority.

"I did tell Yeshua I wanted to go home. And you seem to have made your objections pretty clear. With any luck he'll think I've run back to Egypt and taken you with me!"

The scream of a woman somewhere nearby tore through their conversation as if to sever them from one another's company. Theudas, besieged with confusion, looked at Miriam whose expression remained blank. Instinctively he backed away from her, drawn hopelessly towards the sound of distress. As he turned to run, Miriam grasped his forearm and pulled him back. She tried to speak but some emotion had glued her lips tight shut. Squeezing his arm, she could only shake her head. For a moment, the sheer magnetism of her eyes held Theudas in place, but the ongoing screams of that woman had a sinister gravity impossible to resist.

Speeding from the street into an open, sandy expanse Theudas ran into a crowd, all mesmerized by the spectacle. Fighting his way to the front he saw the woman, still screaming as her ankle was manacled to an iron hook sunk deep into ground. Soldiers wearing the black and gold armour of the temple guard kept the crowd at bay, while a white-robed priestly official lifted his voice above her screams as though ignoring them. The children in the crowd were as impervious to the cries of this young woman as were the men who toyed with the rocks in their hands and the women who looked upon her with loathing.

"Marriage is the sacred bond of God's created order," the official called to the crowd. "Adultery is to break that sacred bond, pouring scorn . . ."

"I am no adulterer," the woman shrieked. On hearing her voice, and seeing the hair pulled from her face, Theudas saw this so-called woman was barely fifteen.

". . . Pouring scorn upon Yahweh himself," the official persisted. "Adultery . . ."

"He is the adulterer," she yelled, pointing at an indignant figure in his thirties, tossing a jagged stone lightly in his right hand at the front of the crowd, in smug knowledge of the inevitable.

"Adultery is punishable by death," the official called to the crowd. He raised an arm toward the condemned girl, "According to the law of Moses, death by stoning,"

"*He* was unfaithful to *me*!" she screamed.

"Yet you have no proof," the official lamented, with the pretence that he wished it otherwise.

"And where is your proof against her?" Every eye fell straight upon Theudas, who was barely aware of his own outburst. The girl saw a glimmer of hope, as the anger directed towards the Egyptian failed to deter him. The crowd was silenced by his impudence. "Where is *your* proof?" he asked again as the official was momentarily stunned.

"This man's word is all the proof we need. The woman is an adulterer, her dignity is forfeit."

Theudas felt his fists clench of their own accord, but kept his voice steady as he taunted the mob. "Every one of you who throws a rock, throws away your *own* dignity."

"She is guilty!" her husband bawled.

"And Yahweh is merciful," Theudas shouted. "Where is your mercy?"

The official lifted his hands to calm the crowd. "Yahweh is merciful, Egyptian," he nodded. "Better to taste justice before the grave, than torture after it." His features overflowed with self-satisfaction. "That, my friend, is the mercy of Yahweh."

"You call that mercy?" Theudas snarled.

The official nodded towards the guard who had approached the troublemaker with drawn sword. "There's always room for one more," the soldier grinned as he thrust the tip of his blade under Theudas' chin, forcing him to step back through the crowd. Having emerged into open space, the Egyptian halted in defiance, calculating whether he could draw his dagger and use it before the soldier would strike.

"Theudas!" Miriam's voice dragged him out of his defiant state. "What are you doing?" her voice rang from behind.

"Get out of my sight," the soldier growled as he sheathed his polished steel and returned to the arena. Even in her distraught state, Miriam had strength enough to drag a bemused Theudas away from the crowd as the stoning began. The girl's screams had ceased with the first rocks hurled, but her quiet was no less piercing.

"What were you thinking?" Miriam words were a cocktail of anger and alarm. "Are you trying to get yourself killed?" Theudas made no sound as Miriam's wrath gave way to sobbing, and she dropped her head into his chest. But the two could not endure the roar of the frenzied crowd reveling in application of Mosaic Law.

"And they call this the 'Holy City.'" Theudas was barely conscious of Miriam's continued embrace as they made their way from the chaos. "What on earth are we doing here, Miriam?"

"Have you never seen a stoning?" she spluttered.

"We don't have this in Egypt."

"She has to prove her husband's guilt, but if her husband accuses her, she has to prove her own innocence. That's how it works."

"How can anyone call that justice?"

"Theudas," Miriam interrupted. "This is Israel," she whispered, close enough for the need to lift her head to look at him.

Cavernous brown eyes, colored with distress, blew the cloud from his mind. He thought for a moment, held her shoulders and turned a full, searching gaze upon her. "Why didn't this happen to you?"

For a moment, they withstood one another's stare in quiet. "My father saved me from a stoning," she breathed in hushed tones. "At the cost of making enemies."

"What kind of enemies?"

Miriam dropped her head. "My husband's family needed to prove how bad a wife I was, how bad a family I belonged to. You and your brother showed up, and it gave them all the proof they needed."

"It really is because of us that Yudah was arrested. Your husband's family, desperate for your blood."

She nodded while Theudas shook his head. "What are we doing here?" His question was directed towards the city, as he gestured toward the stoning. "Overthrowing the Romans to leave Israel in the hands of these people—you could hardly call it liberation."

⫷15⫸

"ARE YOU FEELING READY for this, Yeshua Bar-Abbas?" The rosy glow of Kochba's cheeks radiated warmth through his graying beard.

"What, for fuelling a rebellious crowd using pious words?"

"This is why it has to be you," Kochba smiled.

"And at a festival!"

"This is what the festivals are!" said Kochba. "We re-live the story of our people."

"You mean they remind everyone the land is no longer ours?" Each of the three annual festivals coincided with a major harvest. Passover was the harvest of Barley, Pentecost of wheat, and the Festival of Ingathering for which the city now braced itself celebrated the grape harvest. Each festival spoke of the relationship between the land of Israel and those who occupied it. Gathering a harvest, only to watch it disappear into Roman hands was an insult to native Jews and fed only their exasperation.

"They tell the whole story," Kochba said, as though the Egyptian were ignorant of Jewish custom. "Passover is the escape from Egypt; Pentecost is Moses getting the law on Mount Sinai; this Feast of Ingathering is the wandering through the wilderness on the way to the Promised Land. Whatever you say, you, Yeshua Bar-Abbas, you are living that story." Yeshua's confusion was impossible to hide. He knew well enough that these festivals were packed with nationalistic fervor. He knew how they kept alive the conviction that Israel was God's people: it was their land and their deliverance from oppression was at hand. Surely this was too great an occasion for the cynical Egyptian merchant to be invited to preach.

"Bar-Abbas! Can't you see? You had it all. You have been robbed. You have lost your family and your home. And you're doing something about

146

it because of your love for this land and its people and its God. Your life is the story of Israel. Whatever words you choose will find their mark."

"Kochba, everyone in Israel has a life that tells the story of Israel. I still think Kaleb can do a better job, it's what he does best."

"Kaleb gives the people what they've already heard, sermons they've enjoyed a thousand times before. He'll have his claps and cheers and admiration, but, I have to say, that's the only response he's ever likely to get from most people."

"And what makes you think I can bring anything different?"

"Because, Bar-Abbas, you're driven by something you can't name." The jovial glow had left Kochba's face, but the sincerity remained. "Whatever it is, it drives you to action. I don't think you can say why. You have none of Kaleb's certainty, you make none of his demands, but you have conviction. And that can't be named. It can only be caught. You have conviction, not certainty." A pause. "Just speak. Don't preach."

Yeshua sighed in resignation. He looked at his hands, hearing Kaleb's claim about the hands of God, but thinking only of the blood they had drawn. "Well, Kochba, you'd better be there to defend me when it all goes wrong." This, after all, was a distinct possibility. In the days leading up to any festival, patriotic anger would run high and the synagogues were a melting pot for a passion ready to boil over into violence. That violence was as likely to be inflicted on a Jewish heretic as a Roman pagan.

For every conceivable strand of Jewish belief, Jerusalem boasted a dozen synagogues. To Jews arriving on pilgrimage from distant lands, these places were both a wonder and an oddity. Their roots lay in a failed rebellion against the Babylonian empire several centuries earlier. Jerusalem had been destroyed and its ruling class deported to the empire's capital, hundreds of miles east. Cut off from the holy city, their beloved temple in ruins, the exiles came together to worship, to hear Scriptures, to keep their heritage alive. These synagogues, these communities of faithful Jews, served only those in exile, longing to be at home in Jerusalem.

Yeshua scanned the hundred or so who arrived for worship at Ehud's synagogue. Their faces declared that, despite being here in God's holy city, their hearts remained somewhere in exile. They awaited their homecoming and prepared for the Feast of Ingathering.

After hearing the opening prayers and the eighteen benedictions, Bar-Abbas was invited onto the platform by Ehud. His throbbing heart was almost audible, as Yeshua realized how easily this crowd could be tipped one way or another. This scheme of wanting only vengeance for his family had turned into addressing an entire Jerusalem synagogue desperate for liberation. He saw in every face a hunger for blood, and a readiness to draw it if his message displeased them. "Yeshua Bar-Abbas, of Alexandria! Brother, we welcome you to our synagogue. May the words of your lips and the meditations of your heart be acceptable to Yahweh, our God."

With that the Pharisee took his seat and was replaced on the platform by an attendant carrying the scroll requested by the Egyptian. He had chosen a text unlikely to be appreciated by a congregation eager for a message of rebellion and revolt. Bar-Abbas should perhaps have chosen a war-like image of God, or a portion of Scripture that condoned or even called for violent resistance. Such would certainly have been Kaleb's approach. But for too many Rabbis, the condemnation of Israel's enemies was pronounced with glee, the call for violence delivered too lightly, Yahweh's backing assumed prematurely. Kaleb enjoyed declaring the Romans evil and worthy of expulsion. But the Roman figurine in Yeshua's pocket had not lost its voice. If Yeshua called for violence, it would be through tears not glee.

Tears would come easily as Yeshua prepared to tell his tale. Until now his story had included his brother. But Theudas was gone. Where, he did not know. Theudas had made clear enough his desire to abstain from all that was to take place in Jerusalem, and an obvious fondness had developed between Theudas and Miriam. Perhaps they had returned to Egypt together. Deeply concerned about Theudas' fate, his brother's return to Egypt was the best for which Yeshua dared hope.

His father would have at least one son return to him. Yes, he prayed Theudas would make it home. But without his younger brother, the Egyptian felt alone. He chose a scripture that referred to him alone. He told his story, as though it were his alone, hoping he was now the only one in danger. He unrolled a scroll containing psalms and began to read.

Have mercy on me, O God, according to your unfailing love; according to your great compassion blot out my transgressions. Wash away all my iniquity and cleanse me from my sin. For I know my transgressions, and my sin is always before me . . .

Cleanse me with hyssop, and I will be clean; wash me, and I will be whiter than snow. Let me hear joy and gladness; let the bones you have crushed rejoice. Hide your face from my sins and blot out all my iniquity. Create in me a pure heart, O God, and renew a steadfast spirit within me . . .

Still holding the unrolled scroll, Bar-Abbas lifted his eyes from it, and looked directly at the congregation as he recited familiar words.

. . . Save me from bloodguilt, O God, the God who saves me, and my tongue will sing of your justice. O Lord, open my lips, and my mouth will declare your praise. You do not delight in sacrifice, or I would bring it . . . My sacrifices to God are a broken spirit; a broken and contrite heart, O God, you will not despise. In your good pleasure make Zion prosper; build up the walls of Jerusalem . . .

He returned the scroll to the attendant who snatched it and ran for cover. If this congregation could approve of Kaleb, how would it respond to the implication that those who rebel against Rome are in need of forgiveness?

The Egyptian knew there was room on this platform only for Bar-Abbas, who was now powerful enough to displace the over-reflective Yeshua and his wavering doubts. Yeshua did not want to withdraw, but knew well enough that if there were any hope of success, it lay in relinquishing all decision and action to Bar-Abbas. He decided, in the best interests of all, to take a step back and watch Bar-Abbas at work. After all, this is a place that brings out the best and the worst of everyone. Bar-Abbas was the name for the best and the worst of Yeshua of Alexandria. He looked with confidence into the mass of silent, execpectant eyes arrayed before him.

"I have come to Jerusalem from Egypt . . . I have come to drink your wine," he smiled, and immediately felt the congregation's approval. "The wine of Israel is strong and sweet, a gift from God. Jerusalem is his vineyard. And the harvest of the grape is at hand." He gestured towards the small table at the front of the platform, adorned with a large bowl containing a bunch of deep red grapes. These grapes represented the significance of the forthcoming festival.

"I have come to Jerusalem from Egypt . . . I have come to celebrate the Feast of Ingathering; to give thanks for the harvest, the harvest of grapes; to remember the birth of our nation; to hear again the story of our father Moses, leading our people through the wilderness." The congregation was nodding in agreement.

"I have come to Jerusalem from Egypt . . . and I'm not the first Jew to make this journey." A growing number of chuckles surfaced above the tension. "I would like to say I followed in the footsteps of our fathers. But I did not flee pharaoh or his oppression, nor was I lost in the wilderness for forty years!" Bar-Abbas caught the eyes of Kaleb and Ehud, whose faces were awash with regret at inviting him to this pulpit.

"But oppression is what I have found, here in the Promised Land. Pharaoh is alive and well and living in the holy city. He oppresses the people from the high walls of his fortress." At last, the atmosphere of unease lightened as the Egyptian launched a welcome tirade against their hated oppressors. "He is taking *our* harvest for *his* people. He takes away the fruit of the land," Bar-Abbas gestured again towards the bowl of grapes, "and leaves the people of land hungry and thirsty. He has invaded this vineyard. He has taken our home. And we all are left out in the wilderness."

"I have come to Jerusalem from Egypt . . . I have come to taste your wine. We are the fruit of God's vine," he said, calling to mind a well-known image of God's suffering people. The bowl of grapes was a fitting picture for the story of Israel.

"We are the grapes you see before you." With that, Bar-Abbas moved to the bunch of grapes and, lifting it high, crushed them inside clenched fists. "See what Pharaoh is doing to our people!" His voice trembled, as deep red juice fell from his hands, down his forearms, into a bowl and onto his clothes.

"Oh yes," he said, his composure restored. "I have tasted the wine of Israel. This wine is not sweet and it is not strong. It is the wine of bitterness and oppression." He lifted the bowl of grape juice. "Brothers. You have drunk this wine for long enough. This festival will bring new wine." The Egyptian's listeners could see he was promising more than the usual practice of preparing grapes from one festival for consumption as new wine at the next.

"I have come to Jerusalem from Egypt . . . And I come to this festival with blood on my hands." He lifted those hands for the congregation to see them still dripping with the red juice of crushed grapes, before quoting the scroll. "'Save me from bloodguilt, O God.'"

As he spoke, a surge of energy lifted his spirit as a Mediterranean wave would lift his body. Bar-Abbas felt a mysterious reassurance buoying him up unexpectedly, affirming his every word. Was this the seal of approval from his Father in Heaven? Was this his baptism as Bar-Abbas? For the first time the name Yeshua had never felt worthy of, the name used more in jest than in seriousness, this name, Bar-Abbas, became his. Those listening witnessed the ecstasy taking hold of him. It surprised the speaker more than anyone, as he seemed to be discovering himself in the act of preaching. He waited for the surge to pass, but the pause was not uncomfortable. It was no longer than one of Kaleb's theatrical pauses. But the feeling did not pass, so Bar-Abbas continued to invite his listeners into his monologue, with little care for how it would be received.

"Too much blood has been spilt. Too much of Abraham's blood. And yes, too much pagan blood. Is this how Yahweh achieves his ends? Is this how the Kingdom of God comes? Through violence? Too much blood has already been spilt." He looked down at his hands. "Save me from my blood guilt, O God."

Members of the synagogue now looked confused. Was he condemning or condoning violent resistance? Bar-Abbas sensed he was doing both. "Vengeance belongs to Yahweh, not to us!"

"I come to Jerusalem in penitence because I have lived in freedom in Egypt while my brothers in Israel have lived in oppression. I come in penitence and faith. I come to repent of the act of faith I must soon commit. I do not know if God will approve . . . I doubt he will." He looked again at his hands. "But I act by faith, and entrust myself to his never-failing mercy. The God who saves us, will save us also from our guilt."

Bar-Abbas was lifted by another wave as the words that came to him applied more truly and fully to himself than any of other. The congregation had become mere spectators in a conversation between Bar-Abbas and his Father in heaven.

"The reign of Pharaoh will soon be at an end. The Kingdom of God is at hand. And this is how we must grasp it." One last time, Bar-Abbas showed his red-stained hands to the congregation. "The only way our people will find justice is to take it by force." He paused, motionless for a second. "Save us from bloodguilt, O God who saves us."

Bar-Abbas returned to his seat with no cheers and no shouts of "Hoshannah." None of the excited reaction that Kaleb's sermon in

Narbata had ignited. Only silence. Thoughtful, reflective, silence, surfacing in the occasional nodding head or pensive glance.

∂❧

Ehud had drawn the service to its close and spoken a blessing. The hushed murmuring that followed ascended quickly into chatter as members of the synagogue rose to their feet. Bar-Abbas prepared himself for the inevitable rush of those wanting to tackle him.

He found himself confronted by a young man, angular and angry with an artificial smile. "So, let me ask you, Rabbi, do you think God is punishing us through the Romans? Do you think *we* are guilty?"

"I think we are all forgiven." Bar-Abbas tried not to smile, but his attempt was futile and his smile powerful. "What else can the end of our exile mean but that God has chosen to remember our sins no more!" Though the young man's critique carried more intensity than Kaleb's might, it was far more easily appeased. He nodded in gratitude and made way for the next challenger.

The young man's place was taken by a rough-looking middle-aged man who disguised himself with no smile. "If you think violence is wrong, why condone it? You can't expect forgiveness if you know that you're wrong before you act. It doesn't make any sense."

Before Bar-Abbas had managed to string some kind of answer together, his inquisitor had turned and left.

Bar-Abbas found himself enjoying the exchanges that came his way. He hadn't dared to imagine coping with what he now delighted in. Voices from the small crowd around him continued to question the Egyptian's message and motive.

"Bar-Abbas. Do you advocate banditry? Don't you condemn the violent resistance of the zealots? They use God's name. They speak of justice. But they kill and they steal."

"The only way to find justice in the land of Israel is to steal it."

"But they beat and rob our own people. The bandits in the hills. They do not represent our God." Bar-Abbas thought back to his experience on the road from Jericho at the hands of Simon the Zealot.

"I do not believe the spilling of blood can ever be justified. How can we pray for the seed of Abraham, if we spill the blood of Abraham." His inquisitor looked relieved.

"Well, I didn't really understand what you were saying," he confessed, "but Israel has no room for those who spill Israelite blood."

"And Roman blood?"

The man shrugged and left. For half an hour, Bar-Abbas was besieged by further questions and found himself surprisingly at home in the debate that ensued. Being Bar-Rabbas—the Son of a Rabbi—had stood him in good stead for being Bar-Abbas—the Son of the Father: Years of reading and listening to the Scriptures, years of hearing and engaging in Scriptural debate had enabled him to be at ease with all that he wanted to say as Bar-Abbas. Still he longed to be the Son of his Father in heaven, as one who would act in faith and seek for mercy.

The busyness of the synagogue had subsided, and the queue waiting to address the preacher had disappeared. Bar-Abbas made his way towards the door where Ehud was offering his farewells to the remaining few. As he walked, a white haired Pharisee drew alongside him.

"You made us think today," the old man smiled as he forced the preacher to slow his pace.

"Telling people what to think is just another way of telling them not to."

The elderly Pharisee smiled in agreement and with a mere flicker of his eyes lamented that too many of his pharisaic colleagues were guilty of just this. "Adonai has commanded us to love him with our minds as well as our hearts." He replied.

Yeshua nodded, but as the old man realized they had almost arrived at Ehud, he grabbed Yeshua's right arm with both his hands, forcing him to stop. "Will a second man's blood really wash the first man's blood from your hands?" With that, his face filled with compassion and he withdrew.

❦ **16** ❧

"**H**OW MANY ARROWS DO you want?" Ehud asked.

"If I need more than two you can shoot a third one at me."

Amram's bow, along with two carefully chosen arrows, was placed inside a sack to be filled with grain for feeding the animals housed near the temple. The cart rattled north along the town, beside the fortress and under the gaze of oblivious soldiers. The cart arrived inconspicuously in the street where the entrance to the storehouse was situated. Amram and Bar-Abbas unloaded the grain from the cart and carried it into to the door.

"Can I help you?" A young laborer greeted them before they could enter.

"Animal feed," said Bar-Abbas, reaching into his purse.

"It's part of our contribution to the festival," said Amram.

"As is this," Bar-Abbas added, handing the boy a coin. The boy's face lit up as he stepped back, staring into the week's wages in his hand.

"Thank you, sir," he said, without looking at either of them.

"Perfect! The rafter to the right of the window, up there," Amram pointed. Bar-Abbas remained at the doorway to be sure no one entered while Amram retrieved the weapons from the sacks and climbed onto the platform below the window.

"You sure you'll be able do this?" asked Bar-Abbas.

"You sure you'll be able to keep that doorway free of traffic?" Amram replied as he reached up to the rafter and placed his weapons out of sight and almost out of reach. He peered through the window and up towards the platform where, in just over a week's time, the prefect would meet his fate. "Perfect!" he said, "Perfect!"

Within a minute the companions had left the storehouse, and the boy approached to repeat his thanks. "A gift from my father," smiled Bar-Abbas. "Enjoy the festival."

"And don't spend it all on wine," Amram added, as the benevolent pilgrims made their way back towards the house of Ehud.

"The window is ideal," said Amram as they walked. "It gives the perfect view of the podium but no outlook over the square."

"Why is that ideal?"

"Because it's useless as a watching post for anyone hoping to monitor the crowd."

Bar-Abbas smiled anxiously. The observation brought home the real danger that awaited him, something he had not yet fully grasped. Of course, he accepted that they might be caught and their lives would end. But the particular details of how that might happen, the particular difficulties of the plan had now become real rather than imagined. He had smelt and felt the place where the job was to be done. A new dimension of fear opened inside him as Amram interrupted his thoughts.

"Having men on top of the buildings will give them the view they need," he said.

"On top?" Bar-Abbas asked as his anxiety grew.

"Along the front wall, overlooking the square."

"Are you serious? They'll have soldiers on top of the building we'll be working from?"

"At every festival," Amram frowned, as though it were obvious.

Had Bar-Abbas realized that guards would be positioned along the roof of the storehouse, he would never have proposed the plan that now was taking shape. No wonder everyone had thought him insane when he first suggested it. Amram sensed his fear.

"You've seen the street. They will only see us if they are looking for us. They are watching the square for a riot. They won't be watching these buildings for an assassin." Bar-Abbas was too overcome with the whole new spectrum of possibilities opening up before him to find any reassurance in Amram's words.

"Three of his soldiers died with arrows in their backs," Bar-Abbas mumbled through closed teeth. "They know we have an archer."

"They don't know we have an archer who can shoot straight at this range." Bar-Abbas had no idea how Amram's proficiency measured alongside that of other archers. He glanced sideways as they walked and the hint of a smirk appeared on his face as he was struck again by the archer's abilities.

"They don't know we have a scheme that's as insane as this," he laughed.

"I have to say, this is the most enjoyable display of Roman might I have ever witnessed," Kochba laughed as he watched the spectacle. Bar-Abbas, Amram and Kaleb were the only other faithful Jews smiling as they observed the scene. A train of over a thousand soldiers sprawled along the road that clung to the Kidron Valley east of the city. They were arriving from the west but had circled the city from the south, both to display their numbers and to enter by the safest path, Solomon's Portico, which would allow them safe passage straight into the Antonine fortress. A standard bearer marked the centre of the parade, closely followed by the prefect himself. As they neared his figure could be clearly made out. He was riding a decorative chariot and was endowed with a gleaming breastplate, purple robes and a tall plumed helmet.

"Do you think he has any idea this will be his last entrance into Jerusalem?" said Bar-Abbas, screwing his eyes up as he faced the bright afternoon sun.

"He wouldn't be grinning like that if he had any notion of what awaits him here," Kaleb grunted.

"Welcome to Jerusalem," Amram whispered, as though only the distant prefect would hear him.

"Well, the stage is set," Bar-Abbas smiled. "One more week and Rome will witness the catastrophe."

The cohort from Caesarea was not the only traffic to arrive that day. The city streets began to swell with pilgrims arriving for the Feast of Ingathering.

"Kaleb," Bar-Abbas asked, "is it just me, or does every festival feel as highly charged as this?"

"Anger and hope. You can't have a festival without them."

"Why do you think the soldiers are always here for the festivals?" Amram smirked at Bar-Abbas. "Do you think they're coming to worship God or honor our traditions? They're frightened of a rebellion."

"And for the first time, with good cause," Kaleb nodded.

"I think they're coming to enjoy our wine," said Kochba with a sarcastic frown. "It's worth the journey from Caesarea." He looked at the Egyptian. "I think they'll enjoy our Jerusalem wine," he winked.

"Well we have plenty to do before we sample last year's vintage this evening," Bar-Abbas announced. He had spent the last few days treading the city's streets and alleys, planning one escape route after another. If they were lucky, they would be out of the city before anyone had worked out what had happened.

As he walked the streets of Jerusalem, now and again Bar-Abbas had been greeted with familiarity, and sometimes sensed that those who greeted him whispered his identity with one another. Any hope of anonymity was gone, but the obvious favor that colored the whispers and glances were not altogether unwelcome. And as more worshippers arrived, so the greetings became more frequent and the anonymity lessened.

The streets would be busy, and the assassins should be able to melt easily into the crowds and make their way quietly from the scene. But Bar-Abbas took no chances. Each member of the group was clear about his allotted task. Kaleb would be occupied with instigating the riot, starting on the northwestern corner of the square that would be packed with listeners. He would be waving palm branches, and had a crowd ready to do the same. The gesture might not mean very much to the soldiers who witnessed it, and would not be worthy of much attention. But for the Jews gathered in the square, the waving of the palm branches would speak of the cry for liberty, and the chants of "Hoshannah" would start up automatically. The Pharisee knew how to stir a mob, and would surround himself with reliable friends happy to oblige his inflammatory calls. Kaleb would not begin the moment that the prefect appeared. He would wait until the initial clamor of response to the prefect's arrival had died down. But the moment the prefect began his speech, the palm branches would come out. It would take a few moments for this act of defiance to spread amongst the crowd, and a few more for it to command serious attention from the soldiers lining the square.

The road on the western side of the storehouse, where its main entrance lay, should be relatively quiet. But Amram had advised its access might just be watched by jittery soldiers on a state of high alert. A quiet approach, close in to the walls that lined the east side of the street, would keep them beyond the gaze of the troops on the roof. But if, by some unhappy accident, there were any Roman guard over the street, then Yeshua and Kochba would have their daggers ready.

The jeers of the multitude gathered on the square would indicate clearly enough the moment of the prefect's arrival on his podium. This was the point at which Bar-Abbas, Kochba the farmer and Amram the archer would attempt to enter the storehouse. If the way was not clear, then Kaleb's secondary clamor might just draw attention away from the back street towards the corner of the square.

The noise of any clash with Roman guards would be submerged in the jeers of the multitude. Such was their hope. Once inside the storehouse, Kochba and Bar-Abbas would take their positions on either side of the door, ready to silence any who entered. Amram would string his bow and take his aim. He would loose his second arrow while the first was still in flight.

Bar-Abbas turned his back on the columns of marching soldiers and faced in the direction of the square that would be host to next week's action. "If there are soldiers at the front end of the storehouse, even if they don't see where the arrow comes from, they'll hear you loose them."

"If they're very lucky," Amram replied.

"So let's assume that they are very lucky."

"There may be two or three along the buildings on this street. We'd have to be pretty unlucky for one of them to be near enough to notice anything," Kochba butted in.

"So let's assume that we are pretty unlucky!" Bar-Abbas spoke with a calm that was pregnant with the scheme he had hatched.

"Alright," Amram rolled his eyes, "what do you have in mind?"

"There are two streets that run roughly parallel with the storehouse street, right behind it". Bar-Abbas looked to Kaleb for confirmation, and the Pharisee nodded curiously.

"We find a way of accessing a building on the opposite side of the street that has a door we can bolt behind us and access to the next street."

"In case they try to follow us," Kochba whispered approvingly.

"And once we are in the next street," Bar-Abbas continued, "we do the same again."

"I like it," said Amram. "It would be impossible to follow us."

"We'd be back into a busy street before anyone has any idea where we are," Kochba noted.

Bar-Abbas added his final precaution. "We'd leave our cloaks in the second house, and put them on as we leave."

"Can you arrange that, Kaleb?" Kochba asked.

"Should be able to manage it," the Pharisee frowned. "Probably better if we leave it a little nearer the time though." Bar-Abbas was unable to disguise his haste at having the entire plan in place as soon as possible, so Kaleb elaborated. "We won't want to do it too soon. I'll find out about the houses this evening, so that we know exactly what your route will be. But we'll make the arrangements the day before." Bar-Abbas still did not look entirely convinced. "It won't be a problem," Kaleb assured him.

"Okay. Well, all I'd like us to do now is to secure lodgings in two more places across the town." Again, he was greeted with puzzled frowns and compelled to explain. "Different escape routes, should we need them. Different places to hide in case we are chased or discovered."

"Don't be so nervous about this, Bar-Abbas," said Kaleb, and the expressions of Kochba and Amram suggested their agreement.

"But it will cost us little and might make the difference between getting out alive and not."

"Okay," said Kochba. Amram seemed indifferent to the idea of getting out alive, as did Kaleb as he offered to make the arrangements.

"If we are going to do this, we'd better do it now because the city's filling up with pilgrims."

"So let's do that now, and then we can rehearse the route to each of those houses." Bar-Abbas' final remark evoked little surprise now that the companions were accustomed to his meticulous, obsessive planning.

As the festival began the streets of Jerusalem throbbed with worshippers, soldiers and grapes. Ehud's house was awash with friends, Kaleb among them, who would keep one another's company only at the three annual festivals. As companions broke bread and shared wine, the same conversation—tedious to Amram, Kochba and Bar-Abbas—was rehearsed spontaneously but predictably every evening: The story of Israel and her oppression; someone always with a story of an injustice suffered since their last meeting; others with talk of a would-be Messiah who would defeat the Romans and bring freedom and peace; laments over the widespread ignorance of God's Holy Law; complaints that the rest of the world don't agree with us. Someone would begin singing a hymn, and the rest of the group would join them. The trusted company would now be party to current stories of Yeshua Bar-Abbas, his exploits in Narbata, his escape to the caves of Arbela, his anger in Bethshe'an and at last, his plans for Jerusalem. By the time the conversation had turned to him, he had always withdrawn.

"How long have these people been repeating this turgid drivel?" Bar-Abbas asked.

"It's an age-old tradition," said Amram.

"It goes back centuries," Kochba laughed.

"I suppose it's centuries now since there was a resistance movement that actually resisted," Bar-Abbas smiled. "Judas Maccabeus fighting off the Greeks."

"Kaleb and Ehud see themselves as his heirs," Kochba scoffed. "The Pharisees are holier than your average mortal. Totally committed. They are the living, walking enactment of God's Holy Law."

"Sadly they are also a 'talking' enactment of God's law," Amram grimaced as he sipped the fruit of last year's vine, momentarily halting the nearby pious conversation with a carefully placed impious belch.

On the evening before the prefect's speech only the chosen few were invited to share supper at the home of Ehud. Bar-Abbas, Amram, Kochba and Kaleb reclined at the table of a warm and well-lit room.

Kaleb led a prayer of thanksgiving for their food and drink, and sought God's blessing upon all that the following day would bring. When it eventually came to an end, Bar-Abbas addressed the group.

"Can we spend some time in quiet, remembering those who have fallen because in one way or another, they were caught up in this quest." It sounded like a question but the tone of voice suggested otherwise.

"That's quite a list!" said Amram.

"So let me name them," said Kaleb reverently. He cast his mind back a month, and beginning with the brothers of Bar-Abbas, he named each of those who had been lost, leaving a gap of a few seconds between them. "Yotham . . . Saul . . . Yudah . . . Eliazar . . . we think also of our brother Theudas, and of Miriam, in the hope that God will keep them safe . . ."

The figurine carried by Bar-Abbas exploited the quiet atmosphere and reasserted itself until its shadow eclipsed even the image of his brothers. His imagining was broken by a surprise comment that concluded Kochba's reflections.

". . . we think also of ten Roman soldiers, in the hope that only one more Roman need die tomorrow." Murmurs of respect had fallen with each of the names mentioned but the Pharisee had not finished. "Now, let us drink, and give ourselves to Yahweh, as we each add our name that list."

Amram poured wine from a jug as he issued his warning to the group: "Don't any of you dare ask me one more time whether I am ready for tomorrow."

"Everything and everyone is ready," said Bar-Abbas as the fruit of the vine met his lips. "There is nothing more we can do. We take our step of faith, we entrust ourselves to the mercy of Yahweh."

"Well said," Kaleb nodded. "Six centuries ago our fathers were taken to exile in Babylon. The temples of that pagan land dwarfed Solomon's temple that stood in Jerusalem, just as the pagan fortress dwarfs the temple that stands here now. Our fathers had lost hope, just as our brothers have today. But the word of God came to our fathers as it comes to us now. It spoke of one who dwarfs both temple and fortress. 'In the beginning Elohim created the heavens and the earth.' Everything is in God's hands. And we give our lives into his hands. Our exile is at an end."

✥〈17〉✥

BAR-ABBAS WAS FAR MORE at peace than Yeshua. On his final night in Jerusalem, in the house of the Pharisee, he made an easy descent into sleep. His dream recurred, and somewhere in his subconscious the snake was expected. But the good company and warmth that preceded the snake's arrival was once again impervious to the venom of the serpent. In fact, the serpent was no longer an unwelcome intruder but an invited guest. It no longer had the power to paralyze Bar-Abbas, nor eject him from his dream. It merely sat quietly in the corner. But Jerusalem was the city to bring out the best and the worst of every creature, and on the final night of his visit, the snake became the figurine that lived in the Roman purse from Caesarea. No longer a figurine itself, but the small boy it represented. The boy sat quietly in the corner, listening to the laughter and warmth and said nothing of how this had deprived him of his laughter and his warmth. He didn't have to say it. The recognition alone sank its venomous bite into the Egyptian's spirit with enough force to shake him into consciousness long before sunrise.

"Father, bless all that I must do this day," he muttered as he stumbled to his feet, knowing the futility of any attempt to return to sleep. "Forgive me for what I must do this day. Bring this night to an end."

Eliazar's words returned with the rising sun to Bar-Abbas: the course of the sun and moon and stars would surely be halted by this day. By the time the sun sets tonight, he thought, the heavens will have witnessed the justice for which the shepherd had craved. By God's grace a new era was at hand.

The Egyptian rose from his bed and wandered the streets of the city one last time. The whole being of Yeshua Bar-Abbas reflected the clean air of the young day, unspoiled and full of promise. His tunic clung to him affectionately and his steps were as light as the warm air that rose visibly from the apertures in every flat-roofed dwelling. His cheeks furnished with the charm of a brand new sun, and his eyes boasting of a sufficient amount of sleep and an excessive sense of peace, Bar-Abbas left the narrow streets and entered the open square where the sky was not so hard to find.

The sight of two soldiers looking down upon him from the heights of the Antonine Fortress brought a surge of confidence to the Egyptian. They said nothing, just looked upon him. Bar-Abbas nodded his head towards them with a smile, which they ignored and returned to their conversation. They wouldn't ignore me if they knew all that I am about to set in motion, he thought. Whatever happens today, by nightfall those soldiers will know about me. Their ignorance of his importance quickened his spirit. He prayed as the stone pavement of the wider streets clicked beneath the heal of his studded shoe. His prayer was the hurried repetition of a single request, "Bring justice to this city." Each repetition established more fully the Egyptian's conviction that he was the only means by which that prayer could be answered.

The welcoming smell of broiled fish floated from the house of Ehud as Bar-Abbas returned to it. The companions ate well, and remained in good humor, but little was said. The occasional noises of carts and pilgrims in the street were gradually drowned beneath the growing buzz of activity from beyond Ehud's gate.

Kaleb would be the first to walk out through that gate. He chanted his favorite slogan as he bestowed upon each of his companions the kiss of peace. "No King but God . . . Shalom." With that, the fellowship who had shared one another's destiny for almost six weeks separated to fulfill its purpose. The Pharisee gathered a bundle of palm branches, and a frown. Bar-Abbas thought that Kaleb really ought to have borne a more obvious struggle against the gravity of this day's actions. But then, how was he supposed to look? He appeared as calm as if he were collecting breakfast from the market place. Kaleb of Narbata smiled through his frown, nodded and left.

Amram, Kochba and Bar-Abbas drank only water this morning. Each of them was armed with a dagger. Their cloaks had been deposited in the house secured by Kaleb for their escape. Ten minutes saw little in the way of conversation, despite Ehud's attempts to lighten the atmosphere. The air was heavy with anxious intent and rugged determination. There was no lifting it.

"Shall we go to the temple to make our morning sacrifice?" asked Bar-Abbas eventually.

"I do believe we shall," said Kochba, rising to his feet.

"Shouldn't we pray before we leave?" asked Ehud.

"What do you think we've been trying to do for the last ten minutes?" Kochba growled.

"I don't know," said Amram. "What if we were just a couple of prayerful sentences short of success?" he laughed, and then he belched.

"We'll pray in silence as we walk," said Bar-Abbas with a hand on the shoulder of the Pharisee. That hand was icy cold, but there were no shaking limbs, no shallow breath, no amplified pulse pumping Abrahamic blood through Egyptian veins. Once again the entire created order was his ally, and he knew it.

The walk north across the busy city did not feel unusual. By now Bar-Abbas expected to attract greetings and glances and whispers. Kaleb's propaganda machine had worked well and had made Bar-Abbas into a familiar name if not a face. The assassins walked at a calm pace, as though they were finding their way to the market. They would have some time to wait in the square before moving to the back street with which they were all intimately familiar.

As they approached the market, every person on the road hurried in one direction or another. But even thirty paces away, on a busy street, it became obvious to all that one man stood motionless. He seemed to be awaiting their arrival. Theudas? The image of the snake flashed into the mind of Bar-Abbas and sent a shock wave through his body.

"It's Theudas!" Kochba exclaimed in disbelief. "And he's shaved his face!"

"Where the hell did he come from?" Amram muttered.

"Something's wrong!" Bar-Abbas whispered.

Miriam's brown eyes were fixed on the long column that carried an eagle banner around the Southern reaches of the city. Three men wide, over three hundred long, the last of the soldiers was not yet visible before the first had passed from view. The prefect was arriving in Jerusalem, one full week before he would appear on his podium to address the masses.

"The best or the worst?" Theudas puzzled.

"The best *and* the worst" Miriam replied. "This place will tell you who you really are." She turned her back on the approaching cohort and faced the city. "Even for them."

"I'm not with you at all."

"This mountain has always been the same. It brought out the best in Abraham. He was ready to sacrifice Yitsac, his one and only son! None of us would be here if he'd gone ahead with it. Was that the best of Abraham? Was it the worst? Ready to sacrifice all he had? Or ready to murder his own son because he could hear God speaking so clearly? God had to send an angel to save us all from the best and the worst of Abraham. It's what's always happened in this place."

"What about Yeshua?" Theudas asked. "Will God send an angel to save us from the best and worst of Bar-Abbas?"

"Maybe God sent your brother to save us from the best and the worst of Pontius Pilatus."

"Speaking of which, they're on the move," said Theudas, pointing towards three figures in the distance. "Probably on their way back to that Pharisee's house. What did you say his name was?"

"Ehud!" Miriam grunted. "He's even more of a Pharisee than Kaleb."

The well-dressed couple made their way slowly towards the house of Ehud, distant enough to remain unnoticed by Yeshua, Amram and Kochba.

"Do you honestly think we're going to see anything from this distance?" Theudas asked.

"Not yet," Miriam replied, "but the city's going to be busier by evening. We'll be able to get much closer."

As the days progressed, the crowds thickened and Yeshua's secret bodyguards kept a watchful eye on all around him. The greatest concern were the number of those who entered Ehud's house. Each night the same group would arrive and stay for several hours of drinking, shouting and singing. They became familiar faces, and the task of watching them overtook that of watching for potential murderers.

There were five in all, and the movements of each had been quietly followed by the bodyguards for the entire week of the festival. By the eve of the planned attack, Yeshua's cynicism about the necessity of people watching his back seemed justified. There had been no attempted murder. No movements that raised the slightest hint of suspicion. Apart from Kaleb's disappearances into the swarming streets, which were always going to be important. Theudas and Miriam had guessed that he was securing properties for an escape route. Yeshua's idea no doubt.

"Shouldn't we just go and join them for their last evening? It's an important time for all of us. They don't even know we're here," said Theudas in frustration. "Think how thrilled they'd be to discover we've been watching their backs all along. If anything was going to happen, it would have happened by now. If the Romans are onto them, they would never have got this far."

"Has none of your brother's suspicion rubbed off on you?" Miriam frowned. "Because you could do with a bit of it. Our job is more important now than ever."

"If the Romans suspected anything they would have stopped it by now. What's to stop them marching in and arresting everyone?"

"They're Romans. This is Roman justice. They could be waiting for evidence."

Theudas did not look convinced. "Er—they didn't wait for any evidence before they killed my brothers," he said. But he agreed that caution would do little harm, even if it meant postponing celebration with his brother for one more day. That day was to arrive soon enough.

For Theudas and Miriam, it began by almost having their cover exposed. As they stood on the corner of the street on which Ehud's house was situated, Yeshua walked straight past them.

"Where on earth has he been this early in the morning?" asked Miriam, once he was safely out of distance.

"Probably wet the bed worrying about later on!" Theudas laughed.

The bodyguards walked nearer to the house, and found a place to share bread inconspicuously. This became easier as the streets became busier. Another full hour had passed before Kaleb emerged, carrying one of his beloved parchments.

"We should follow him," Miriam grinned mischievously.

"Both of us?"

"I'll stay here," she said. "You find out where he's off to." With that he stood up, and looked her in the eye.

"You keep praying," she said as she pointed to him. "If I'm not here when you get back, it's because your brother's left."

Theudas nodded.

"And if anything happens, I'll stay at the lodgings," she added as he began to disappear. He turned, ran back to her, kissed her forehead and disappeared into the crowd.

Theudas kept a safe distance behind Kaleb's hurried pace, but wasn't entirely sure why he was following. Kaleb was clearly going off ahead of the others because to build momentum for the riot. Eventually he found himself in the square underneath the garrison, where the Pharisee was greeted by a young man that Theudas recognized too well. Sol, Kochba's elder son. What was he doing here? Why was he meeting secretly with Kaleb? Theudas' surprise was displaced by confusion, his confusion by anxiety, and his anxiety by dread. Kaleb and Sol exchanged agitated and hurried conversation for about two minutes, before parting company and rushing away in opposite directions, the parchment now in Sol's possession.

Without knowing why, Theudas chose not to follow Kaleb. He followed his conversation partner, whose pace was hurrying, breaking here and there into a run before returning to a less conspicuous walk. Occasionally Sol would glance behind him, forcing Theudas to leave a greater distance. Kochba's son seemed to know he was being followed. The Egyptian's ears began pounding with fear, and as his own pace increased in tandem with his target's, the covert tracking was gradually displaced by open pursuit. The fear on Sol's glance over his shoulder confirmed to Theudas that he must not lose this chase, which had now hit full speed. Onlookers did not have time to verbalize their astonishment before the pursuit had passed, as the race weaved its way through silent spectators. The distance between the two was a mere ten paces, three or four quickened heartbeats, no time for prey to slip predator. And that distance was rapidly closing.

A further glance behind him was enough to tell Sol that his pursuer would soon be upon him. The parchment was thrown up into the air in a deliberate gesture, as though its importance were obvious to all. Theudas ignored the gesture, but only for a moment. The chase ended. Within a couple of seconds the sound of his target's footsteps merged into others. Theudas turned to gather his breath and stooped to retrieve the parchment from the dusty street. The Egyptian's heart sank. Unaware of the looks he drew from those who had witnessed the chase, he propped his back against a wall to read the scroll. It began like just another of the Pharisee's prayers, but the words on this scroll began to stab at Theudas, each one of them wounding him further as their purpose became clearer. As he read, panic seized his limbs and forced the parchment to shake in his hand. "Yeshua," he muttered.

Theudas forgot himself, and was barely aware of the speed at which, again, he was able to move through busy streets. Would he make it back to Ehud's house before his brother and the others had left? Five minutes brought him back to the place where he and Miriam had shared their breakfast. But Miriam was gone. Theudas could only assume she was following the others. He was too late.

His pace became more frantic as he pushed back towards the square by a different route. Each time Theudas saw a soldier in the crowds he would slow his pace so as not to stand out. But his frenzy was growing. How could he find his brother?

He arrived at the corner of the street on the final approach to the square, and his eyes fell straight onto Amram. He stepped into the middle of the street, directly into the path of his brother and his friends. He released an extended sigh of relief, and stood motionless in the crowd as though he were standing in a river facing upstream in a strong current. His companions laid eyes on him, but he knew how much danger they were all in. His alarm was obvious enough to Yeshua at least, and he could see that Yeshua, still twenty paces away, had taken note. Theudas walked slowly towards Yeshua, Amram and Kochba, but did not look at them. The urgency of his eyes was directed towards the ground as he repeated the phrase, "It's a trap, it's a trap, it's a trap." He bumped into Amram, as though by accident. "Use your escape route now," Theudas whispered loudly, "they're onto us," and kept walking, his back turned upon his companions. Was he the angel staying the hand of Abraham? He was certainly preventing an act of sacrifice.

A few paces later and his eyes fell straight into Miriam's, who had been walking behind the companions and could read him well enough to render whispered warnings unnecessary. She kept walking, as did he. When he had reached the top of the street he dared to stop and look behind him. He could see no one he recognized. Theudas took this as a good sign. He turned again to walk forward. That was the last thing he remembered before his head fizzed into a concussion. He lost consciousness before his body had hit the ground.

"A trap?" said Kochba

"No need to discuss it now," whispered Bar-Abbas calmly. "Let's just use our escape routes. We should split up and go." The crossroads near the square arrived quickly, leaving the companions to take three separate routes. Bar-Abbas walked against the crowd and away from the square. Several men seemed to give him curious stares, and he began to see every pilgrim as a disguised soldier like the ones who had carried concealed canes under their tunics to beat the prefect's enemies to death. He managed to weave his way through the crowd, with his eyes fixed on potential escape routes which he had spent the last week studying. But still there was no need to run. Until the horn sounded. Echoing down the street from less than fifty paces behind came three blasts. Like everyone else, he looked in the direction of the horn, only to see three men in civilian clothes but obviously soldiers, closing in on him. As he looked forwards, more undercover soldiers emerged from the sides of the street, but had not yet registered who they were to arrest.

Bar-Abbas made straight for the side of the street within six feet of a soldier who was still ignorant of the Egyptian's identity. He leapt upon a five-foot high wall and onto the roof of a house that gave him easy and quick access into the next street. If nothing else, it meant that those in pursuit were now all behind him rather than lining the street ahead of him. Bar-Abbas knew exactly where he was going. He knew how to get there at speed. This second street was much quieter. It allowed the Egyptian to break into a good sprint. Only one of the soldiers chasing him was any serious danger, the rest had already and thankfully lagged some distance behind. Bar-Abbas used the smallest streets to avoid running into any more soldiers, uniformed or concealed. But he could still hear the breath of the soldier chasing him down. Again he glanced behind. His satisfaction at having evaded all but one was tempered by the fact that this one was managing to stay with him.

The gap between the assassin and the soldier was less than five seconds, and the Egyptian could sense it shrinking. But Bar-Abbas was as good as on home territory. He made for the labyrinth of slum dwellings that had been their home on his arrival at the city. He leapt onto another high wall knowing that he could make it quickly over another wall into the adjacent street, and then double back through a small alley way and return to his current position. He had completed the move and made it back to the street from which he had leapt before having time to think about it. He threw another glance over his shoulder. Still the soldier was with him, but thankfully much further behind. At least he had gained some space. How was he going to shake this pursuer? He felt unable to run for much longer.

As he slowed to take a tight corner to the right, he threw his back against the near sidewall and drew his dagger. As the soldier appeared he did not see his target immediately and slowed to scan the street before him. By the time he was aware of the Egyptian's position, eight inches of dark, sharpened iron had been sunk deep into his neck. Bar-Abbas did not stop, even to watch his victim fall. He ran straight for the safe house that had been so carefully arranged the week before. He entered into the building near to the lodgings where the companions had rested on their first night in Jerusalem. He had opened, closed and bolted the door before turning to see who was already in his room.

Armored soldiers carrying spears emerged from the shadowy corners of the chamber. Another armed with only a sword, but obviously with some authority sat on a bench at the back of the room, sharpening his drawn sword. "And you would be . . . ?" Bar-Abbas turned towards the door. "It's no use. You missed the guards who so kindly let you in, but will not be so ready to let you out. So let me ask you again, what is your name?"

"How could you possibly know I was staying here?"

"Your name."

"My name is Yeshua Bar-Abbas."

✥18✥

THEUDAS AWOKE IN A dark, cold cell. He sat up and looked around, his vision still blurred. The cell was about twelve feet square, lit by a single torch hanging on the wall next to the door. There were no windows, and no sounds. The cold of the stone floor seemed already to have penetrated his bones. A noise came from the corner of the room, where a Roman soldier, having seen that the prisoner was waking, had risen to his feet. He said nothing, but the disdainful look he threw at Theudas was unmistakably Latin.

"Felix," he called. "He is awake." The door opened and the soldier took the torch and left. Theudas was left in confusion, alone with his thoughts, trying to retrace his steps. This is how it had ended. He didn't know whether his brother or companions or even Miriam had been caught. All he could be sure of was the fate that inevitably awaited him. Kaleb had betrayed all of them, he thought. The words on that parchment that read so much like a prayer forced Theudas into thinking back through all of Kaleb's written prayers. For how long had he planned to hand them over? Footsteps echoed down the corridor, as more than one person approached, and someone was carrying a torch which brought light back to the room. The door opened and the soldier entered alone.

"Up!" grunted the soldier in Greek.

Theudas rose slowly to his feet. He was still dizzy and not quite able to stand firmly. The torch was thrust within a few inches of his face, so that all the Egyptian could see was a flame.

"Is this one of them?" asked a voice in the corridor, again in Greek. Theudas heard no answer. "Are you sure?" the same voice asked. "Good." The door was opened again and the soldier left, along with the torch.

The room was left dark, but the image of the torch had been burned into the eyes of Theudas. He sank again to his feet, sweating, shivering and wondering how long it would be before he vomited. Less than two minutes and the footsteps echoed again, this time only one man. The soldier entered the cell and placed his torch on the wall. "Blankets" he said, and dropped a bundle next to Theudas. "Rest."

"Thank you" he replied automatically. He lay one blanket beneath him, covered himself with the other and lay down. I must be in the garrison, he thought. But why are they treating me with this kindness. Was that Kaleb in the corridor, answering the pagan captors silently? But Theudas was unable to think, and fell again from consciousness.

❧

"Is that him?" Unbeknown to him, Bar-Abbas heard the same voice and the same question his brother had heard. Again there was no reply, just one set of footsteps echoing down a corridor, as the door to the Egyptian's cell opened. Three men entered, two guards who remained silent, and a centurion, unarmed but the most menacing of the three. His voice was deep, his words precise and his demeanor indifferent as he took his seat, making the rickety wooden chair behind the table look far more comfortable than it could have been.

"We have all of you now, Yeshua Bar-Abbas," said the Centurion with affected fatigue, "Even your little brother." He gestured for Bar-Abbas to sit upon the chair his guard was placing at the desk. The Egyptian complied.

"Theudas had nothing to do with any of this," Bar-Abbas protested, hoping that his brother would recall the conversation in Narabata's market place. He had thought that they might be caught that morning, and that if he claimed the lives of both soldiers maybe they would let Theudas off the hook. But much time had passed, so Bar-Abbas could only hope his brother would remember.

"Any of this?" asked the soldier who appeared agreeable if perplexed by the figure before him. "Well perhaps you can tell us about . . ." he voiced slowed for a gesture, "'this." With his clean-shaven, rosy countenance, the Centurion had an air of childlike simplicity. But though his appearance was gentle, the child resembled was the kind who would refuse to tolerate anything but the simplicity he demanded.

Bar-Abbas considered denying his intentions. There was no proof against him. He had done nothing. But if nothing else, the Romans knew his and his brother's name. And they couldn't know who he was or what he was doing without knowing about the deaths he had already caused. Regardless of what his plans for the prefect might have been, Bar-Abbas decided he was a condemned man. He may as well boast of, rather than deny his intentions. It would change neither his own nor anyone else's fate. But he would not tell them everything about Caesarea. If he could claim both of those kills as his own, which they very nearly were, then Theudas might be released.

"Where would you like me to start?" asked Bar-Abbas, surprisingly buoyant.

"I'd like you to start in Caesarea."

Bar-Abbas shook his head, in confusion rather than refusal. "How do you know about all this?" he asked. "Who told you? Who was that with you in the corridor?"

The centurion threw one leg over another, folded his arms squarely and repeated himself. "I'd like you to start in Caesarea."

Bar-Abbas sighed. "What began in Caesarea began here first of all. It began with your prefect."

"Go on."

"At the festival of Pentecost." Bar-Abbas spoke in subdued tones. "I'm sure you know what happened." The centurion nodded. "Innocent members of that crowd were battered to death by the prefect."

"He was trying to prevent an uprising. And let me assure you, Egyptian, that an uprising would have led to many more deaths."

Bar-Abbas ignored the Centurion's attempt to justify the massacre. "Two of those innocent worshippers were my brothers. Pilatus killed them."

"So, you were out for revenge?"

"Yes."

"You lost two brothers," said the Centurion as he closed his eyes and nodded in artificial sympathy. "And tell me, how many Roman lives have you now taken? I make it three."

"Four."

The inquisitor watched his opponent steadily and remained quiet. Bar-Abbas did likewise, refusing to break silence or eye contact. Echoes of Amram's instruction sounded in the Egyptian's mind. "*The tip of your*

blade should touch the line between your eyes and your enemy's." The centurion turned towards his soldiers as he continued. "And you thought
you could kill the prefect himself?" The soldiers laughed. "For revenge?
And when we add to your own death toll the work of your accomplices,
it comes to twelve! For your two brothers! Were their lives worth that
much more than my soldiers' lives?"

"There were more than two deaths at Passover. And we all know
you've had more than your fair share of revenge for any losses your cohort has incurred."

"We are not interested in revenge, we are interested only in justice."
Now it was the Egyptian's turn to laugh.

"Roman justice? I took two lives for two lives. That was justice. And
you avenge it by killing random innocent people. I killed only soldiers. I
know about justice. We are driven by justice," said Bar-Abbas, unable to
suppress his anger.

"Well be thankful, Bar-Abbas, that justice has now come to you."

"But not to my people."

"Rome has made more concessions for your people than for any
other people. Your people should be grateful for the justice and the
mercy of Rome. Caesar has been good to the Jews. Had your own little
dream come true, your people would have tasted only wrath . . ."

"I thought you said that you weren't interested in vengeance," Bar-
Abbas interrupted.

"Be grateful, Egyptian. Caesar's wrath would be just . . ."

"Because it is Caesar who deals it out?"

"And your quest for justice, Bar-Abbas. Dealing in death as you do.
Do you call it justice simply because you do it in the name of your God?
You have hidden your bloodlust behind the name of Yahweh. We have
saved you from profaning the name of your own God. We have saved
your people from wrath. We have saved this city from destruction. Be
grateful, Egyptian, and tell me of Caesarea."

Bar-Abbas paused and shook his head. "I killed two soldiers outside the city."

"Two soldiers for two brothers?"

Bar-Abbas nodded. "I brought my brother Theudas with me, but he
wanted no part in the bloodshed."

"Too scared?"

Bar-Abbas feigned anger. "His refusal to shed blood is courage not cowardice. Theudas is no coward. He came with me and tried to talk me out of this at every stage."

"But you wouldn't listen to your own brother."

"I might have, early on. But the death toll continued to climb."

"And . . . ?"

"We arrived in Narbata, just ahead of the cavalry. They executed an innocent trader in cold blood, and were about to kill a second, had a Pharisee not stepped in."

"Kaleb? The collaborator? He's been most helpful. In fact, we are all here today only because of him!"

Again Bar-Abbas displayed his confusion, forcing the Centurion to continue. "It was Kaleb that came to us. Or at least it was his father." His voice slowed. "His long lost father. That Pharisee would do anything to be reunited with his father." The Egyptian's eyes moved sideways. Was the Centurion playing tricks, probing for more information? Or had Kaleb really betrayed them. The Romans had, after all, stopped this plot before it had begun. Someone must have told them."

"Kaleb hated his father. He wanted nothing to do with him. His father . . ." He slowed down. "His father was . . ." The words of Bar-Abbas petered out into silence as the Egyptian withdrew to his thoughts.

"It was the Galilean Prophet that changed his mind. Yeshua of Nazareth. That's what he told us. Rebelling against Rome wouldn't bring happiness to anyone. But being reunited with your father . . . The Pharisee was desperate for that. Yeshua of Nazareth led him to that."

"Doesn't make any sense!" Bar-Abbas frowned and continued to shake his head. His anger shook his voice as he repeated himself. "That doesn't make any sense."

"How do you think we found you? His father's a Sadducee. If there's anyone with nothing to gain from rebelling against Rome, it's a Sadducee. And to provide us with a foiled assassination plot . . . Well. Kaleb's father has done himself no harm."

Silence. "Why are you telling me all this?"

"Part of your punishment."

"Well, I don't believe you."

"You will. When you've had long enough with your thoughts, you will." The centurion reached into a case and produced the parchments penned by the Pharisee. "Oh, and these might help," he frowned, handing the letters to Bar-Abbas.

The Egyptian read back through letters that had been written as early as their time in the caves. Letters by Kaleb's hand, reading like prayers but tracing his intent from the moment he was turned by Yeshua of Nazareth. The centurion failed to conceal his glee as Bar-Abbas was conquered by dismay. Leaning forward, he continued. "Letters addressed not to his Father in heaven, but to his father in Jerusalem . . ." Bar-Abbas seemed not to hear. "You might find this one interesting," he grinned as he passed a damaged parchment across the table. "Your brother was carrying it."

> *Father,*
>
> *The day of justice is upon us. The purchase of peace by the sacrifice of my company.*
>
> *Everything is set for this morning. They will leave the house of Ehud, and begin their quest for justice. They will pass by the fortress, and enter the storehouses as we discussed. Their weapons have been prepared in the place I described. I have shown you their safe houses, and their plans for escape.*
>
> *I will try to prevent the riot, and I will trust in the pardon that you have bought for me. These were my friends. I ask once more, that you do your utmost to secure mercy for each of them.*

A snake's bite sent its venom throbbing violently through his bloodstream. Had Kaleb really done this? Sacrificed all he had once held dear, to be reconciled to the father who had forsaken him? He began to sweat and shake. Being caught was one thing. But being betrayed like this. The thought was impossible to entertain, but the betrayal filled his body with terror, and left him sinking already into Sheol's empty darkness.

At length, Bar-Abbas looked down at the veins on the backs of his hands, just as he had done whilst lying in the scrubland outside Caesarea. He turned his hands over, staring at them in disbelief, running fingers over the calluses made out of swordplay, knowing they were soon to be pierced with nails."

"The hands of God?" the Centurion smiled.

"Yudah? Where is he?" Bar-Abbas replied without any apparent interest.

"Awaiting release."

"He's not dead?" he asked, as his spirit returned.

"We're not as barbaric as you think. He's no rebel. His only crime was dreaming of rebellion. But we couldn't release him until this episode was complete."

"That's how you knew of Eliazar's house?"

"You did well to evade us when we came for Eliazar," the Roman conceded, with a hint of admiration. "Although I understand that your god or your archer brought justice to the shepherd in the end."

Bar-Abbas lifted his hands to support his head as it dropped. "Is this too much to take in?" No answer. He turned to one of the soldiers. "Bring the prisoner some wine to loosen his tongue."

The soldier returned before any word had fallen from the lips of Bar-Abbas. "Thank you," he said.

"So you decided you'd like to kill Pontius Pilatus, our prefect. I was delighted to hear that news."

"Why?"

"Because by then we knew you would come to us. And more importantly, it helps us politically. It's sometimes difficult for Jewish people to understand why some of our more forceful expressions of justice are necessary. But when we catch rebels with murderous intent and proof, what choice does the prefect have but to continue coming down hard?" The centurion raised his hands like a child feigning innocence whilst denying some misdeed. "What's more," he added as the expression left him, "catching you lot in the act shows the people of this land that we see everything. It tells them that plots like these are a real threat for us. *And* it tells them that plots like these are futile. Or at least, it will if we crucify you."

"If?" asked Bar-Abbas, thinking his fate was inevitable.

"If you survive the afternoon. You have a visitor who's been looking forward to meeting you. If you're still alive tomorrow, then we might even take you to meet Pilatus."

Theudas heard more footsteps. The door opened, and a centurion entered, flanked by two soldiers in black amour.

"So you are Theudas?" the Centurion asked, as the prisoner rose to his feet.

"Yes."

"And what were you doing this morning, muttering to your companions."

"I . . ." Theudas stopped, unaccustomed as he was to interrogation.

"What were you doing, Theudas of Alexandria?" came the question a second time.

"I . . . I was trying to stop them."

"Stop who from what?"

"My brother, his friends, they were going to try and start a riot. I was going to stop them."

"Is that all they were going to do?"

"I don't know, I hadn't seen them for nearly two weeks."

"Why not?"

"Because I couldn't get them to listen to me."

"How many soldiers have you killed, Theudas?" the Centurion asked.

"None," he answered instinctively, as though Yeshua's panicked demand in Narbata's market place had been voiced only that morning. "I've killed none, and I've tried to stop them from killing."

"And who were your companions?"

Theudas listed the names and told the story of everything that had happened since Caesarea. He had told them that Yeshua had killed both soldiers at Narbata, and he over-emphasized his protests about killing any others. He denied receiving any of the money from Bethshe-an. Nobody would know how much there was anyway, and the Centurion didn't seem too interested. In fact the questions that the Centurion asked were straightforward, and after only half an hour the interrogation was over, and the soldiers had departed.

"You will receive your sentence within the hour."

Theudas sat, shaking and alone, not knowing whether his companions had been caught. Might they even have been successful in killing the prefect? Probably not. Could their escape route have worked? Prayers to Yahweh were mingled with the agonized thoughts of Kaleb's deed. And what had Theudas done? Had he confessed prematurely? Might his desire to speak so soon and so openly have harmed his brother's fate? Guilt began to displace all other feeling until his entire spirit was numb. Within only ten minutes' time, the Centurion had returned.

"Theudas, having considered your case the Legate has recommended ten lashes."

Theudas was expecting only crucifixion. Ten lashes was a fearful punishment. But it meant he would be walking free soon after.

"However," the Centurion continued, "you are in no fit state to receive them today. In the morning you will be flogged and released." With that, the prison door slammed shut.

ॐ

Bar-Abbas was led into a room with a table and chair at the center. He was taken to a wall beyond them and his arms chained above his head. "Your visitor will be along shortly," the soldier grinned.

The prisoner did not even try to guess who might be coming, but his body was seized with fear when the footsteps shaking the stone hallway approached. They came to a halt outside the door, and Bar-Abbas heard a lowered voice.

"I'll be right here. Just you remember to give him what he deserves."

With that the door opened slowly, and a young Jewish woman carrying a large wooden club entered. She closed the door quietly behind her, and walked softly towards Bar-Abbas and looked into his eyes. Still without a word, she turned and placed the club on the table. The heavy, clunking sound of wood on wood echoed round the cell. She then sat on the chair, facing Bar-Abbas and still saying nothing.

The Egyptian just looked at her, still unsure as to why she was there. She then looked in her pocket and produced a small wooden object that she placed on the table. Bar-Abbas looked more closely and recognized it with horror.

"Would you like to know who this is?"

Bar-Abbas was paralyzed at sight of the figurine.

"Would you like to know who it is?" she shouted.

"Your son?" he whispered.

"This is Benjamin, my son. My only son. And he is six years old." Silence took over. This was a Jewish woman? Was that soldier he killed married to a Jewish woman? If he was, then that boy would be Jewish. And what were the Romans doing allowing a Jewish woman into their garrison?

"How have you got in here? They wouldn't let a Jewish woman into a Roman prison cell."

"My husband's centurion is a member of our synagogue," she answered. More silence. "And he loves Benjamin. And my Benjamin is grieving. Why do you think my Benjamin is grieving, Bar-Abbas?"

"I killed his father," Bar-Abbas answered, but no sound had come out of his mouth.

"Why?" she asked again.

"Because I killed his father," he said as he dropped his head to look at the stone floor.

"Wrong. You didn't kill him. You murdered him," she said in hushed tones as she rose from her seat. "My husband's name was Markus. He loved our nation. He supported our synagogue. He never harmed anyone. Why did you kill him? Why did you make an orphan of my son, Son-of-the-Father?"

"Because I am grieving too."

"And you took it out on an innocent father?" Bar-Abbas kept his eyes toward the ground. He raised them only in response to the sound of the club being lifted from the table. "Who were you grieving?" she asked as she walked towards him.

"My brothers. Murdered by soldiers from Caesarea." Meeting her gaze, he continued. "Soldiers who never harm anyone."

"And you wanted revenge?"

"I did then."

"What do you think I want, Bar-Abbas?" she said, walking nearer to him, and appearing all too comfortable with the deadly weapon in her hand.

"I don't know."

"What do you think my son wants?" No answer. "Do you think we want revenge?"

Bar-Abbas looked away. She touched the Egyptians chin with the end of the club, forcing his eyes back into hers. "I am Abraham's daughter, but what I do now, I do for my son," she said, taking a step back and raising the club above her head, ready to strike downwards onto the prisoner's skull. He closed his eyes. The sound of falling wood bounced throughout the chamber as the club clattered on the stone floor.

"Revenge is the coward's way of dealing with pain," she said. "Wealthy merchant boy, not used to pain. Not used to injustice or suffering. So when it comes to you, instead of dealing with it, you try and pass it on to someone else. Try and hand your pain to them. Get them to grieve so you don't have to. But it never works does it?" She looked at him as though she were trying to show her whole self, and see into his whole self. "I will pray that God grants you the time to live with what you've done."

She turned and walked over to the door, knocking for the guard to open it. As the door opened, she looked back towards Bar-Abbas. "Take that as a lesson in Jewish justice," she said as, for the first time, her will showed signs of giving way to her emotion. And then she left.

"Are you ready for Roman justice?" The door opened, and two soldiers marched quickly towards Theudas.

Ten lashes, he thought, how painful can it be? As he was carried along the corridor he reflected on the maximum number allowed being forty. That was supposed to be as much as a human being could bear. I'm only getting a quarter of that, he thought. It'll take less than a minute. It won't be that bad. But Theudas' body was not convinced by the reasoning of his mind. He emerged into daylight for the first time in twenty-four hours, and screwed his face up as he looked around the small courtyard.

At its centre was a low thick post, with metal hooks. He was carried towards it and his hands tied to the hooks with such speed that there was little chance to prepare himself mentally, although he did have time to reflect that this was probably no bad thing. And then the flogging began.

He felt life draining from him with the first strike. The second hit him from the other side before he had opportunity to realize that it would probably kill him. Still, he made no sound. The third struck him, and then the fourth. At which point Theudas lost count. Soldiers looked on from inside the veranda that lined the courtyard, fascinated by this ordeal. The victim was oblivious to their jeers. He was hoping that his back would become numb, but with each strike the agony was multiplied. He began to wince, and then to cry out as the lashes continued.

Before he realized that the flogging had ceased, his wrists were released and he was lifted to his feet. Grabbed by his arm, he was led quickly through the garrison, struggling to stay on his feet. A small door within a larger one was opened, and Theudas thrown onto the street.

Within seconds an arm was around him, lifting him gently to his feet. Miriam made no attempt to conceal her tears.

"I preferred the guest house we stayed at the other night," Theudas laughed.

☙19❧

"I CAN'T BELIEVE THEY let you go" Miriam stuttered with a hand to her mouth.

"You call this letting me go?"

"Compared to what will happen to the others . . ." she said, breaking into something that was not quite laughter. "Can you walk?"

"I can walk away from here," he muttered, limping slowly away from the fort.

Barely able to speak, and unable to touch his back, Miriam somehow transferred silent energy to Theudas as they made their way across the city.

"What news of the others?" he grimaced.

Her face dropped. "They have your brother, and Kochba, and Amram." Theudas had assumed it, but hearing it spoken brought more pain that he expected. "Theudas, I'm sorry." She wanted to embrace him, but his wounds were open. She contented herself with touching his arm and smiling.

Theudas looked at her, and turned away with a pensive nod. "We failed," he said as a muscle twitched in his back forcing him to screw his face up in pain.

"But you knew it was a trap. How? What's happened to Kaleb?"

"I followed Kaleb—he found Sol and handed . . ."

"Sol—you mean Kochba's son."

Theudas nodded. "Kaleb gave his parchment to Sol. I forced him to give it up."

"And?"

"Kaleb's parchments were not messages to his father in heaven. They were to his father in Jerusalem."

"What?"

"Kaleb betrayed us. For the sake of being reconciled to his father. And Sol. What the hell was he doing, plotting against his own father?" Miriam did not look too surprised, but then surprise didn't suit her. She sat quietly and eventually nodded with a sigh. "What will happen here, Miriam?"

"You already know that. They'll all be crucified."

"When?"

"At the next festival."

"At Passover? That's months away."

"If they do it now there's still the risk of a revolt. If they crucify resistance fighters with this buzz in the air, they risk trouble. It's better for the Romans if they wait."

"Well I'm not going to complain about that," said Theudas before his thoughts returned to Sol. "Kochba—he came with us for the sake of his sons—and his sons have betrayed him!"

It was a full week before Theudas was able to walk with ease, but the discomfort did not prevent him from trying to visit his brother every day. Each time the reply was the same. "No contact before sentencing."

"And when will the sentencing be?" Theudas' question had now tested the full range of a Roman soldier's capacity to say, "I don't know" without speaking and without making eye contact. The festival had ended and the city had emptied of pilgrims. It was then that the prefect, presumably because of the reduced risk of uproar, chose to announce the sentence of Bar-Abbas and his associates. He delivered his brief message from the platform where his life should have ended. Three Jewish bandits, Yeshua Bar-Abbas, Kochba of Capernaum and Amram of Narbata, were to be crucified for insurrection at Passover next.

It came as no surprise, but Theudas felt a wrenching in his abdomen, as all that he could see and sense instantly withdrew from him. He did not hear the jeers from the small crowd that had gathered in the square. He did not sense Miriam's tactile attempt to bring comfort. He did not see the delight concealed in the prefect's dispassionate expressions. He felt nothing. But it was a nothing that had a forceful presence. Sheol had entered into the Egyptian, disorienting him from his world, leaving him disengaged, untouchable, numb. He could speak and respond only mechanically. His body set off a few paces ahead of him, and Theudas paid no attention to where it led him. In fact, it led him back to the Roman guards at the garrison, who by now were expecting to see him. For once, they addressed him first.

"No visitors for the crucified."

Theudas' body offered an involuntary response. "May the crucified write and receive letters?"

The soldier turned and whispered to someone out of sight. Turning back to Theudas, he replied, "In Greek text only."

Theudas neither moved nor spoke nor even appeared to have heard the answer, so the soldier continued. "So that we can read what's going in and out." Still there was silence, and the soldier's stern exterior was at odds with his readiness to provide further information to one who ought to have had to beg for it. Theudas wouldn't usually have noticed such tiny details, but in his current state, he could see that the soldier was not just relieved to be releasing information after a week of withholding it. A faint streak of compassion was detectable in his cold voice. "And you'll need to bring writing materials."

Theudas then heard Miriam address the soldier. "Sir," she said, "The other two prisoners, Kochba and Amram. May we bring letters and writing materials for them?"

The soldier did not look at her. Nor did he turn to his unseen colleague inside the fortress. He just looked straight in front of himself and in his deliberately cold voice declared, "You may." Theudas saw himself nod in gratitude, and heard Miriam thanking the soldier as though he had granted the prisoners pardon as well as letters.

The couple left, and walked to the hill south of the city where they could watch the sky and smell the olive trees.

Miriam and Theudas were all that remained of the fellowship that had grown close in the caves of Arbela. They established a rhythm to their days, writing letters of encouragement to their imprisoned friends, gathering what luxuries the soldiers would allow to pass through the gates, and visiting the garrison to deliver their support and to collect what letters might be sent to them. The soldiers themselves became more than familiar faces. Tullius was the name of the guard with the cold exterior. As the weeks progressed, that exterior remained intact and his refusal to make eye contact was undiminished. But the divulgence of information continued, and expressions of concern along with advice about how best to support the prisoners were smuggled through the soldier's apparent disinterest. His detached, disinterested appearance became a strange source of warmth in the routine of Miriam and Theudas, whose visits were shaped around the shift patterns that he worked.

Letters that came spoke of humane treatment at the hands of the Romans. Theudas had assumed that this was a necessary lie when the letters were obviously being filtered through guards. But increased exposure to Tullius, along with the mood detectable in the letters suggested that whatever cruelty the Romans inflicted was being stored up for the execution of the sentence that awaited them. Until then, the prisoners were treated in accordance with Roman law. No cruelty. No kindness. Only justice.

The letters from Yeshua, Kochba, and Amram poured out of the prison. Yeshua's were read and sent to Alexandria. Kochba's went only to his family in Galilee, but no reply ever came. Amram's were sent only to Theudas and Miriam. And so the three prisoners, held within a single garrison, heard of one another's fate. Yeshua's messages to Ely were hardest of all to arrange, since crossing my sea during winter months was so treacherous. Letters traveled with traders, and would take up to a month to exchange.

> *From Yeshua to Ely of Alexandria*
>
> *Shalom to you my Father, from a place where there is none. And neither is there justice.*
>
> *I know you warned us against coming here, and I am sorry that it has resulted in the loss of another son. I wanted justice and nothing more. But it has eluded me. I thought that Adonai would bless our cause. It is a just cause. I believed it would be a service to our people. But our attempts were foiled before they had begun. God has not blessed us. All I can see is his hand of judgment directed towards no one but me.*
>
> *You are a Rabbi. Does Adonai not see what happens here? Or is he helpless? Or has he just abandoned justice? There is no justice for his people here. No justice for my brothers. All is darkness, and Adonai has withdrawn from it to the safety of heaven. As far as the east is from the west. As high as the heavens are above the earth. Adonai has abandoned this land. He has abandoned justice. The only justice left here is Roman justice. It has conquered this land, and like a coward, Adonai has withdrawn from it.*

> *At Passover he will withdraw from me. You know of my sen-*
> *tence, and I only wish it were sooner. I cannot live in this world*
> *where justice is defeated and Adonai hides his eyes. It is unbear-*
> *able. I only want this to end.*
>
> *I do take some consolation from Theudas. I am grateful at least*
> *for the commitment he shows to me and the support he brings each*
> *day. I am also grateful that he will return to you and that you may*
> *find comfort in one another. This is my only comfort. Let this be so.*

Theudas himself, having read the letter, added to it one of his own.
Yeshua's letter alone would bring only further distress to their Father,
but the younger brother was still compelled to deliver it. His own letter to Alexandria was more optimistic in its tone, and tried to hint at
how Yeshua's letter was to be interpreted. It was six weeks before a reply
arrived, the first word the brothers had heard from their father since
leaving Alexandria three months earlier. Their Father, Ely, had written a
letter to each son, in the knowledge that Theudas would read both.

> *From Ely of Alexandria, to Yeshua.*
>
> *Shalom to you, my beloved son. A shalom that may penetrate*
> *the walls of a garrison to reach your inner being.*
>
> *You are where you are because of your hunger and thirst for*
> *justice. Suffering and grief were yours long before you heard your*
> *sentence. This is not the first time that your sense of justice has*
> *caused you to tackle Romans. My friend Caius (he sends his greet-*
> *ings, and asked me to remind you there never was a safe path to*
> *victory.) Caius remembers when you were five years old. He was*
> *teaching you and your older brothers how to fight with wooden*
> *swords. But you, being smaller, got less attention than the others.*
> *Usually you could cope with this. But he had made a promise. He*
> *had promised to play with each of you in turn, and you lost your*
> *turn. It was a little injustice, but you were a little person. You threw*
> *yourself at him in a rage and tried to stab him to death with your*
> *stick. Your protest could have been heard all the way from Rome.*
> *But he conceded that you were right, and said "this little man is a*
> *veritable warrior for justice." How true he spoke! And now your*
> *protest will undoubtedly be reported in Rome.*
>
> *You believed your cause was just, and even as a child, when*
> *you believed your case to be just, there was not a man under the*
> *heavens you wouldn't challenge.*
>
> *But listen to me my son, when I say there is no such thing as*
> *justice. She is a Roman goddess. Adonai does not obey her.*

There is no invisible force of good and evil, no timeless rights and wrongs for Yahweh himself to obey.

Justice means nothing outside of a relationship. And if a relationship is based on justice then it is no relationship, just a way of conducting transactions between people. As merchants, we know this well enough. It is how merchants should relate. But the children of men are more than merchants.

The justice of Adonai is rooted in the lives of people. If we honor him we act justly; if we grieve him we do not. Justice is merely the process of seeing God's will done on earth, the process of seeing Adonai's loving character manifest amongst his people. There is no justice outside this. As far as you are able to do so, let go of whatever you think of as justice and seek the mercy of Adonai. His mercy is renewed every morning, and I pray that it renews you every morning.

Our God is a compassionate God, a God who suffers with us. I pray that you feel his presence even as I write this, and that you feel my love as you read it. Let this be so.

Ely's letter enjoyed some of its desired effect upon Yeshua, who could hardly believe how his father seemed to have acquired such wisdom in the course of only three months. The newly acquired power of Ely's words was magnified by forty days of quiet self-reflection in a dimly lit cell. His confinement was not as cruel a punishment as it might have been for others, since Yeshua was thoroughly at home with his own thoughts. The Egyptian knew well enough that this was probably because his thoughts did not settle readily into concrete conclusions but remained active. Whilst often frustrated by his own wavering, his mind remained alert in such a way as to bring comfort as well as disturbance to the core of his being. The constant letters from his brother and limited news of the outside world, helped to root Yeshua's musings in the real world, keeping him sane and strangely hopeful. By the time he received his letter from Ely, he was ready to respond immediately.

From Yeshua to Ely of Alexandria

Shalom to you my Father, from one who deserves none.

You know why I write to you from this cell, and why I deserve to be here. In this cell, I am receiving all that I have asked for, save the grace to write this letter to you.

We came here against your wishes and your pleas, but it took this journey and these experiences to learn what you had already foreseen. I wish we had been able to hear you, because the wisdom of your advice has now been proven.

It was justice that brought me on this quest. It is justice that will soon end it. I don't think justice is an idea. And I sought justice as I did when I was a child. Because I was hurt by injustice. Relationships have always been at the heart of my desire for justice. It is pain that cries for justice. But I was unaware of the pain that my justice brought for others.

We have avenged our brothers. But vengeance brought no relief and no comfort, only further bloodshed and further vengeance. I have been unable to draw together the deaths of my brothers and the deaths I have caused. They feel utterly unrelated. There is nothing to link them but the chain of violence. But the violence will cease with my own death. Justice will come at last to me. It will come at the hands of pagans, but it will be the justice of Adonai. This is how Adonai has always judged disobedient Israel. I am an incarnation of that disobedience. And justice will come on the cross that awaits me.

Father. I have sinned against all my fathers, from Adonai to Abraham to you. "Bar-Abbas" they call me, "the son of the father!" But I am no longer worthy to be called your son, nor anyone else's son.

I have shed blood that brought no comfort. I have dishonored my older brothers and misled my younger. And I have dragged your name through the failure and filth of my actions. I dare not ask for your forgiveness. I ask for nothing, but that you remember me as the son I was before you lost your others. Let this be so.

Jerusalem plunged into the depths of winter, leaving only three months before the executions. The possibility of three more letters from his Father ignited the Egyptian's hope. The prospect of Ely's reply had begun to colonize Yeshua's spirit. He waited for news from his father in Alexandria as though his words would be penned by his Father in heaven. The desire for some means of reconciliation with the father whom he had so tragically failed began to outgrow all other desire or anxiety. But the end of this hope was beyond his control. He could not force it, nor manipulate it. It would come only with the grace of his father. All the Egyptian could do was to hope and pray, until the letter finally arrived.

From Ely of Alexandria to Yeshua, my son.

Grace to you, and Shalom, from Adonai, our Father.

Every day that I spent with you, I treated as an undeserved gift from Adonai. Still I thank him for every moment until the present.

My beloved son. If you need any forgiveness from me then you have it. A condemned man needs no more condemnation. But I offer you my affection and forgiveness for no other reason than my love for you.

Death is always our enemy. But when death announces the day of its arrival, at least some of its power is robbed. I pray that you use your days well. That you pray to Adonai. You are still his son, just as you are still mine. If I am desperate to forgive whatever needs forgiving, how much more is Adonai ready to offer the same?

You now feel yourself under God's judgment? That justice has now been visited upon you? When I heard this, I prayed and was reminded of a psalm, which could have been written for you.

"Adonai, do not rebuke me in your anger, or discipline me in your wrath. Be merciful to me, Adonai, for I am faint; Adonai! Heal me, for my bones are in agony. My soul is in anguish. How long, Adonai ? How long?"

"Turn around, Adonai, and deliver me; save me because of your unfailing love. No one remembers you when he is dead. Who praises you from the grave? I am worn out from groaning; all night long I flood my bed with weeping and drench my couch with tears. My eyes grow weak with sorrow; they fail because of all my foes."

"Away from me, all you who do evil, for Adonai has heard my weeping. Adonai has heard my cry for mercy; Adonai accepts my prayer. All my enemies will be ashamed and dismayed; they will turn back in sudden disgrace."

Once again, when the letter arrived from Alexandria, Yeshua was ready to pour his spirit into an immediate reply.

From Yeshua to Ely of Alexandria

Shalom, from Jerusalem to my Father

This will be my last letter to you, and I hope that you feel something of the Shalom that now rests in this place. Anxiety, fear and guilt are my constant companions. I fear the beatings I must endure, the shame of carrying my cross, the agony of the nails, and the slow torture. But even amidst the torment of my fears, is a persistent presence of Shalom. Sometimes it is only a flicker, sometimes a raging furnace. But constantly now it burns.

I have made this psalm my own. And I have taken possession of my crime. It was not concerned with my violence. I thought I acted for my people, for my brothers. An eye for an eye. If I multiply the number of my brothers, I justify the multiple vengeances I took. Had it not ended here, there would only be more spilling of blood. The fact that it is now my own blood to be spilt is just, and from that justice true Shalom can blossom.

My shalom was robbed when I placed justice higher than love. It was just the same for Adam and Eve. They treasured justice, they wanted knowledge of Good and Evil so they could know better than Adonai, and because they grasped at it, they lost their Shalom with Adonai. The devil offered justice, and it is alluring. When I put justice first, life is easy because the questions cease. But putting justice first robs us of Shalom.

Adonai restores our shalom, not only for Adam's race, but even for me. And somehow, in this place, I do feel a part of my people. Even in the loneliness of my cell I feel the comfort and promise of Adonai. I don't know for sure if God will forgive me. I face justice now, but pray that I find mercy before Adonai. Let it be so.

Theudas read this as every other letter to Alexandria. But he did not send this letter to his father in Egypt. Ely of Alexandria would collect the letter by hand when he arrived in Jerusalem.

❧ 20 ❧

S PRING HAD COME UPON Israel all-too-soon. As at every festival, the city was rife with whispers of freedom and rebellion, talk of another uprising. Bar-Abbas was almost forgotten, and the whispers of the new rebellion revolved around a new figure, the prophet from Galilee. As the festival approached, the talk was less covert as people began to speak openly about the coming Messiah from Nazareth.

Four pilgrims in Jerusalem were sick of such talk, and had no stomach left for uprising or rebellion or revolution. It would all become very sobering for the over-excited masses of Jerusalem once the crucifixions took place at the end of the week. Bar-Abbas, Amram and Kochba were to be crucified the day before Sabbath, on the hill of Gol-Gotha, east of the city wall.

The four companions walked through the afternoon streets of the holy city. Behind Theudas and Miriam, two old friends and trading partners walked side by side. Ely of Alexandria and Yudah of Narbata. They were there to see the condemned men one last time, and to accompany them as they carried their crossbars through the city and out to the execution stakes that awaited them on the hill. But on this Passover, the more people talked about the Galilean prophet, the more Theudas suspected that this poor fellow would be destined to share his brother's fate.

On the evening that the prophet was due to arrive, Theudas and Miriam stood in the place where, several months earlier, they had watched Pontius Pilatus enter on his chariot for the Feast of Ingathering. Now they watched a crowd of similar size following their would-be Messiah into the city. But this Messiah was not dressed in purple robes, and was not riding a chariot. He was dressed in a peasant's garment and riding a donkey. It did not prevent the cries for liberation as the word, "Hoshannah" echoed around the valley below. People had thrown their cloaks on the road before him, and were shouting psalms about David's royal descendant, the true King of Israel, the Messiah, coming to set them free in the name of Adonai.

"Do you seriously think he's going to storm the garrison?" asked Theudas. With several others, they walked along the wall to watch where he would go after he entered through Solomon's Portico. But he marched straight past the Antonine Fortress and into the temple precincts.

"He's going to the armory," said Theudas in amazement. "It's where the nationalist Lestai keep their weapons. We have got to see this."

Miriam and Theudas hurried into the precincts to arrive at a chaotic scene. The Galilean was not collecting weapons. He was performing a prophetic act. The temple courts were busier than usual, as the city was full of pilgrims for the Passover. The animals that were sold for worshippers to make their sacrifice littered the eastern end of the precincts. The Galilean clambered onto a table in the midst of them and raised his voice, quoting an ancient prophet.

"My house will be a house of prayer for *all* nations . . ." he bellowed, emphasizing the "all."

"Ouch" said Theudas. That's just what the nationalists wanted to hear, he thought. He and Miriam smiled, entranced by what the prophet would say next.

". . . But you have turned it into a den of Lestai". Gasps of horror filled the precincts. This was God's holy temple. This was where the hope of all Israel was focused. The prophet was supposed to be liberating Israel. Not condemning those nationalists who treasured hopes of liberation more fully than anyone.

"Why doesn't he just tell the Romans that the armory is hidden away here?" Theudas whispered.

But the prophet was far from done. He leapt from the table and threw it over. He then did the same to every table within his reach. The birds and animals screamed and squawked amidst the chaos. Coins were thrown onto the floor, leaving the moneychangers scrambling after their takings. But for all the fury amidst the disgusted onlookers, there were also cheers. For Israel's poorest, for those who were outcast and marginalized, the Temple and all it represented was as much as symbol of oppression as was the fortress.

More confusion ensued at the precincts' entrance way. Those who were blind or disabled had never been allowed in the temple. It was King David's fault. A thousand years ago when he first laid siege to the city, its defenders laughed at him from the walls, saying, "You'll never capture this city! The blind and the lame will keep you out." From that moment, King David and all his descendants had cursed them and barred them from the temple. But in the midst of this chaos, the blind and the lame were now entering the temple precincts and the Galilean invited them to him. He was effectively rejecting this "Son of David" title.

"I have never seen anything like this," said Miriam, covering her mouth to hide her amusement.

"So much for Israel's liberation," sighed Theudas.

"At least there's no danger of him joining your brother on a cross," said Miriam.

"There'll be other dangers for someone doing that kind of thing," Theudas lamented. "This is going to get unpleasant."

The chaos in Jerusalem that surrounded her newly arrived Messiah continued to increase over the next few days, but the excitement washed over the grieving companions. Ely and Yudah, Miriam and Theudas watched the days pass with anticipation and dread. The conversation between them lessened, but their fellowship did not need to be bolstered with words. The communication between them was inarticulate comfort.

When the time came, they prepared to share the Passover meal only in one another's company. As the senior member, Ely recounted the story of Moses leading the escape from Egypt, and in accordance with the tradition, he used the different parts of the meal to highlight different elements of the narrative.

"Liberation for our people was all that our friends wanted," Ely declared tearfully. "And here today all Israel is gathered to relive that experience, and our friends who tried to make it a reality are already forgotten."

"All eyes are on the Galilean now," sighed Theudas, shaking his head.

"I'd like to see how he brings liberty without using force," Miriam complained.

"Father, do you think Yahweh approves of what we tried to do?" Theudas asked.

"From what you've told me, it sounds as though your brother was not far from the truth," Ely replied. "We can't know for sure. But we can't be condemned for taking a step of faith, even if it was the wrong one. You genuinely tried to please Adonai, and he won't condemn you for that."

"But we are condemned," said Miriam. "Half of our group is going to die."

No one tried to ease the mood or lighten the spirit. This was a dark day, and any attempt to experience it differently would be a dishonor to their companions.

⁊♥

Light morning mist was filled by a distant clamor. Long before sunrise a noise similar to and yet distinct from the competing squawk and cry of waking birds, echoed from the heart of the city. Theudas awoke from a light sleep to discover that he was the last in his company to do so.

"What's going on?" he asked. Ely and Yudah were already wrapping themselves in their garments to go and investigate. That crowds were busy shouting was clear enough. But what they were shouting was unclear.

"Yeshua still managing to cause trouble," Theudas yawned.

"Unless it's something to do with the Galilean," said Miriam.

As the four neared the temple it was clear that something close to a riot had begun. Fewer than a couple of hundred were present. But amidst the crowds were senior priests and members of Jerusalem's nobility. This was no rebellious gathering. Something different was taking place, and outside the walls of the garrison.

"What's happening?" Ely asked a priest.

"The prophet from Nazareth. We are securing his death sentence," said the priest, looking down his nose at the Pharisee.

"For what?"

"Haven't decided yet," said the priest dismissively. After a moment he looked Ely in the eye, and added "Blasphemy!" before turning towards the heightening commotion at the gate of the fortress. Soldiers began to stream out. The sight animated Theudas' memory of the day when these soldiers had attacked the crowd that he was part of.

"We need to get away from here," he said, as more and more soldiers spewed out through the gate. The crowds raised their voices in a rage, even as they backed away from the soldiers. The soldiers moved quickly but were more interested in making it through the crowds than attacking them. They continued to pour into the square until they outnumbered the crowds themselves, forcing some of the shouting to subside. The soldiers were tightly packed around a figure in their midst, and headed west across the city. This was obviously the Galilean who was now being taken to Herod's palace. The companions followed the crowds at a distance through the full ten-minute journey before some of the soldiers entered the palace, whilst the majority took up defensive positions around its gates.

"What is this man's crime?" Theudas asked one of the mob.

"Blaspheming Adonai!" he replied.

"So when is his trial?"

"It was during the night," came the reply, "and now he'll get what's coming to him." The sky behind the eastern hills was turning into a lighter shade of clear blue, and the young man of the mob turned away, disinterested in anything but baying for blood.

Blasphemy is no Roman law. This must be why they've brought him to Herod, Theudas thought. "Why the nighttime trial?" he asked his companions. "You can't have a trial in darkness. It is not lawful!"

"You can for a master manipulator of the people," said another priest in disgust.

In less time than the journey from the garrison had taken, the journey back had begun. The soldiers emptied from the palace, the Galilean with them. By the time the crowds had arrived back at the fortress, the birds were adding their voice to the clamor. But the crowds continued to grow.

"I'm not staying here to watch this," said Ely. "It will be lunch time before my Yeshua emerges."

"Can you eat?" asked Yudah.

"We're Jews," Theudas smiled, more than happy to distance himself from the crowds. A light breeze brought the smell of jasmine as the companions broke bread together and awaited the fate of their friends. Nearby the shouts had now ceased but the crowds had continued to grow. The chatter from the square was the only talk that was heard as the pilgrims ate together. Eventually Miriam broke the silence.

"Do you think we might be missing something important?" she said, nodding in the direction of the square.

"Or something fatal?" Theudas said as he raised his eyebrows.

"Something unusual is going on. If they're trying to get him a death sentence, then it's going to make it very difficult to see our friends. They'll be swarming around them all the way to Gol-Gotha."

"Well I can't just sit here," said Miriam. "I'm going back to the square." She was joined by the others but with little enthusiasm.

The square beneath the prefect's podium was packed with spectators, but the platform was empty. It was mid morning, and the heat of a spring day was gaining strength. The sky was hazy, and the hills around the city could be seen only in their outline. The garrison towered silently and clearly above the gathered multitude, and there was no telling what was happening inside.

Packed in by the crowds, there was little room to move. But Theudas felt alone. All he wanted was to see his brother. The waiting had been too long, and every moment was lengthened by the dread of what would soon take place. Eventually two soldiers appeared, carrying a large wooden seat, upon which the prefect would sit to pass judgment. Having placed it in the centre of the podium, they took a step back. The prefect himself appeared. This was the first time Theudas had seen Pontius Pilatus so close. About forty years of age, he wore a compassionate expression that ill suited him. This man hardly seemed worthy of the hatred or the energy his action had evoked among Theudas' friends. Little charisma emerged from the deep sockets hiding his eyes within the dark recesses of his skull. His stance was hardly that of defiance, and his voice lacked any authority. Polished plate amour and purple robes concealed his un-athletic frame, as he looked down upon those who had gathered to hear the sentence pronounced on the Galilean. Then he turned, took his place on the seat of judgment, and nodded to the person next to him.

Two soldiers appeared carrying a disheveled man in manacles. The quality of the robes in which this man was dressed could hardly escape Theudas' attention. The robes of fine, beautifully woven purple were those befitting royalty, but they hung on this pathetic figure only in mockery. His face was swollen and bloodied. He could barely stand un-aided. His head hung, staring at the stone of the podium rather than the people in the square. Those people shouted and jeered at the Galilean. Theudas thought about how, only a few days earlier, these same people had been shouting "Hoshannah", and hailing this figure as the Messiah.

"People of Judah," the prefect shouted. "You want me to condemn this man to death." The crowds irrupted in a chorus of angry bellowing, which the prefect allowed to subside before continuing. "You condemn this man, but I find no crime in him. By Roman law, by Jewish law, this man is innocent." The crowds returned to their frenzy, too numerous now to feel threatened by the prefect's soldiers.

The roar only subsided as two more soldiers appeared with another manacled figure. It was his brother. What was Yeshua doing here, paraded in front of crowds who had forgotten who he was? Why was he on display? What was this spectacle?

"People of Judah," he shouted. "You see before you two rebels. Yeshua the Messiah . . ." The crowd resumed their jeering so the prefect waited for it to fade. ". . .Yeshua the Messiah," he repeated, "and Yeshua Bar-Abbas." Again he waited for the noise to die down before continuing. "Roman justice is compassionate. In honor of this festival, it is my custom, as you know, to release to you a prisoner. Your leaders suggest you might want this man?" He pointed to Bar-Abbas. At this moment a small note was handed to him, and a visible fear gripped him as he looked intently at the Galilean. The Galilean looked back, through his swollen eyes. Eventually, Pilatus managed to regain his composure before turning again to the crowd.

Yeshua obviously had not seen daylight since the Feast of Ingathering. His skin was white, and there was little between that skin and the skeleton to which it clung. He had aged several years. He was utterly bemused by what was happening. The crowds were already cheering him. The people favored him over the Galilean. Pilatus clearly had in mind to release one of them, but it could not possibly be Yeshua of Alexandria. He was a rebel against Rome. Theudas prayed it would be his brother, but if the crowds asked for this assassin to be released, then it would give the prefect all the excuse he needed for a mass slaughter. Although, the crowds were numbering thousands. Perhaps the prefect would be afraid of something far bigger than any rebellion Bar-Abbas could have caused. But the prefect was unpredictable.

"Which of the two do you want me to release," he shouted, "Yeshua Messiah, or Yeshua Bar-Abbas?"

The crowd chanted almost as one, "Bar-Abbas, Bar-Abbas . . ."

Pilatus nodded and raised his hand. "What then, shall I do with the Yeshua who is called 'Messiah?'"

Again, the crowd began their chant. "Crucify him, crucify him . . ."

Again Pilate nodded and raised his hand to speak. "For what crime?" he asked.

But the crowd simply repeated the chant. Pilatus spoke to one of his soldiers who hurried away. He reappeared with a bowl of water, allowing the prefect to make a prophetic statement in true Jewish style. He stood and washed his hands in the bowl that his soldier held. As he dried them he shouted to the crowd, "I am innocent of this man's blood." He did not linger to hear the crowds respond, and neither did he look at either of the prisoners on the podium. Within just a few seconds, the podium was empty.

The crowds were too dense to make it off the square in a hurry. "Does that mean he's going to be released?" Theudas shouted in disbelief. "Are they going to free my brother?"

"Come on," blurted Miriam already rushing away. They pushed their way slowly round to the gates of the fortress through which Theudas had been released several months earlier. It was five minutes before they got anywhere near the doorway.

"Has it opened yet?" Theudas asked one of those present.

"Not yet," he replied.

Theudas abandoned his companions to the crowd, and forced his way towards the front where he could see the gate clearly. And he waited. Why was his brother suddenly so popular? It soon became clear that the numbers present were too many and too excited for any Roman in his right mind to open the gates of the garrison simply to release one prisoner. And so Theudas waited.

Twenty minutes saw many who were present abandon waiting and return to the square where they could wait to see the Galilean emerge with his cross. Theudas was joined by his companions. The crowds at the gate slowly dissipated, and still Theudas awaited his brother. None dared believe that Yeshua would emerge alive from that garrison. They stood and watched the silent gate, barred and locked for all eternity it seemed, the prefect's promise a cruel joke. Scuffles over to the right end of the crowd drew Theudas' attention away from the gate. A company of soldiers was forcing its way through the crowd as the troops positioned themselves in front of the gate. Behind them, the top of the door could be seen to open and close. The soldiers parted, and Yeshua of Alexandria walked into a crowd that exploded in cheers.

Yeshua's only expression was confusion, as he scanned the crowd in disbelief. Theudas made eye contact with his brother, and walked quickly towards him only to be overtaken by Ely who locked him in his embrace. Theudas joined them, amidst rapturous cheers to which the three remained oblivious.

Once again, Yeshua Bar-Abbas had failed. Once again he had been frustrated by circumstance. Once again, he had succeeded in reconciling himself to the turn of events that were to shape his life, only to be overtaken by circumstances beyond his control. He had prepared himself even for death. He was ready for this fate, and the journey to that state of readiness had been agonizing. But once again, he had been the victim of circumstance. His preparation, even for his own death, had been in vain. Yeshua Bar-Abbas had lost the very conception of control over his own fate. At every turn his plans were thwarted. Maybe his release should have brought more gratitude to the doomed Egyptian. But it did not. His newfound freedom brought only grief, a grief that was to be drilled deep into his psyche by the manner in which his release was granted and the events that he now had to witness. Bar-Abbas should have felt joy. But it had forsaken him.

ʕ❧

"Less than an hour ago I was a dead man," Yeshua wept, shaking his head. "What on earth has happened here?"

"Justice?" Theudas grinned.

"I don't know what we call this," Ely laughed tearfully.

"Mmmmarvelous," said Yudah as he joined them.

"I'm not the only one back from the dead!" said Yeshua putting his hand on Yudah's shoulder. "Is this the resurrection?"

Yeshua Bar-Abbas, still unsure that he was walking as a free and celebrated individual, moved through the crowds with his family and his friends in search of a place where they had more room to weep. "I should be carrying my cross," Yeshua shouted as they pushed their way through the packed street that led away from of the square. "What is the Galilean's crime?"

"His crime was not being you, apparently," said Miriam.

Yeshua turned towards Ely. "And mine was not being him" he said. "Has he really done nothing wrong?"

"He's been trying to get himself killed since he arrived," Theudas laughed, but no one else did. "Although technically, no, he's committed no actual crime that we've heard of."

"Amram and Kochba?" Yeshua asked. "Is there any news of them?"

"No miracle release for our friends," Yudah lamented. "They'll be joining the Galilean on Gol-Gotha."

Bar-Abbas stumbled to the ground, and not only because of his weakened limbs. "I wish I was with them," he cried. "I should be with them."

Ely embraced his son, as he had been accustomed to doing a generation earlier, on every occasion that his toddler stumbled beneath his own tiny, clumsy limbs. The old rabbi uttered no words, but tried to absorb some of the trauma into which his son had plummeted. The companions found a hostel and brought beer at Yeshua's request.

Yeshua sipped his drink before inspecting it more closely. "I understand now," he said, addressing the bottom of the cup that contained his beer. He looked at his companions, who were all eager for him to speak. "I understand why Noah got utterly bladdered when his ark landed on dry ground." Yudah frowned in confusion, looking towards Ely. Yeshua stared back into his cup. "He wasn't full of joy at being released. He came out of the ark into a place of death."

✄≪21≫✄

HALF OF JUDAH'S SOLDIERS were dispatched to line the streets en route to the western gate of the city that the criminals would take on their way to Gol-Gotha. The city's passages, already swollen with pilgrims for the festival, became a tightly packed, noisy chaos. Many spectators didn't even know why they were there, but had been drawn by the guards sent to control them. When the gates of the garrison eventually opened for the criminals to emerge, they were tightly packed in by a company of soldiers, who in turn were hemmed in by an impenetrable crowd of onlookers.

The companions hurried to a position on Via Delarosa where they might be able to glimpse Amram and Kochba as they carried their crosses. The moment arrived before Yeshua was ready for it. Kochba shared the pale skin and withered features that Yeshua had acquired in his cell. The companions called his name as he came by. Kochba looked at them, but if he recognized them he failed to show it. He looked exhausted, and as confused by the crowd as Yeshua had been two hours earlier.

Behind Kochba was the Galilean. The prophet from Nazareth could barely walk, let alone carry his own cross. A makeshift crown of camel thorns had been thrust onto his head and cut deep wounds. If his face were not devoid of expression, then that expression was undetectable through the swollen and bloody bruises of his beatings. Following him was an unfamiliar face, no doubt drawn from the crowd by the soldiers. He was neither pale, nor had he been beaten but he carried a cross on his shoulders, since the Galilean he followed could barely carry himself. He shared the looks of confusion and exhaustion as the soldiers pushed him along the narrow street.

Last in the procession was Amram. He looked just as he had looked six months earlier. At sight of him, the companions called out his name.

The archer nodded at them, and winked unmistakably at Yeshua, with something of a smirk. Through the shouting that surrounded the entire company, Theudas thought he heard a belch.

The companions followed at a distance. From Gol-Gotha they heard the agonized screams mixed with the sound of bolts being hammered into hard wood. Kochba was the first to become visible as he was lifted high. The clunk of the crosspiece to which he was nailed falling into its allotted groove on the execution stake was followed by a wince as the farmer dropped his head. The Galilean followed soon after, but without the clunk since the prophet's body, already weakened by beating and flogging, would have been unable to cope with too harsh a drop onto the stake. He was placed more carefully onto his ill deserved cross. Finally Amram appeared, and the now expected clunk thrust a dark terror deep into Yeshua's spirit.

Three would-be rebels now took the strain between the nails and Sheol beneath them. Had they no use of their legs, they would have suffocated soon enough. But the single nail that pierced each pair of ankles gave them something to push against in the attempt to lift their bodies higher and enable them to breathe. Yeshua had witnessed this horror before, but never for friends. And the fact that this should have been his fate, that the center cross had been reserved for him flooded him with horror and gratitude simultaneously. But Yeshua's cross was still not visible beyond the crowds that continued to surround the Galilean. It was a curious sight. Senior priests, over-privileged Sadducees, the Jewish ruling class, all had gathered to insult and jeer this peasant. Once his fate had become inevitable, the satisfied onlookers spat and withdrew, and the crowds began to move.

A company of soldiers had established a cordon around the crosses, and once the most hostile onlookers had left the companions forced their way towards the front. The spectators who remained were mostly followers of the Galilean who awaited some miracle or mighty act. If he really were Israel's Messiah, then Adonai would not abandon him. The prophet would be delivered. His followers were not alone in their hope.

Betrayed by the family for whose benefit he had tried to act, Kochba's was a look of utter dejection. Surrounded by hostile crowds but without his family, no one could appear more profoundly alone. He was far from ready for his fate, and looked across towards the Galilean. "Where is our liberation?" he called. "Where is *my* liberation?" The soldiers laughed.

This was the basic taunt that had been thrown relentlessly at the crucified Messiah. But from the lips of Kochba it was a genuine plea, and not without a grain of hope. The farmer gathered his breath, since the brief shouts had consumed much of his energy. "You're our King, why don't you do something?" The soldiers continued to laugh, but Kochba's humor had long since deserted him. "Save yourself!" he shouted and paused again to gather his breath whilst looking at the soldiers who pitied him. "Save us!" he cried in desperation, and then dropped his head.

All was silence as the crowds awaited the Messiah's response. But it was the archer who shouted in reply. "Kochba! Brother!" he cried, commanding the crowd's attention and drawing them into the spectacle. "Leave him alone!" he gasped, "Our way has failed." Kochba lifted his head to hear his friend. "You fear God don't you?" Another pause as Kochba nodded silently if vacantly. "You share this death sentence . . ." he called, ". . . and let's face it . . . we earned it." The ghost of a smile sped almost imperceptibly across Kochba's lips. The Galilean now turned towards Amram who, unlike the prophet's hecklers back in Galilee, did not avert his eyes. "You wanted justice . . ." Amram continued, glancing down towards Yeshua and Theudas, "This is our just reward" he called, somehow gesturing towards the crosses.

Amram was uninterrupted as he paused for breath, since he was clearly not finished. Looking back towards Kochba he nodded his head towards the Galilean as he continued, "This man has done nothing wrong." The soldiers had stopped laughing. Amram had expended all of his energy for now, so his shout dropped in volume as he turned to address the Galilean whose own gaze remained fixed upon the archer's.

"Yeshua!" said Amram. "Remember me when you become King." The sniggers began to spread once again, but then the Galilean prepared himself to speak, and once again silence fell.

"I tell you what," the Galilean spluttered through swollen, bloody lips, "today, you'll be an honored guest in my walled garden." The laughter that ensued had no effect upon the archer, who, for the first time, did not look as though he was late for his own grave. How could he possibly have known about Amram's deepest and vainest hope? And how could he promise to fulfill the archer's dream from this place of death?

❧

The sun was approaching its noonday strength, and the crowds were dissipating further. But the atmosphere rapidly became one of early evening. The temperature dropped with extraordinary speed and the sun was losing its light as the condemned men were losing their strength. The darkness of the evening had arrived at least six hours early, and many of the crowds disappeared to find warmth.

"Just when I thought this day couldn't get any more bizarre . . ." said Yudah to no one in particular. Bar-Abbas thought of Eliazar. Had the courses of sun, moon and stars finally ground to a halt in the way that the shepherd thought they must? Had Yahweh commanded the entire creation to halt in order that they might witness the horrors of this injustice? Whatever the reason, Bar-Abbas was so captivated by the spectacle before him, the fact that the rest of the universe stood still, entranced by the same horrific events, could hardly surprise him.

The companions found a space near to Kochba. Their companion, now a disheveled, pathetic figure, bore little resemblance to the successful, rotund farmer of Capernaum. All the life had gone from his eye, leaving nothing but hopeless fatigue, but on seeing his companions a trace of comfort appeared briefly on his grief-stricken face. "I can't bear this agony," he cried, writhing in pain. Bar-Abbas closed his eyes, and felt in his own body all that he saw in Kochba's face.

"For God's sake," Kochba called, "don't let anyone else try what we tried." The companions did not try to verbalize their compliance. "Yahweh has abandoned us," he wept. "He has abandoned this land," he said, raising his eyes to the inexplicable night. He summoned up the strength to continue, "He has abandoned this people." The companions stood in silence and waited. After a few minutes the farmer lifted his head again. "But you . . . My friends . . . You have not abandoned me," he said, before releasing a long breath which spoke something of the small comfort he felt at their presence.

The shallow darkness remained, leading some who were present to see a divine hand at work. For Yeshua of Alexandria, this now suggested what Kochba had articulated. That God himself had withdrawn from this horrific place. Were it not for Amram, Yeshua might well have been convinced of this. The Galilean obviously was some kind of prophet.

The squawk of early morning birdsong alerted those present to the slow return of warmth and light. But this afternoon sunrise brought little comfort. A delegation of priests was conversing with the centurion at the cross, complaining that the Sabbath was approaching and that they did not want dead bodies visible for pilgrims at the festival. The Centurion's reluctant nod suggested that more horror was soon to follow.

Within a few minutes, a soldier appeared carrying a large iron hammer. Kochba lifted his head in confusion and then began to shake it. "No," he called, "No!" The soldier swung the hammer straight into the farmer's shins, three times crushing the bone until it was visibly shattered. Kochba could no longer use his legs to push himself up, and a renewed look of fear gripped him as he began to suffocate.

The soldier then moved to Amram. The archer lifted his eyes, closed them, and awaited the blows that would end his life mercifully quickly. Yeshua and Miriam rushed to Amram to call shalom down upon him as he breathed his last. Theudas, Ely, and Yudah remained to offer what comfort they could as Kochba met his end.

The soldier approached the Galilean, but the prophet seemed already dead. The centurion gestured towards another soldier who brought a spear and thrust it into the prophet's side. Blood and water gushed out. The prophet was dead, and by the time the flow of his blood had ceased, those who were crucified with him had also breathed their last.

Yeshua was present, but somehow dislocated from these events. The horror of them was obvious enough, but on this day he had been exposed to so much that he could not reconcile himself to each new atrocity. He felt in his entire spirit, the sheer horror of this place, but it failed to impact him as he had expected. He had been prepared for his own death, but death had eluded him this day, leaving him unable to cope with any reality that followed. He had seen his father, his brother, his friends as never before. His resurrection was full of pain. He had witnessed two of his closest friends for the first time in months, only to see them face the agonizing death that he should have shared. And worst of all, his own place of torment was occupied by an innocent man condemned to so violent a death. As the warmth of daylight reappeared, a darkness entered Yeshua's being and thrust him from consciousness.

After Sabbath, at dawn, on the first day of the week, five companions took the western road from Jerusalem. The first stage of their journey home would be towards Narbata, but from there they would not travel directly to Alexandria. From Caesarea, Theudas, Miriam, and Yeshua sailed west rather than south.

Miriam and Theudas had not spent all of their time in Jerusalem writing and delivering letters. The difficulty of tracing Kaleb's whereabouts was hardly surprising. They had only wanted to confront him, to question him, to find out why he had handed them over. Those guilty of such crimes rarely conducted them without some compulsion. All who served Rome in this way did so under blackmail. They knew well enough that Jewish nationalists did not usually treasure ambitions of becoming Roman spies. And why Kaleb's sudden desire to be reconciled with his father? After years of hatred from an abandoned son, why now should he long to return to him? They, and even Yudah, wanted only answers from Kaleb, but Yeshua Bar-Abbas wanted far more than answers.

The couple had waited for several weeks before going in search of Ehud. He was not difficult to find, although—quite predictably—he denied all knowledge of the plot at hand. What was more, under the threat of Theudas' dagger, Ehud had withstood Miriam's interrogation. The Pharisee had suggested that Kaleb would have traveled deep into the region of Decapolis until the repercussions for his actions had died out. There he might find some anonymity. But Ehud was not the only man in Jerusalem subjected to Miriam's questions. A single visit to the synagogue where Bar-Abbas had preached was all that was required to find others of Kaleb's friends whose craftiness, courage and loyalty to Kaleb were all inferior to that of Ehud. They gave a different story. Theudas and Miriam returned to Ehud's house, but Theudas entered alone.

"So you think Kaleb went to Decapolis?"

Ehud looked more afraid than he had on the previous occasion. What had Theudas learned in the mean time? "I told you I wasn't sure."

"But you were sure that he was far more likely to go elsewhere!" said Theudas calmly. "And you do know, that if we can't find Kaleb, we'll have to hold you responsible for his actions."

Ehud's fear was palpable.

"Are you going to be honest with me this time?" asked Theudas. The Pharisee nodded.

"Thou shalt not give false testimony," Theudas warned.

"Thou shalt not commit murder," Ehud answered tentatively, realizing as he backed towards the wall that it was a mistake.

Ehud did not see Theudas draw his dagger, but felt its blade pressing on his neck.

"Who said anything about murder?" said Theudas, in a voice that was angry but quiet. "We want answers, not revenge."

"Okay, Okay!"

Theudas backed away.

Ehud sighed and shook his head at the ground. "Cyprus. You'll probably find him in Lefkotheia."

"We'll be back for the Feast of Ingathering, Ehud," said Theudas, still looking at his dagger, and trying not to show the relish he felt at his success. "If I have to visit you again," he added, lifting his eyes to the Pharisee, "it won't be to ask questions."

Spring was beginning to give way to summer when Theudas, Miriam, and Yeshua landed on the island of Cyprus. The companions had tried to talk Yeshua out of going in search of Kaleb. But there was no dissuading him. Yeshua Bar-Abbas, for all his talk of abandoning the quest for justice and revenge, had claimed that he had only one more life to end. He would never be able to rest until it was ended.

"Lefkotheia," said Theudas as they approached the city. "At least we're outside the jurisdiction of Pilatus!"

"But they have real soldiers here, Yeshua," Miriam grinned, still unable to understand why Yeshua was determined to take another life.

The companions found the synagogue and waited for the afternoon service. They had not laid eyes on Kaleb for over six months. Did he know anything of what had happened in Jerusalem? Would they recognize him? The companions took up a position in a quiet corner of the street opposite, and scanned all who approached.

"I'd recognize that frown anywhere," said Theudas, tapping Yeshua on the shoulder and gesturing discreetly towards the Pharisee. His robes were as white as ever, his walk was as confident and his frown was as proud. He disappeared into the synagogue.

Two hours had passed before he re-emerged, and made his way back through the dusty streets of the city. He walked into a small house. Its stone walls took the light from the evening sun and gave it back to the city with a warm, red glow. After a few seconds a light appeared through a small aperture in the stonework, confirming that the Pharisee was alone in his house. Yeshua Bar-Abbas pulled from his cloak the dagger of dark, sharpened iron that had been the cause of immeasurable suffering.

Theudas shook his head and repeated words that Yeshua had heard a thousand times since his release. "Are you sure you want to do this? You've been given a second chance."

"One more death, and it is finished." Theudas' eyes began to fill with tears. "Trust me. It will be okay this time. But I must do this." With that, he disappeared into the house.

Yeshua had endured more violence than he could bear. Over-exposure to bloodshed had not immunized him to it, as might be expected. Nor had it enlarged his appetite for blood, as he had been accused. It had poisoned him. For the sake of his fallen friends, and for the sake of his own freedom, one more life must end. It was a conviction impervious to the reasoned and impassioned pleas of those nearest to Yeshua Bar-Abbas. This life had to end: the person that had brought down misery upon them all, the one who had led the companions to their doom. Once this man, who deserved to die, had met with his end, Yeshua would be at peace.

The sound of a dagger's tip being buried into the table that occupied the centre of the room caused Kaleb to turn in shock. The frown disappeared from his face, and he adopted the same pale complexion and fearful confusion that had marked the condemned companions in Jerusalem. "Bar-Abbas!" he whispered in disbelief. He took his seat at the table and dropped his head. It was the first display of humility Yeshua had seen from the Pharisee. "How did you get away? I'd known all along that this would come back to me. I didn't dream it would be like this."

"Someone else took my place. The Galilean prophet."

"He's dead? . . . They let you go?"

"It is a custom of Pilatus. You know that."

"To release a prisoner yes. But to release a Lestes awaiting crucifixion . . ."

"So you thought you'd got away with it?"

"I know it doesn't work like that," said Kaleb, still unable to lift his head.

"Why did you do it? They say you became a collaborator. That you wanted to be reunited with your father—a Sadducee—the very thing you detest . . . Why?"

Kaleb lifted his head and looked straight at Yeshua.

"Why did you do it?"

"I had no choice," Kaleb said.

"No choice. That phrase is a pathetic cop out for cowards," Yeshua replied. "No choice! It means you can't find the courage to make the right choice. You can't be bothered with the pain of facing yourself and your world. Tell me the truth, Kaleb."

The Pharisee's head sank again.

"And don't even think about quoting any Scripture at me," said Yeshua. "If you try that I'll bury this blade where it belongs."

Kaleb said nothing.

"The only time you're lost for words is when you're forced to be honest," Yeshua grinned.

"What do you want me to say? I can't justify myself can I?"

"I don't want you to justify yourself. I want you to explain yourself."

"It was you! It was the prophet from Galilee."

"And . . . ?"

"To hear of you and your brothers. To hear, every day, of you, your family, your Father . . . You're not privileged because you're wealthy." Bar-Abbas looked unconvinced. "To hear that prophet talking over and over about our father in heaven. A Father who made it sound like it was alright for me to love my father in Jerusalem. To be loved by him. You have a father, your own father, who loves you . . ."

"Many people have a father, but it . . ."

"Not me. I didn't have one. Can you even begin to understand that?" Kaleb's confidence was returning. "I know what my father is. But what crime is it to be reconciled with your own father? . . ."

"You condemned your friends to death."

"They did it themselves. That plan was never going to work, you knew that."

"Not with a traitor in our midst. Why did you not just leave us? Why not just go to your father?"

"With what? He wouldn't have listened to me if I'd gone to him with nothing."

"A father who requires blood to be satisfied by his own son? Is this a father worth having? And where is he now, this great father of yours?"

"I have proven myself to my father. By giving him all I had, and all my plans . . ."

"And all your friends, Kaleb," the Egyptian interrupted, "I read your letter."

"I saved your brother's life!"

"What?"

"In the garrison. I identified him as one who had nothing to do with any of it. I pleaded for his life."

"Theudas was innocent anyway!"

"There were going to be four execution stakes, not three."

"And what about all the other lives? Did you plead for any of those?"

"I pleaded for mercy for all of you. But your lives were over. You were going to join Eliazar. And who's to blame for his death? I warned . . ."

"Don't even try that!" shouted Bar-Abbas. "You betrayed us all for the sake of some collaborator you hardly knew."

"He is my father."

"In name only," Bar-Abbas scoffed.

"What would you know? What do you know about being father-less? What do you know about being ignored by your own father? You still have your father. You still have your brother."

"What about Kochba—your friend? You encouraged his own son to turn against him!"

"Kochba had already lost his sons."

"So, Kaleb, you have committed no crime. You were just being a faithful son, betraying your friends, and for God's sake, betraying your-self. Betraying all that you are, all that you stood for."

Kaleb remained silent, and then he mouthed something.

"What was that?"

"I know," he whispered.

"What!"

"I know," he shouted. They were the only words that could be heard by Theudas and Miriam. "I knew this day would come," he muttered and lifted his eyes, "and I am ready to face it."

"So, Kaleb of Narbata. What does justice now demand of you?"

Kaleb remained silent.

"Answer me," Yeshua raised his voice as he pulled his dagger from the table.

"I deserve that blade," he said, looking boldly at the Egyptian.

Miriam and Theudas watched Yeshua as he came from the house of Kaleb. His face streamed with tears as he stared at the dagger that had been his companion for almost a year. He did not look up at his other companions, so they followed him behind the house where a small dusty hill concealed the light of the falling sun. His eyes moved from the dagger to the top of the hill. He stepped forwards, lifted the dagger high and threw it as hard as he could. It spun across the ridge of the hill and fell silently beyond their sight. Its blade was dry. It had drawn no blood.

Yeshua turned to Miriam and Theudas and whispered to them. "Bar-Abbas is dead."

Epilogue

A Message From Bar-Abbas for the Followers of the Galilean:

At that time they had a well-known prisoner whose name was Jesus Barabbas. (Matt 27:16)

A man called Barabbas was in prison with the insurrectionists who had committed murder in the uprising. (Mark 15:7)

Barabbas had been thrown into prison for an insurrection in the city, and for murder. (Luke 23:19)

Now Barabbas had taken part in an uprising. (John 18:40)

IT'S NOT MUCH TO go on is it? But that is all the information you have about me. Everything you can ever know about me is found in these four sentences, and they are all different versions of only one sentence. So no. You don't know much about me. You know that I was condemned for insurrection and murder by the cowardly prefect who represented a barbaric empire. You know that the crowds called for my release so that the Galilean would be condemned. Have you ever wondered why? Or have you condemned the crowds as you have condemned me? And let's be clear. You have condemned me.

You have condemned me because you have managed to distort even that one sentence that you did know about me. You know that I was a "lestes." A thief and a murderer, you call me, as though I were a mugger, a thug or perhaps a cat burglar, out to get rich quick with minimal work and minimal concern about the pain it may bring to others. But it is far more likely that I am far more virtuous. Try to imagine yourself living in the shadow of a ruthless empire. How would you live? If your family were battered to death by the empire, what would you become?

There were many "lestai" in my day. Some of them might rob from the rich and give to the poor; others might simply rob from the rich and beat up the poor. Some would be choosy about their victims; some would not. Such a life is never the fruit of career aspirations. "Lestai" are made out of sheer desperation. If you faced the life that my countrymen had faced, you would not be so quick to brand me a thug. But this is no simple mistake on your part.

Whether you like it or not, you represent the empire. My land and my people know what it means to live under the shadow of the empire, and even two thousand years after my passing, I continue to live under the shadow of yours. It is not, after all, only my land that has been colonized. Since my day it had been colonized by the Romans, the Galileans, the Moors, the British, the Americans. Some conquered with sword and spear, some with semi-automatic rifles and bombs, some with plastic seats and coffee shops. It is a precious land, and all who lust for power lust for Jerusalem. But it is not only my land that has been colonized. My time has been colonized, and you are guilty. You may not realize it, but you represent the empire that continues to oppress my people and me.

You have not simply misunderstood me because you misunderstood. Your mistake is a guilty one. You have tried to put a great moral distance between us, because if you look too closely at me, you will see something of yourself that frightens you. And I am the one who suffers. Your quest to conquer my time is your refusal to face yourself. And you have colonized my time.

My time has been colonized by those who have sought to tame the disruption my people inflicted upon history. Colonized by those who are forging the past in their own image. Colonized by smug assumptions that those of us you deem "good" are just like you, and those you deem "evil" are nothing like you. But the sun is setting on your colonies.

It all went wrong when the empire made an idol out of the Galilean. Eventually, the emperor himself took the Galilean and turned him into a puppet for his own purposes. And what happens to me when the empire worships the Galilean who took my place? Those who suffered from the empire had once seen me as a hero. But what will that empire do to those like me who gave their lives to oppose that empire? Will they hear me for who I am? Will they present me as the person I was? I was and remain their enemy. If the Galilean became their idol, then I became their Voodoo doll. But the doll was so unlike me I am immune to the pins you continue to stick in me. You are part of that empire, but I dare you now to join me now in rebellion. If you have the courage to see me as I am, then the rebellion has begun.

And let me assure you followers of the Galilean, that the Messiah himself won't mind. Do you think he was happy to be turned into an idol? Do you think he was happy that his image has been recast to reflect the empire's ambition? I saw this Messiah. He took my place. What do you think he was up to? Do you think he was just performing some dirty transaction between his beautiful self and a heavenly father who was baying for human blood? Do you think he was doing this just to wipe your slate clean so that, relieved of the effort of facing who you really are, you can follow my friend Amram to paradise?

The Galilean has always had followers who glimpsed something of what I saw. But he has had many more who worshipped his idol. The test of which group you belong to is whether you straightaway assumed that you belonged to the first. If you did, then you can be assured that you belong to the second. I dare you again, to look at me. You cannot know much about the Galilean until you know a little of me. And please, none of that patronizing nonsense about your inability to know me because of the centuries and the languages that separate us. Please, none of that false humility that says you can't possibly know much about me at all because you are afraid of imposing your time, your culture, your assumptions and prejudices upon me. It looks like historical humility, but it is a very modern invention. "Historicism" you call it, as you marvel at "the great ugly ditch" that separates us. But this is not humility. It is pride of the most self-deceptive order.

You don't want your comfort, your assumptions, your prejudices to be rattled by someone as disturbing as me. So you put your fingers in your ears and pretend you can't hear me. Like Pilatus who washed his hands before the Galilean, so all who pretend to be too humble to hear me are only washing their hands. But we are humans, you and I. We both use language. We are born, we learn, we love, we breathe air, we fear death, we drink wine. Your wine is better, mine is cheaper. But we can share a glass now if you have any. Just don't pretend you can't hear me.

Sure, you bring your assumptions and prejudices to anything you read, about me or about anyone from my time. But you bring those assumptions and those prejudices to anything you read from any time, and anyone you meet from your own time. To be human is not to free yourself of your assumptions and prejudices. To be human is to allow those things to be reshaped through the course of your life. You can never escape them, and you modern people look ridiculous to us, your ancestors, because you think yourself superior enough to have achieved this. What makes your plight all the more pitiable, is that your empire requires you to obey your prejudices and your assumptions—keeping you subject to the whore every bit as much as did the Romans before you. So once again, I call you to rebellion.

Again, I ask you why the crowds called for my release. Why the crowds supported rebellion. Please understand, it was not because they were pure evil. They called for my release because I opposed the empire that was crushing them. The Galilean did not appear to do this. Everyone expected him to do it, even his mother. But he did not. He had failed; she had been mistaken. He did not bring the liberation he should have done. Instead of entering Jerusalem to overthrow the Romans, he went into the temple and overthrew the tables. He offered none of the liberation for which the people longed. I did. That is why they eventually rejected him, and called for my release. They wanted action, not simply words. None of them realized what the Messiah was really up to. No one would have dreamed how subversive his word would be, how it would eventually overthrow that empire. But that empire has sought its revenge.

The centuries that followed have seen the Galilean's followers gazing at an idol, forged by the empire to add to their credibility. According to the empire, the Messiah's passive. He's spiritual. He's apolitical. He's nice. He's nothing like the Galilean. The truth is that when you throw stones at me, you are in danger of hitting your beloved Messiah. You have distorted this Messiah into his own exact opposite. If you don't believe me, then ask the Galilean's priests why they still wear the robes of a Roman leader.